The
QUEEN GEEK
Social Club

The QUEEN GEEK Social Club

Laura Preble

BERKLEY JAM BOOKS, NEW YORK

THE BERKLEY PUBLISHING GROUP
Published by the Penguin Group
Penguin Group (USA) Inc.
375 Hudson Street, New York, New York 10014, USA
Penguin Group (Canada), 90 Eglinton Avenue East, Suite 700, Toronto, Ontario M4P 2Y3, Canada
(a division of Pearson Penguin Canada Inc.)
Penguin Books Ltd., 80 Strand, London WC2R 0RL, England
Penguin Group Ireland, 25 St. Stephen's Green, Dublin 2, Ireland (a division of Penguin Books Ltd.)
Penguin Group (Australia), 250 Camberwell Road, Camberwell, Victoria 3124, Australia
(a division of Pearson Australia Group Pty. Ltd.)
Penguin Books India Pvt. Ltd., 11 Community Centre, Panchsheel Park, New Delhi—110 017, India
Penguin Group (NZ), Cnr. Airborne and Rosedale Roads, Albany, Auckland 1310, New Zealand
(a division of Pearson New Zealand Ltd.)
Penguin Books (South Africa) (Pty.) Ltd., 24 Sturdee Avenue, Rosebank, Johannesburg 2196,
South Africa

Penguin Books Ltd., Registered Offices: 80 Strand, London WC2R 0RL, England

This book is an original publication of The Berkley Publishing Group.

This is a work of fiction. Names, characters, places, and incidents either are the product of the author's imagination or are used fictitiously, and any resemblance to actual persons, living or dead, business establishments, events, or locales is entirely coincidental.

PRINTING HISTORY
Berkley JAM trade paperback edition / September 2006

Library of Congress Cataloging-in-Publication Data

Preble, Laura.
    The Queen Geek Social Club / Laura Preble.—Berkley Jam trade paperback ed.
        p.   cm.
    Summary: Seeking more of their own kind and wanting to shake things up at school, fifteen-year-old Shelby and her new best friend, Becca, start a club, but geek solidarity may not solve their problems with weird single parents, guys, or popularity.
    ISBN 0-425-21164-9
    [1. Popularity—Fiction.   2. Clubs—Fiction.   3. Best friends—Fiction.   4. Friendship—Fiction.
5. High schools—Fiction.   6. Schools—Fiction.   7. San Diego (Calif.)—Fiction.]   I. Title.
PZ7.P9052Que 2006
[Fic]—dc22   2006006422

PRINTED IN THE UNITED STATES OF AMERICA

10   9   8   7   6   5   4   3   2   1

CONTENTS

ACKNOWLEDGMENTS

I've been writing since I was sixteen, so I have a lot of people to mention. I'm grateful to my parents, Dick and Therese Preble, who always read to me and encouraged me to do anything I wanted to do, and to my three sisters, Linda, Barb, and Ann. Thanks to my husband and partner in chaos, Chris Klich, and our two wonderful boys, baby Noel and Austin, my first proofreader and reality checker. Thanks to the great staff at West Hills High School, especially to the English department and Sue Arthur, our awesome librarian. Thanks to all the English, drama, and journalism students I've had over the years who made for the best character studies a writer could ask for. Special thanks to Kym, Patrick, Twink, Jasmine, Gilbert, Leina, Queen Bob, West Hills GSA, Becca, Fletcher, Samantha D., Alyssa, and Laura B., who will inherit Euphoria upon my untimely demise. Also thanks to my friends, Becky, Stacey, Shaun, Kayak Boy, Jackie H., Joe N., Diana S., and all those who encouraged my writing. Big,

big, big eternal thanks to Susan McCarty who said yes at a Writer's Conference, and to Tova Sacks who picked up where Susan left off. Thanks to all my teachers; to Virgil Mann, thanks for the Kafka. And a shout out to God, the Universe, and Everything, including the number forty-two.

1

A GEEK IS BORN

(or 101 Creative Uses for Silly String)

The original meaning of the word *geek* was a person in the circus who bit the heads off live chickens. Let me say up front, I'd never do this, because I am a strict vegetarian. However, in more modern terms, I guess I fit the definition.

If you say the word *geek* to people today, they think of a schlubby kind of misfit, usually young (I don't think geeks live to a ripe old age—must check this out) and almost always single. My theory: The universe in its wisdom tries to keep geeks from mating to keep the geek population in check. In this way I sort of mess up the averages, because I date with a vengeance.

I'm actually on a date right now. It's ten-thirty at night, I'm sitting in a parked '68 Mustang in front of my house, which is dark, but I know my dad is still awake because I can see the flickering lights of the television in his bedroom. Dustin Garrett is staring at my breasts at the moment, and if it were possible to have a small, inflatable thought bubble orbiting his head, it would be filled with the word *Yum*. For about the tenth time tonight, I mentally kick myself for going out with someone who has an IQ in the negative digits. I know better, I really do. But sometimes your hormones get the best of you. Even if you're a geek.

"So what about going to the dance next week?" Dustin is stretching his arms and yawning, using that classic move to put his arm around me, all the better to get a grope at my boobs. "I mean, I know you're a freshman and all, but don't let that stop you. I don't care what people think."

"That's very considerate." I wriggle around to avoid the grope. Dating is like a fine country line dance without the funny hats. "But I have a science fair coming up, so I think I really need to spend some time on that next weekend. And you know, I really need to go. My dad's waiting up for me."

The mention of my dad has the chilling effect I was going for. Dustin shrinks a little and throws a cautious glance at the front door as if my father is going to appear, crazed, with a shotgun, demanding that this boy marry his daughter and make her boobs honest.

"Well, yeah, it is getting late." He changes focus and smiles his expensive-orthodontia smile. "Got a tennis match tomorrow after school. You coming?"

"I'd love to. But I have a study session after school. Sorry." I fumble in my purse for my keys.

"Study session? Why? You have, like, straight As, don't you?"

"Yeah. That's why." I produce the key and hold it up like a magic talisman. Begone, oh feeler of boobs! "I better go. Thanks for the movie. I'll see you at school." I lean over and give him a peck on the cheek. Sensing his options disappearing, Dustin pulls a wrestling move and I'm lying face up in his lap, the steering wheel digging into my scalp.

"Hey! That's hot!" His face is hovering above me, his eyes wide, nostrils flared with the scent of girl. "Let's do it."

"My dad is right in the house," I remind him. "He has a shotgun."

"Oh." For a nanosecond, common sense flashes across Dustin's face. Then lust takes over again. "I'll be quiet."

I sigh, pull myself up by levering my weight against the steering wheel, twist, and open the door in a lightning move calculated purely with physics that would make my science teacher, Mr. Rich, extremely proud. "See ya."

"Shelby!" He's frantically rolling down the window, cranking the handle. "Wait!"

"'What satisfaction canst thou have tonight?'"

"Huh?"

"*Romeo and Juliet*. Anyway, thanks for the movie. I'll see you at school, okay?"

"Shelby!" He's yelling now. Not cool.

I go back, lean in the window. "What?"

He swallows hard, as if he has honest words caught in his throat. "I love you."

"You do?"

"Yes. I think so." He grips the steering wheel and concentrates on it. "It's kind of annoying."

"Dustin. You don't love me. You're just feeling desperate."

"Don't sell yourself short. You're really hot." He turns to me, smiles again, and I realize it was all a ploy to get my boobs back to the car.

"Thanks again. Gotta go." As I scamper across the lawn, I hear scuffling behind me.

"Shelby!" I turn, and Dustin is standing next to the passenger door of the car, his shirt open to the waist, his arms outstretched across the car, his head upturned like an underwear model on a Times Square billboard. He has a great upper body since he plays tennis, and I guess he must feel like it's his secret weapon. I have no choice.

I rummage in my purse and pull out my own secret weapon. I shake the can of Day-Glo pink Silly String, take aim, and decorate Dustin Garrett's gorgeous chest with sticky strands of embarrassment. "Good night!" I whisper as, horrified and confused, he plucks absently at the mess entwined in his scraggly chest hair. I cleanly make my escape.

Tomorrow, no doubt, he'll have to try to explain that to the tennis team.

My dad usually stays up until at least three in the morning working on various hobby projects. By day, he is a well-paid researcher for some company you've never heard of, and he gets to do a lot of his work at home, which is nice. They even built him a lab in back of the house so he could have all the equipment he needs. At night, though, he works on his eccentric ideas that the company wouldn't necessarily want to fund.

On the night of Dustin's humiliation, Dad is in the lab, as I suspected. He leaves the TV on in the house so it looks like we're sort of normal. He never watches it. Okay, except for the old *Star Trek* episodes.

I go through the dark house and out the sliding glass door in back, to the steel door with a keypad. I key in the password, and it swooshes open with a satisfying *Star Trek* hiss. Dad didn't really need this; he paid extra for it himself so he could feel like Mr. Spock hunting for Klingons or something.

"Hey." The room is dim, as usual, except for the glow of computer screens and some equipment radiating green neon in the corner under a huge portrait of Mom. It makes Mom sort of look like that princess from *Shrek*.

Dad is wearing goggles and is staring at something through a huge magnifying glass on a hinged arm. It makes him look like a big-eyed insect. He doesn't look up. "Oh, hey, Shelby. How was the movie?"

"Okay."

He hears the catch in my voice, looks up, and slides the goggles up into his wild nest of salt-and-pepper hair. "What? Wasn't he nice?"

"Hmm." I perch on a tall stool and swing my legs back and forth. It makes me feel little again. "He was a jerk. Just in it for the boobage."

"Hmm." He's back to the magnifying glass again. "I found some really intriguing properties on this—"

"I'm going to bed. See you in the morning." I kiss him on the forehead. "Don't stay up too late."

He doesn't really notice I'm leaving. Dad is literally the absentminded professor if he's on a project. He does care about me, he really does; but if I disappeared while he was working on something juicy, I don't know that he would notice for, like, a week. When my mom died three years ago, he threw himself into work, and that helped him deal with the loss, I guess. Now it's just a habit.

"Night," I hear him say as the *Star Trek* door swooshes behind me. Well, nothing left but to go talk to Euphoria.

Euphoria is the robot my dad built for me. She (I call her a she, but actually, she has no real gender) is sort of a combination diary, best friend, playmate, nanny, and baby monitor. She's about five feet tall, with a brushed-nickel finish. Dad gave her sort of a face, but it's kind of like the robot maid on that old cartoon *The Jetsons*. She's a very simple machine, really, but he did program her to be able to talk to me and respond. She's also sensitive to temperature and humidity, so if I'm angry or crying, she knows it, and she knows the proper response to make. I know this is all fake, the right combination of zeros and ones, but I have pretended that Euphoria is really a person for years, like most kids pretend their teddy bears are real, or that the imaginary friend in the couch cushions is real.

"Good evening, Shelby," she whirs as I walk into my bedroom. "How was your date?"

"It sucked." I kick off my black Vans and dig my toes into the carpet.

"Oh. Sorry to hear that, baby." Her voice is kind of like a grandma, but also kind of Southern-sounding. I think this is because Mom was from Georgia, but Dad claims it was totally accidental. Her green eye-lights blink in the darkness.

"Yeah, well. That's what I get for dating a jock."

"A jock?"

"Yeah. He's a tennis star." I sit on the bed and click the remote for my stereo. Classical music. Ahhh. "I had to Silly String him."

"I think you need to find someone who thinks like you do."

"You mean, someone who thinks too much?" I pull off my plaid knee socks, shimmy out of my black, pleated mini, and pull my red sweater over my head, which leaves me in my underwear. "Check it out." I stand in front of a full-length mirror attached to my closet door. "I'm attractive, right? I'm smart, right? And yet I have no real friends and boys bore me."

The image looking back at me isn't bad. I have long auburn hair, straight as a stick, and huge eyes that look like aggie marbles swirled with shades of blue. And there are those darned boobs. They get me in so much trouble. I mean, in seventh grade, I had nothing. Suddenly this year, they've puffed out like rice cakes in water. I have to constantly watch my posture, Euphoria says, because I tend to hunch over to hide these huge monstrosities. Okay, well, they're not *that* big, but they feel pretty obvious, and when guys look at your chest instead of in your eyes, it sort of makes you feel like the dollar-a-pound special at the butcher shop. Anyway, moving on . . . high cheekbones, delicate lips, a slim but curvy figure . . . all pretty good. So why am I so miserable? Isn't this supposed to make me happy?

"You are a pretty girl, but you are way too picky." Euphoria rolls to the stereo and changes the channel to a rock station. "And you're just too much of an egghead, if you'll pardon my opinion. You need to get in touch with your rebellious teenager side."

I punch a button and change the music back to Mozart. "Time for bed, Euphoria. Good night."

The light goes off. Daddy has rigged it to Euphoria's central control, so she can turn it off and on all by herself. "Night-night, Shelby. Don't let the bedbugs bite."

"Wouldn't you kill them if they showed up?" I snuggle up under my covers.

"Absolutely." Her lights blink off too.

Green Pines High School, in beautiful San Diego's North County, is best known for its high percentage of tanned students, and for having one of the only surf phys ed classes in the country. It also has a huge number of teenagers who think they are better than everyone else. I suppose I'm one of them.

I don't have a lot of friends at Green Pines. I've gone here for nearly a year, and I've made some acquaintances, but nobody I'd consider a best friend. I don't know if I've ever had one, to be honest; I hung out with a girl named Jane in junior high, but she and her family moved to North Carolina or some other state with a *North* in it, and I haven't heard from her since last summer.

Here's the thing about friends, I mean *real* friends: You can't just put up a poster at school and advertise for somebody and hope you find the perfect one. It might work, I guess, but you'd look so pathetic and desperate that no one would want to be your friend, and so it would be kind of pointless. And if you're somebody like me—smart, witty, charming, humble—it's even more challenging to find that special someone who becomes your Best Friend. Plus, it's even harder than finding guys, because Best Friends are much more important. You can date anybody, but you can't just tell anybody about the time you threw up milk through your nose at the seventh-grade honors lunch, or about the time you got your period in the middle of the baseball game while wearing white jeans and a tank top, sitting in the front row.

It's February, it's Friday, and it's the middle of my freshman year, so I'm pondering what I'll do this summer, all alone, with no Best Friend. Dad wants me to go to a summer science camp, and I guess I might, but I don't know. I could also try out for a play, write a book, or do about half a dozen other things. The bottom line is: Whatever I do, it will probably be alone.

First period English, I sit next to Jennifer Crist on one side, Taffy Burton (her name is really Taffy) in front of me, and Ted Trinidario in back of me. He kicks my chair all the time and smells like firewood. The seat next to me is empty. At least, it was until today.

The class is, as usual, engaged in trivial conversation, this time about the upcoming dance. Dustin is in this class too, and across the room I see him talking to some friends; he says something, looks over at me, and they all laugh. I wish Euphoria was here.

While we're waiting for Ms. Napoli to start our fascinating discussion of British boys who mount pigs' heads on sticks for fun, a new girl walks into the room. I can't hear what she's saying over the din, but she shows the teacher a paper, Napoli points to the seat next to me, and the girl walks down the row toward it.

What a poser. She's tall, unusually tall, freakishly tall really, and to make her seem even taller, she's wearing those high platform sneakers in shocking green. Her ridiculously short blond hair has green streaks in it that match her shoes, and she's styled it so it sticks straight up in about fifty little points. It looks like a microscopic close-up of one of those Bioré pore strips.

Her outfit, not that I care: pink gauzy shirt over a knee-length tight black skirt, pierced ears with Celtic crosses, a whole batch of silver bracelets wound around her forearms. As she glides into the desk, her long praying-mantis legs fold up under her in the cramped space.

Napoli starts class. "I'd like to introduce you to a new student," she says, squinting at the paper. "Becca Gallagher. Becca, could you tell us a little about yourself?"

I get a good look at her profile, and she looks kind of intriguing. "We just moved down here from Los Angeles," she says.

"Swimming pools, movie stars!" Dustin yells from across the room. I wonder if he got all the Silly String out of his chest hairs.

"Thanks for that, Dustin." Napoli shoots him a look. "Go on, Becca. You're from L.A.?"

"My mom and I just moved here two weeks ago."

"Well, welcome. I'm sure you'll find Green Pines a great school. Let me get you a book. We're reading *Lord of the Flies* . . ." I tune out at that point because I am fixated on Becca Gallagher's leg tattoo. Now, lots of kids have tattoos and piercings. But hers goes from ankle to knee in this intricate design, a dragon or something entwined with a feather. It is in multiple colors, and there is some sort of metallic ink in it that makes it sparkle when she moves. I spend pretty much the rest of the period studying that tattoo, wondering how her parents let her get it, wondering what it means. Even when Napoli asks me to explain why the British boys went savage, I make something up about dragons and get laughed at. Dustin laughs the loudest. Big shock.

The day goes by as it usually does, and it's finally lunchtime. As usual, I have no one to sit with, and neither does Becca Gallagher, whom I spot parked against a window in the cafeteria, sucking on an iced latte.

"Hey," I say casually. "Can I sit here?"

"Free country." She sips loudly on the remainder of the crushed ice. "Aren't you in my English class?"

"Yeah." I park my tray and start to open a yogurt. "Aren't you eating?"

"Already did. I don't have a fourth period yet, so I came over early to avoid the crowds. I hate crowds."

"Me too."

She turns to really look at me, and I notice she has eyes that are almost identical to mine, except they're green. She's looking through me, with that kind of intense gaze that freaks people out when I do it to them. No one's ever done it to me before, so now I know how it feels. Weird. "What's your name?"

"Shelby Chapelle." The look is making me feel kind of blushy and embarrassed, because she never takes her eyes away. "I was born here."

"Oh, yeah." She finally looks out the window. "San Diego. Must be nice."

"Not so much."

She turns her eyes back to me. "Why not? It's so much more laid back than L.A., and there aren't as many posers. Plus, you have some killer beaches. Everybody loves it here."

"Not me. If I could get out, I would. Nobody here likes to think."

She laughs. Now, this laugh was really out of character for her, because she looks kind of gazelle-ish and elegant, but her laugh is like this donkey honk. It makes me immediately bust up too. My mom used to tell me I sound like a chicken, so I guess we have a regular barnyard symphony going on.

"Yeah, that's the way it is in Los Angeles too. It's all about the movies. I always felt like I was the only person who'd ever read a book for fun. You like to read?"

"Sure." I finish up the yogurt and turn around to face her. "Who's your favorite author?"

"That's tough." She takes another long slurp from the cup, pops the lid, and starts to tip it toward her to get at the ice, but it sticks and then comes tumbling out in a big chunk all over her pink gauzy top. "I've got a drinking problem."

"Let's go outside. You'll dry faster."

Our school is on some huge bunch of acreage, and there are lots of trees and shrubs everywhere, nice landscaping, even a big patch of roses that are blooming. Becca walks toward the middle of the campus, where most of the other kids hang out on benches and under trees. She's going toward the panther sculpture.

"Now, I've never heard of a school having a big art project in the middle of the campus." She touches the nose of one of the panthers. "Although since we were so close to Hollywood, we had a great theater at my school."

"Theater? Were you in drama?"

"I had the lead in *Romeo and Juliet* in the fall. And I'm only a freshman."

As we walk past the panthers, I notice that Dustin and his pack of boob-addled friends are stalking us. "Oh no," I mutter.

"What?"

"That guy. I just had a date with him. He went all octopus on me, so I had to take him down."

By this time Dustin and his gang had caught up with us, and I was expecting the worst.

"Hey, Shelby. How's it going?" They had casually surrounded us, Dustin and five of his tennis-star buddies, chests rippling. "Thanks for the date. I had a blast."

"Yeah, me too. Thanks." I try to walk past him, but he blocks me. Not cool.

"I was wondering about something, though." I see him wink at Jeremy Friend, a sophomore on his team who is standing behind me. "I just thought I'd ask you about it."

"Yeah?"

Through all of this, freakishly tall Becca Gallagher just stands, arms crossed, watching everything play out. I glance quickly at her, and even though we've just met, I feel anger brewing under those fifty green little spikes on her head. I have a feeling you wouldn't want to be in the way if those little spikes blew.

"Yeah, I just wondered. Is it true what they say?"

"I don't know, Dustin. What do they say? And who are *they* anyway?"

The boys snicker. Dustin's eyes are checking the reactions of his friends, unaware of the ticking time bomb that is Becca Gallagher. "That you're a lesbo. That's what I heard."

The guys cackle. I guess the fact that I didn't plow helplessly into Dustin Garrett's pants makes me gay. "Actually, no. That's not true."

I turn to go, trying to brush past Dustin, but again he blocks my path. "See, because I heard that rumor, and I asked you out anyway. Because lesbos are hot, you know?" He turns to give Becca a long appraisal. "In fact, if you're the new resident lesbo, maybe we could all get together—"

It happens so fast that I don't consciously see it. Later, Becca would teach me the trick, her own personal move she had dubbed the Titillating Tit Twist, but just seeing it for the first time was an amazement, a thing of beauty. Because what she does is lunge forward quick as lightning, grab Dustin's right nipple, twist it in a 360-degree turn that nearly rips it off his chest, and then takes her original position as if nothing has happened.

Dustin is so stunned he just stands there and blinks, unconsciously rubbing his abused nipple. Becca pounces then and sidles up to him slowly, towering over him by at least three inches in her green platform sneakers. "If you're an example of what there is to pick from in the dating pool," she whispers in his ear, "what choice would a poor girl have, sweetheart?" She licks his ear, stands back, and gives him a grin that reminds me of an overly enthusiastic Wal-Mart greeter on massive doses of caffeine.

From that moment on, I know that Becca Gallagher and I will be Best Friends.

2

DINNER AND A MOVIE

(or Bald Obese Aliens Ate All My Popcorn)

After two weeks of hanging out with Becca during every lunch and break, I come home one Friday afternoon and find my dad getting ready to leave for a business trip. He won't take me with him; it's boring, he says, and I'm totally safe here at home with Euphoria. I announce, "I really like this girl Becca at school. She's new."

"I know it's been a long time since you had a friend you could really bond with," he says as he packs his suitcase. All of his clothes, by the way, are exactly the same. He just finds a pair of pants he likes and buys them in every color there is, then does the same thing with shirts. His suitcase looks like the stock room at Macy's. When Mom bought his clothes, he had some small hint of style. Now he's just a Ken doll with frequent-flier miles.

I suppose you want to know why my dad would leave me home alone when I'm only fifteen. It's a good, logical question, and the best answer I can give is that my dad doesn't realize I'm fifteen. This can be a good thing, but it can also be bad. Being home alone on the weekends he's away on business trips is very restful. The several weeks he usually leaves during the summer is great, because I can stay up late, eat Oreos for breakfast, listen to very loud music, and spend time doing anything I want—cooking, reading, creating an evil army of robotic sea monkeys. It's bad because, well, I miss my dad, to be honest. Whenever he goes, I always have this little tiny voice in the back of my head telling me he might not come back. I know this voice is wrong, because he always has come back, but I guess when you lose one parent, you worry about losing the other.

Another thing you might not have thought of: Euphoria. Remember how I said she was also sort of a baby monitor? I wasn't kidding. I have a microchip in my watch, and it's synchronized to her main system, and has a Global Positioning System component too, so there's no way I can go anywhere without her knowing my location. That's kind of comforting, actually; the only problem would be if I were kidnapped by a rogue band of watch thieves, but that doesn't happen too much, even in movies.

"Am I going to get to meet this Becca?" Dad is folding his all-the-same pairs of underwear and tucking them into the side pocket of his suitcase.

"Sure, I'd like you to. Want her to come to dinner before you go?"

He whips out his Palm Pilot, his connection to life, the universe, and everything, and flicks it on. "I'm going on Tuesday. So, what day?"

"Saturday? Like, tomorrow?"

"You don't have a date?" He frowns. I usually have dates on Saturdays, but of course now nobody's asking me out because Dustin has managed to spread it all around school that I'm a lesbian. It's actually been quite a nice break.

"No." I don't tell him about the rumor. I don't want him thinking Becca and I are kinky or anything. If I were a dad, I wouldn't want to even have to think about that while I'm away building robotic rhinos or whatever he was going to do. "Let me call her."

I had Euphoria rig up a speaker and voice command to the phone in my room. I'm perfectly capable of punching numbers on a phone; it's just cooler to be able to speak your command. "Dial, please. 555-2298. Becca. Program, please."

"Is that your new friend?" I hear her electronically selecting the digits. "Is she a nice young lady?"

"She's from Los Angeles. She has a tattoo."

"Well, well! That's nice."

I arrange for Becca to come over for dinner, and to spend the night, and the next day Euphoria and I spend a long time planning a great meal full of vegetarian delights. Fresh green beans almondine, mashed potatoes, and my own personal recipe, sham ham. Euphoria always clicks disapprovingly whenever I make it, insisting that humans are, by nature, meat eaters, and I'm fighting my natural urges. But it's really good, and with a nice glaze and some well-placed cloves, it hardly tastes anything like tofu. Dad spends most of the day in his studio tinkering with something expensive, and surfaces only occasionally to use the bathroom or get a drink of water.

"So, your friend is coming over tonight?" he asks between gulps.

"Yep. We're making dinner." Euphoria beeps in agreement as she chops onions. "You need to be cleaned up by six."

He grunts as he downs the rest of his water, bangs the glass on the counter, and flies out the door to his lab.

"That man needs to get out of that workroom." Euphoria has moved on to piecrust rolling. The onions are already simmering in a pan with garlic and some other unidentified ingredients. "He needs to get a life."

"I suppose it's easy for you to say." I am trying to pincushion the sham ham with little cloves so it will look like the ones in ladies' magazines. It looks more like an aerial map of scattered terrorist compounds.

Becca arrives on time, wearing jeans, with a plaid carpetbag overflowing with clothes. Her hair is spikeless, the green faded to a faint chlorine shading over her bleached-blond pixie cut. A purple Jeep drops her off, and she doesn't even wave to whoever the driver is. "Is that your mom?" I ask.

"Yeah." As I close the door behind her, she surveys the front room. "Wow. You have a really nice house."

"Thanks. Hey, come in here and meet Euphoria."

"Euphoria?" She laughs as she drops her bag in the hallway. "Is that your dog or something? What a cool—" She stops, and, in my opinion, squeals a very un-Becca-like squeal.

Euphoria has rolled up to her from the kitchen, and she's dusted lightly with flour from working on the pie. I had put an apron around her so stuff wouldn't get into her inner workings, so I guess it did look pretty weird. "Hi there. You must be Becca." She extends a claw.

Becca looks wide-eyed at me. "Is this a joke?" She looks at Euphoria's claw, and then at me again.

"No. She's our robot."

"You have a robot? Do you have any idea how weird that is?"

"Yes." I gesture toward Euphoria's still-extended grabber. "Please shake her hand. She's easily offended."

Becca gingerly touches the tip of one claw, then grips it a bit tighter, finally shaking it with some enthusiasm. "Well, pleased to meet you, I guess."

"And pleased to meet you too. Welcome to our home."

I think Becca's kind of stunned because she just stands there squinting for a couple of minutes, slowly shaking the claw. Then she turns to me. "You know, I kind of figured you were unique. I guess I didn't realize how truly out there you are."

"Is that a problem?"

"Not at all." She grins and puts an arm around Euphoria, whose green lights sparkle in what I guess is the robot equivalent of happiness. While she finishes cooking dinner, I take Becca to my room. I haven't actually had a friend over to my room since the previously mentioned Jane (my junior high friend who moved), so it feels sort of scary exposing my stuff to a stranger. But she just moves right in, plops on my bed, kicks off her shoes (just flat Keds this time), and starts to look at the books on my bedside shelf.

"You have all the same books I do." She lies down on my pillow and stares up at the Day-Glo stars on my ceiling. "I was afraid I wouldn't meet anybody here at all. I'm glad you came up and introduced yourself."

"Well, I could tell you weren't like everybody else." I sit in my desk chair and swivel. "What's with the tattoo?"

"Oh, this?" She rolls up her pant leg. "This is the dragon of the East. It's some Buddhist thing or something. My parents are big Buddhists."

"Yeah?"

"What are your parents?"

I don't know how to answer this question. First of all, I haven't had any real friends since my mom died, so nobody has asked me stuff about them, really. I also don't think we ever had a religion to speak of. Unless you count science.

"I guess we're not religious."

"Nothing?" Becca is picking at my bedspread, looking at the patterns of constellations on it.

"Well, I think my mom was raised Catholic."

"Oh, well, once you're Catholic, you're always Catholic. That's what my mom says. She went to parochial school. Had to wear uniforms. It drives her crazy when I wear used uniforms I buy at Goodwill." She laughs that donkey laugh again. "I don't know. I think it's all kind of just a way people make themselves feel good about dying eventually."

"Wow. You're cheery. Remind me to take you to lots of parties." She throws a pillow at my head, and then the fight is on, and we're lobbing projectiles through the air until feathers are popping out.

When we finally finish demolishing my room with feathers and pillows, we collapse in a heap, laughing. "I haven't done that for a long time."

"I don't think I've ever done it." She scans my room silently, looking at all the stuff hanging on my walls, at my dresser, at my photo gallery. She jumps up off the bed and points to one of the pictures. "Is this your mom?"

It's my favorite photo. It's Mom and me when I'm about ten, and we're in the park, riding on the carousel, and Dad is taking our picture. We're both hanging off our horses like they're going wild, pretending to gallop off into the desert.

"Hey." Becca nudges me slightly. "Are you okay?"

"Yeah." I smile, a pale, anemic smile.

"My parents are divorced," she says bluntly as she plops back down on the bed. "It just happened. That's why we moved here."

I don't answer her. I'm not really sure what to say. It's always awkward, that conversation where you have to talk about what happened—

"Your mom is dead, isn't she?"

Dead. Nobody ever says that word—it's always "she passed away," or "we lost her," as if she just read a map wrong or something. I like Becca even more for using the word.

"Yeah. Okay," she says, sensing that I'm not ready to go into details. "Let's go get something to eat, huh? Maybe your robot lady can whip us up an appetizer like on *Star Trek*, where they have a food replicator and you just tell it what you want."

"I told my dad to invent that . . ." And we walk off to the kitchen, the small shadow of the idea of death tucked back in its little box where it belongs.

Dinner with my dad is not like eating with other human beings. For one thing, as I've said, he cannot concentrate on anything that's normal. Eating, I think, reminds him of Mom, and so he tries to get it over as quickly as possible. This is why we don't usually have people over. In fact, I don't think anyone has been over for almost three years.

We sit at the dining room table, something that hasn't seen much use lately. We usually eat alone, and we get whatever we want: He takes his to his workroom; I take mine to my bedroom or to the den to watch TV. If it weren't for

Euphoria, I'd eat baked beans out of a can seven days a week. Of course, that would also solve my dating excesses, wouldn't it?

But tonight, in honor of Becca Gallagher, Euphoria has set the table with a linen cloth, nice china and glasses, and silver. Dad comes rushing in from the workshop, still in his white lab coat with his goggles nesting in his hair. I suspect Euphoria has had to nag him to come in.

"Well, I can't help it that I have to leave in a few days and I'm supposed to have this design at least workable," he grumbles to no one in particular. "You must be Becca. Hi." He extends a hand and she shakes it, checking to see if it too is a claw.

"Hi." Suddenly, Becca seems kind of shy. I guess my dad is intimidating, what with the mad-scientist lab coat and the total lack of social grace. "Nice to meet you."

"Yes." He pulls a chair out and eases into it, so Becca and I scramble to sit too. Euphoria clicks and whirs disapprovingly. "Well, well. A formal dinner. I had no idea our guest was a V.I.P." He picks up a crystal goblet, turns it in his hand, and then sets it down quietly.

"Becca just moved here from Los Angeles," I offer.

"Los Angeles? Really? Which part?" Dad is slicing angrily into a stick of butter on a blue china plate.

"West Hollywood." Becca is looking tense. I don't blame her. Most people's parents don't attack dairy products with sharp knives. "My mom and I just moved here—"

"Euphoria!" Dad has officially turned into Dr. Jekyll, or

Mr. Hyde—whichever one was crazy, I can never remember. He has stopped slicing the butter and is now onto the ham glistening on the platter in the center of the table. "I need the electric carving knife!"

"The dinner looks really great," Becca says nervously. "It's been a while since I've had a really good home-cooked meal. We've been packing and moving for—"

"Euphoria! Where is my carving knife?"

"Keep your pants on, Mr. Chapelle." Euphoria has rolled up next to him, holding this huge electric knife. It's like, *Come see the Jetsons' maid star in* Psycho: Revenge of the Appliances! If it weren't my life, I'd think it was funny.

"Thank you very much." He's calmed a bit, and he takes the knife, thumbs it into action, and begins carving up my map of terrorist activity in the greater Cleveland metropolitan area, also known as the cloves on the sham ham. "This does smell delicious."

"Yes, it does." Becca, great freakishly tall tattooed Becca, looks scared. I could almost smack my father with a dinner roll. The first friend I've had in forever and he's going to scare her away!

Euphoria has taken a bowl of potatoes to our guest, and Becca is serving herself. Dad has moved on to the casserole dish of green beans, and he's digging at it as if he expects to find hidden treasure. For a few minutes, the only sound is the clank of serving spoons on porcelain, then the metal utensils on the plates as we all start to taste the food. It does taste good, by the way; I hadn't really realized how much I missed real dinner. Mom used to cook.

Dad seems to have chilled out a bit; he breathes heavily and sinks into his chair. He deliberately lays his fork down and turns to Becca. "So, what brings you to sunny San Diego?"

She pauses a moment. "Mom and I came alone. Dad stayed in Los Angeles." She hesitates again. "For work."

"Did you mind moving?" I ask, finally glad for a conversation that isn't about my family.

She shakes her head and reaches for a roll. "I sort of did, but I really didn't have any good friends there. Nobody there likes to think." She smiles at me; it's our first inside joke!

The rest of dinner goes about the same way, but Dad is uncomfortable the whole time. He doesn't even stick around for dessert. The pecan pie, though, is amazing, and I have three slices. Euphoria clucks at me; she likes to help me watch my weight.

"So," Becca says as she collects all remaining piecrust crumbs on her plate and scrunches them together with the flat of her fork, "what are we going to do tonight?"

"What do you want to do?" I try to be very sneaky about plucking an exposed pecan from the remaining pie, but Euphoria grabs it and pulls it away to the opposite side of the table. She has fast reflexes.

Becca considers as she licks the fork. "What do you usually do for fun?"

"You really want to know?"

"I think I do. Unless you tell me you go shopping. I hate shopping."

"Me too." I nod. "I usually just read, or I work on projects I have, and I do usually date a lot. Of course, Dustin has sort of stopped that for the moment."

"Right." Becca stretches. "Want us to clear the table, Miss . . . uh . . . Euphoria? Should I just call you Euphoria?"

"That's my name. And yes, you can clear the table. Miss America over there thinks she's too good to do that, so maybe you can influence her a little bit."

I make a face at Euphoria, who ignores me.

I discover that Becca shares one of my favorite hobbies: watching bad science fiction movies and talking back to them. We decide to do that for the evening, and we choose one of my favorite bad sci-fi films, *Plan 9 from Outer Space*. If you've never seen it, you have to find it because it is an absolutely unplanned riot. It's about this guy who looks like Count Dracula (well, it's the same actor, Bela Lugosi, from the old black-and-white *Dracula*, but half the time it's not him because he died right in the middle of the movie) and he hunches all around a graveyard and a UFO lands, and some lady who looks like Elvira, Mistress of the Dark, floats around for no good reason.

It feels so amazingly good to do this normal thing (okay,

I know you're thinking it's not that normal, but normal for me) with another person. We turn off the lights and huddle up on the big purple velvet couch in our pajamas. Mine are flannel with rubber ducks and hers have retro coffee cups on them. Euphoria rolls in with a vat of popcorn.

"I've never watched *Plan 9* here in this house," I say as I grab a handful of fluffy kernels.

"Oh. I thought you grew up here." Becca fishes in the bowl and scoops out the largest handful of popcorn I've ever seen. It's because of her freakish big hands, which go with her freakish tallness.

"Nope. We lived in a different house for most of my life. We just moved here a few years ago."

"Hmm. Did your dad get a different job or something?"

"No." I don't feel like talking about What Happened. It's nice to have just a normal conversation that doesn't involve that. Since it's been mostly me and my dad, it seems like What Happened just hovers there between us all the time, like a third person in the room that never says anything. But right now I don't want to deal with that. I want to watch crappy science fiction like any other normal geek. "Let's watch the movie."

For those of you who have never seen *Plan 9*, let me explain the point, or nonpoint, of it. It's about a bunch of aliens who come to earth to raise an army of dead people to do their evil bidding. Their best secret weapon is a dead bald police detective who weighs like three hundred pounds, and who, when he died, got white contact lenses. The aliens go around in flying aluminum pie plates and terrorize people by walking so slowly their victims fall asleep while being pursued. The aliens, who meet in their spaceship in a room made of black curtains, use laser electron guns to control the dead people.

We're watching the scene where the astronaut's wife is scared when Bela Lugosi comes into her bedroom to terrorize her by pacing with a cape over his face. He has a cape over his face because the guy in the movie is really not Bela Lugosi, who, in a fit of good planning, died before the movie was finished. So anyway, this lady is hysterical with fear, so she covers her mouth with her hand and runs past the slow vampire dude and runs into the graveyard. What else would you do?

"Why didn't she take the car?" Becca asks between munches.

"I think the astronaut has it. They never had two cars back then."

"Hmm. So, let me get this straight: The guy in the cape, who was short and is now tall, is chasing the woman, but she runs much faster, and he still catches up to her? Is that possible given the laws of time and space?"

"It is if you buy the fact that aliens would pick dead obese people and old guys to be their army of choice, I guess."

Now Vampira, the cheap ancestor of Elvira, Mistress of

the Dark, is stumbling around in the graveyard too, with her impossible teeny-tiny waist and ripped-up black shroud. "Who would get buried in a black Elvira dress?" Becca asks.

"I guess Vampira."

"God, she's got the tiniest waist ever. What is that, like five inches?"

"I think she had her ribs removed."

"The fat guy probably ate them. They had a barbecue. Hey, got any hot chocolate? I love popcorn with hot chocolate."

We go to the kitchen to forage for the gourmet powdered chocolate, and while we're microwaving the milk, Becca says, "So, tell me about school. What's it like at Green Pines?"

"Hmm. Hard to describe." The microwave dings and we take the mugs out. "It's a good school, I guess. Kids are kind of snobby, rich. I don't really have any friends there. I mean, I get along with everybody, but I just don't know anybody who's—well, who's—"

"Like you?" She grins as she spoons heaps of chocolate into her warm milk.

"Exactly."

"You said you date a lot." She sips the cocoa. "Mmmm. Perfection."

"Yeah, I do. I did. Before the lesbian thing."

"Yeah, what's that about?"

We pad back into the living room, where *Plan 9* is flickering, time stopped for the moment on the alien invasion of the overweight cue-ball heads. "Okay, so here's the story. Dustin asked me out, and I went, which was stupid."

"Why? He's cute. Obviously a jerk, but cute."

"Yeah, well, not so obvious before I went out with him. Anyway, we went to a movie and when he brought me home, he wanted to hook up, and I didn't, so he pulled some lame wrestling move on me."

"Which you obviously broke out of," she comments, taking another sip.

"Of course. But then, I'm walking to the door and he yells my name, so I turn around and he's, like, draped across the car with his shirt open."

"Ewww. Chest hair?"

"Oh yeah. Like the stuff that clogs up the bathroom drain."

"Yuck."

"So I Silly String him."

She chokes on her hot chocolate laughing. "Huh?"

"Silly String. I keep it in my purse as an emergency tool. Day-Glo pink."

"That works? Crap, my mom spends money on pepper spray!"

I set my mug down on the coffee table. "It works on high school guys because they don't expect it. I also have a mini airhorn canister and a cell phone for more pressing emergencies. Dustin was low-level. Definitely Silly String. The problem is now, because of his amazing inflated ego, he thinks I must be gay because I wouldn't give in to his 'charm.'"

"I could see that. Anybody else worth pursuing?"

"I don't know." I sigh. "I've gone out with a lot of guys, but most of them are either really shallow and self-absorbed, like Dustin, or they're boring, or they're hormone-addled idiots who don't see me as anything other than a walking pair of boobs." I've switched the movie back on.

"Hmmm. Maybe you could get a date with the aliens. I bet they have some interesting stories."

We watch the rest of the movie and then decide to go to bed. Dad has not resurfaced, so I take Becca out back and show her the swooshy lab door. "Are you sure we should go in there?" she asks.

"It's just my dad. He's not crazy or anything."

She says nothing. I don't blame her.

"Look. I think he's just . . . uncomfortable . . . because we haven't really had company over since . . ." I let the thought trail off, unable to finish it. Even after time has passed, I can't say the word.

Becca just nods grimly. "I get it. My dad's therapist would say it's something like an avoidance technique." I stare out onto the patio, and I can sense her watching me. Then she smiles, and says, "Then again, maybe he just doesn't like my hair."

I smile and shrug, thankful for the silly comment. "What's not to like?"

Inside the lab, Dad is tinkering with some electronic

components, and I have to admit it does look sort of mad-scientist in there: Something smells sort of burned, and there's a small sheet of some kind of metal on the floor. It has a big black scorch mark on it. "Dad, did you blow something up?"

"Hmm?" He looks up, just noticing us. "Why are you in here?"

"Wanted to say good night. We're going to bed."

"Oh. Well, okay."

Becca has hung back behind me, because I think my dad scares her. He'd scare me too if I didn't know him. He weaves his way through the mess in his lab (and believe me, that idea of creativity being messy is sure true of my dad) and gives me a kiss on the forehead. "Night, sweetie." He turns his attention to Becca. "Good night . . . uh . . . Brenda?"

"Becca." She extends a hand shyly. "Nice to meet you too."

"Right. Becca. I'm bad with names, ask—uh—" he gestures to me, looks confused and says, "What's your name?" He hugs me, smiling.

"Dad—"

"I know, I know. No corny jokes in front of friends. Sorry. Anyway, see you in the morning at some point."

Back we go through the space door, into the house, and to my room. Euphoria blinks to life and turns on the lights for us and Becca jumps, nearly hitting the ceiling. Literally.

"Holy crap! Does that thing just turn on by itself?"

"I'm sensitive to light and humidity," Euphoria says, almost apologetically. "I didn't mean to startle you."

"Does it—sleep in here too?"

"She's not an it," I whisper. "She's very sensitive."

"Would you like your music turned on, miss?" Euphoria's voice barely masks her annoyance. This could be a long night.

"Sure. Classical, please." The strains of Beethoven fill the room and Becca plops down on my bed, looking astounded.

"You have, like, this whole Disneyland life, Shelby," she marvels. "It's like a movie or something."

"You want the right or left side?" I pull down the comforter of stars and moons. She hops in on the left and snuggles up under the covers. "Okay, lights, please." Euphoria dutifully dims the room lights until they are out altogether, leaving only the glow-in-the-dark ceiling stars and my lava light to illuminate us.

"This is a cool room," Becca says as she tucks the quilt up under her chin. "It feels very safe."

I'm lying on my pillow with my hands folded behind my head. "I guess."

"What do you mean, you guess?" She rolls sideways so she can see me.

"It's safe. I just feel sort of isolated a lot of the time. I mean, like you said, my life is not ordinary. I couldn't just bring anybody in here. Most people wouldn't understand. They'd think I was a freak, and that my dad was an even bigger freak. Little Freaks don't fall far from the Big Freak

Tree, and all that. I guess maybe that's why I haven't really invited anybody over for a while. I just didn't want to deal with the questions and the arched eyebrows."

"Haven't you brought your dates home?"

I snort. "Yeah. Can you imagine Dustin Garrett coming into my house? 'Hey, meet my robot, Dustin. Oh, and this is my dad's secret lab, so don't touch anything or you might lose an arm.' I'm sure that would go over real big."

"Yeah, I see your point." She turns over and stares up at the ceiling, arms folded over the top of the sheets like a mummy in a museum. "Why aren't there more people like us?"

"I think there are. I just think they tend to keep to themselves."

"Can you blame them?" Euphoria chimes in snottily. I think she's jealous.

"Nobody asked you," I reply.

3

PRETTY IN PRANKS

(or Shopping for Trouble with a 10-Percent-Off Coupon)

Ever have one of those mornings where you wake up and something is really different but you can't quite remember what it is? Like, maybe you won an award, or got a phone call from this guy you have a crush on. But right at first you just remember that it's something good, and it makes you tingly, and like waking up is somehow worth it.

That's how I feel the day after Becca stays over. That morning, we wake up pretty early, but Dad's already out of the house and gone, so we act like mature teenagers and eat cookies for breakfast.

"They're oatmeal cookies," I point out to Euphoria, who is clucking her disapproval at my substandard dietary habits. "I mean, if I made a bowl of oatmeal, I'd put butter and sugar and stuff on it, so what's the difference?"

Becca dunks her cookie in a big mug of milk, takes a huge

chomp out of it, and then wipes the dribble of milk from her chin. "Do you drink coffee?"

"Of course." Dad didn't even bother to make any before he left, which is typical. I don't think I've seen him eat breakfast for several years, and I'm not sure he even knows how to turn on the coffeemaker, which is weird considering he's like a mechanical genius. The only time he drinks coffee at all is when I make it.

While the brew is brewing, we decide to do a crossword puzzle with all made-up words. It's not as easy as it sounds, because you actually have to make something up that fits what the meaning really is in the crossword, and then make up other words that fit where that word is. Okay, well, it's not as hard as actually doing the puzzle, but when you first wake up, it's plenty challenging.

"Okay, five-letter word for a river in France." Becca has launched into her third cookie and is furiously erasing our previous answer to 6 down, a fourteen-letter word for an actor from Austria. "It can't be the real answer," Becca insists as she smudges out Schwarzenegger's name. "It only works if we totally make it up, but still fits the definition in some way."

"How about Von Trappist? You know, for *The Sound of Music*? That was in Austria."

"Too short. But clever."

We go along like that for a while, but we get bored eventually. "Let's go to the mall," Becca suggests, and I get this weird cold shiver, like she's some alien parading around in a cool person's body and she's just made a huge mistake. How can it be that someone I have begun to think of as my best friend wants to shop? I guess she can tell that I am creeped out by this suggestion, because she drops her cookie. "No—" she stammers. "I didn't mean—I don't want to *shop*, for God's sake." She looks insulted.

"Nothing wrong with shopping," I offer reasonably. Will she take the bait? Is she really an alien in disguise?

"Oh, no. I know what you're doing. You're trying to make me say I like shopping, and I won't do it. I like new clothes, but I detest stores. I buy most of my stuff at Goodwill. No," she sighs heavily. "I only go to the mall for one thing, and one thing only: practical jokes."

"Practical jokes?" This is not where I thought the conversation was going.

"Sure. We go to the mall, and of course that's where everyone else hangs out, so we'll run into people we know. Well, people *you* know. I haven't been here long enough to know anybody except you. Anyway"—she speeds up in her enthusiasm—"anyway, we spot some likely victims, like cheerleaders, and we stalk them and play some really interesting, mind-bending practical joke on them."

"And you've done this?"

She smiles deviously. "Oh yes. Many times."

Hmmm. Now, this to me is interesting. This is a true insight into what Becca is all about, really; depending on her definition of what a practical joke is, she could be a benign and clever prankster or a twisted-genius criminal mind, the

Hannibal Lecter of my high school. Since I don't know her well, it's a bit of a risk to agree to anything, I think. However, since I need Silly String anyhow, I suppose a trip to the mall won't hurt, and if she has anything criminal in mind, I can always fake a felony conviction or something.

Dad is still not back by the time we get cleaned up and ready. Euphoria is not particularly pleased that we're leaving unescorted, and I have to explain to her why it wouldn't do to be seen in front of the other kids with my electronic nanny. Besides, I tell her, people might mistake her for a Bissell and try to get her to do a carpet-cleaning demonstration or something. That changes her mind. She hates caustic cleaning agents.

Since I cannot drive (and I believe this is discriminatory), we have to take the bus to the mall. I hate taking buses anywhere, but the one that goes to the shopping center is particularly gross, especially on weekends. Today, the bus is stuffed like a pepper with the spicy smell of unwashed people mixed with old beer. Yuck.

We find a seat in back, me on the aisle, and Becca begins to outline her prank plan. "Okay. I tried this once, but it didn't work really well—"

"Okay. That inspires a lot of confidence."

"Just wait! So, we find a couple of girls who look really popular but not very smart. We pretend that we're from England—can you do a British accent?"

"Not very well. I sort of sound like Mary Poppins with a bad head cold."

"Okay. Well, maybe we can be French or something. Anyway, we pretend like we're royalty, and we get these two girls to believe us. We have to follow them carefully, then sit down where they sit and then make sure they overhear our conversation."

"Won't they recognize us? From school?"

She snorts. "Are you kidding? We are barely a blip on their radar screen. If you act like what you're saying is the truth, people believe it. So our conversation must be convincing."

"And it will be about?"

"How we're looking for American cheerleader girls to come with us to England to be part of the queen's fiftieth birthday celebration!"

"I think the queen is older than fifty."

"Exactly!" She beams. "Because they're dumb, they won't know that. And why would the queen of England want American cheerleaders?"

"Fashion advice?"

Becca laughs her donkey-honk laugh, and sits back to give me the details of this hideous plot to humiliate popular blond people. "Okay, so I'll be the Duchess of . . . of . . . what's an English-sounding place?"

"England?"

"No, no. Something fancier. What about Barrington?"

"Duchess of Barrington," I try it on my tongue. "Not bad."

The bus lurches around a corner, spilling a raggedy man

in a trench coat into us, and then the vehicle readjusts itself, sending the man back to his spot like the stuff in one of those snow globes that gets shaken and then set down.

"But what about me? My accent stinks."

"Hmmm." Becca squints out the window, concentrating very hard on my possible role in the duping of the divas. "I know. You can be my American agent. Like, my companion or something, somebody who was hired to help me."

"No! Your bodyguard!"

"Yes!" She squeals in delight, which causes half a dozen cranky people to turn around and frown, sneer, or spit in our general direction. "Now you're thinking. A bodyguard. But why would you be so young?"

"I have some weird growth-stunting disease?"

"You don't look ravaged by disease. Not at all."

I frown in thought, which is unfortunate because a really toxic-smelling guy in a Raiders shirt has loped onto the bus and is checking out the seats in front of us. He sees me and decides I'm trying to pick a fight with him. Maybe I *do* look like a bodyguard.

"Hey, girl, you got a problem?" He lurches forward as the bus continues, and he nearly stumbles into my lap.

"No. Not really." I look down into my lap, the position I've adopted for any encounter with any threatening insane person. You meet a surprisingly large number of those in high school, actually, so I've used it a lot.

"She does have a problem, sir," Becca twangs next to me. "She lost her glasses, and she thought you were Brad Pitt, but I don't think you are, because he doesn't like football, and you're wearing that Raiders thing. Otherwise, you do look a lot like him, so I can see how she'd be confused. Sorry 'bout that."

"Oh," he says, sounding confused. I keep squinting, hoping to look really blind to reinforce Becca's story. "Brad Pitt?"

"Yeah. You have the same—uh—cheekbones?" I squeak. "Were you married to Jennifer Aniston?"

He frowns, but unsteadily takes a seat in front of us. Becca tries to contain a giggle that slips out and she passes it off as a violent cough. The Raider guy's eyes appear, bulgy and bloodshot, over the top of the seat.

"Tuberculosis," Becca chokes. "But I think I'm okay. Did I get any on you?"

"What the hell—?" Raider Man is flapping wildly at his greasy hair, trying to get rid of the imaginary TB germs, and then gets up and quickly moves to a seat farther up in front.

I can't help but laugh, so I slump way down in my seat and Becca does the same, so our faces aren't visible. We shake and vibrate with contained laughter. "That was genius," I whisper in an awed voice.

"Yeah," she hisses back. "But we should've gotten his autograph!" We both start laughing out loud, and when the Brad Pitt anti-clone turns around, we both start coughing instead, soul-racking coughs that cause him to pull the stop bell frantically until the driver lets him off.

Finally, we arrive at the mall: a huge concrete monument to stupidity, in my opinion. I mean, it's like a church, sort of; people go there because they have some need they want filled, but the more stuff they buy to fill the need, the more room there is to fill, so it becomes something designed to comfort them and make them feel less alone, like a religion. A religion with corn dogs.

As usual for a weekend, the mall is crammed full of teenagers, everybody from the spike-haired punks to the popular kids to the goths to the druggies. They tend to hang in clumps, and it's pretty much predictable where they'll orbit: punks outside Metal Mayhem or Tower Records, goths outside the Crypt, druggies near the food court. Popular kids, at least the girls, tend to go to the clothing stores. Not the regular ones, like Penney's or Sears, but the cool ones, like Wet Seal or Lady Slipper or Slutwear Unlimited. Okay, I made that last one up. But some of the clothes they buy really look like they belong on a downtown hooker rather than on a kid barely into puberty, in my opinion.

Becca moves slowly to a neutral position: left of the food court carousel, where most of the small kids and their parents tend to go. From this vantage point, we can see the herds of cheerleaders grazing on hot pretzels and smoothies. In her best Crocodile Hunter Australian accent, Becca says, "See how they stick together. We've tracked them all the way to this watering hole, and we're hoping to snare one of them right quick. Crikey."

Two girls, both blondes, separate from the group and choose a seat in the food court with their jumbo-size drinks.

"It's time," Becca whispers, whipping out a pair of sunglasses from her bag. "I know you're new at this, so just follow me."

She ambles over to a table near the girls, and sits, regally, crossing her long legs, peering over the tops of her shades. "I tell you, Sybil, it's simply *exhausting* trying to accomplish this in one weekend." Her British accent is flawless.

I am sort of confused as to what my role here is, except that I'm Sybil. I figure just nodding can't get me in trouble, so I do that. I nod. Vigorously.

Becca goes on. "Regardless, it simply won't do for us to come back empty-handed, Sybil. We absolutely must find someone. The queen won't tolerate failure."

I nod again.

By this time, Becca has been speaking loudly enough for the two blondes to overhear us. I can sense that they are now listening to us because their conversation has stopped in between sips of Razzleberry Blasts. "All in all, my dear, it's simply too difficult to find two cheerleaders who are willing to travel. We were really counting on you, Sybil, to help us find some, since you are so familiar with the high school milieu."

I see one of the girls mouthing the word *mil-yew* with a questioning look on her face. The other girl shrugs.

Becca is arching her eyebrows at me. I do not know what this means. She does it some more, and I begin to wonder if it's some latent form of a nervous tic that only comes out when she's lying. But then I figure it out: She wants me to talk too.

"Ummm. Well—*Duchess*—I think that if we were to approach some young ladies and propose the . . . proposal . . . that perhaps we could find what we're looking for."

"Absolutely!" Becca, aka the Duchess of England or whatever, practically screeches. I cannot believe the girls are buying this, but they seem to be. They are now staring at us without even trying to hide it.

Becca acts as if she has just noticed them. "Now, Sybil, just look at these two young ladies. Perhaps fate is on our side after all. You, girl." She crooks a finger at Blonde #1. "What *is* your name?"

"Brittney." She smiles with perfect white teeth offset by her equally perfect tan. "So are you from England or something?"

"Brittney, how delightful!" Becca sweeps over to their table and scoots up a chair. I follow, feeling absolutely amateur. I figure I'll watch the Master (or, more technically, the Mistress). Clearly, Becca had had a lot of time on her hands when she lived in Los Angeles. "That is an absolutely exquisite name. And your friend?"

"Ashley." Ashley's dark blue eyes are half-closed with cool boredom. "Brit, let's go. This is lame."

"Wait," Brittney hisses loudly under her breath, as if Becca's accent would also impair her ability to hear. She turns to us. "What were you talking about cheerleaders for? We're cheerleaders, you know."

"Are you? I'd never have guessed," Becca gushes. The

girls look confused, trying to decide if they'd been insulted or complimented. "Well, you see, I was sent on a little excursion to find two young ladies to assist us in England at the queen's fiftieth birthday. We've simply been *scouring* the Victoria's Secret stores all over town and haven't found a single cheerleader! Sybil here suggested we look in the Barnes & Noble bookstore, but I told her, no, dear, cheerleaders are much too busy to *read*."

I feel that if I don't actually laugh out loud my head will explode. "Excuse me, Duchess?" I cough to cover it. "I believe I'm having a bit of that tuberculosis we contracted on the . . . uh . . . jet. Will you pardon me?"

Becca squints at me over her sunglasses. "Well, Sybil, certainly. We do have a pressing schedule"—she says it *sheh-jool*—"anyway. Dears, it's been lovely speaking with you. Do give my regards to the rodeo riders and the gunslingers when next you go to Dodge. Long live America! God Save the Queen!"

Becca grabs my arm a little bit too hard and escorts me off away from the food court, leaving Brittney and Ashley to mumble between themselves about whether we're legitimate English people looking for cheerleaders or simply tinfoil-wearing crazy people who left their Reynolds Wrap at home.

As soon as we're far enough away from the food court, we duck into a phone alcove and laugh so hard we slump against the tile wall. "That was so good!" I manage to squeak. "Where did you ever think that up?"

"Oh," Becca giggles, wipes a tear from the corner of her eye. "I used to do that at the Galleria all the time, only I mostly did it by myself. It's so much more fun with somebody else. But you have *got* to work on your poker face!"

We spend the rest of the afternoon at the mall and the highlights go like this: We convince a punk kid with magenta spikes in his hair that the clerk at the medical supply store is a talent scout looking for the next Insane Clown Posse; we do a conga line up the down escalator; and we pose with half-naked mannequins in a casual-wear display at the main door of Macy's. That is the hardest, because we can't laugh and we have to stand still for so long. Some lady who works at the store finally comes up and tells us to leave.

"All this pranking has made me hungry," I say. I have to walk fast to keep up with Becca's long strides. "Wanna stop for some food?"

"What I'd really like is to eat for free." She stops and I almost run into her.

"Yeah. And I'd like to quit school and magically become independently wealthy."

She turns to me and puts her hands on my shoulders. "Shelby, if you never ask, you never receive."

"And if you never commit a crime you don't go to jail. What's your point?"

"I'm not talking about *stealing* food, for God's sake!" She looks offended, and her green eyes are blazing. "Do you think I'd do that?"

"Well, I don't think so, but—"

Becca puts a hand up to silence me, and I get the sense that we've reached our destination. We've made our way to the food court again, and it's busier than ever now that it's lunchtime. It's crawling with kids, like a bunch of ants, wearing the uniform of brand names and perfect orthodontia, perfect all-the-same hairstyles, perfect hang-out attitudes. And they all eat the same stuff: fast-food crap.

"To be honest, I don't eat this stuff." I look with what must be disdain at a couple of boys wolfing down nasty drippy hamburgers and a tub of French fries that could grease all the cars in Paris.

"I know. Vegetarian." She turns to me and frowns quizzically. "Is that, like, a moral thing? Like you don't eat anything with a face?"

"No, not really. I just think meat is gross."

"Did you ever eat it?" She has started to scout out possible targets for our free-food scam, gazing across the horizon like a bird of prey.

"Yeah. Mom used to—we used to eat it a lot. Especially chicken. But now—I don't know, I guess it just seems too mean to eat something that's been part of a family. That sounds totally stupid."

"No. *Be kind to your web-footed friends / For a duck may be somebody's mother . . .*" she sings under her breath to the tune of "Stars and Stripes Forever." If you've never heard that (and I have because my dad is old) it's that song they play every Fourth of July for the fireworks: *Duh-duh duh-da-da duh-da-da*. I didn't think anybody else knew it but me and my weird family. Of course, if anyone else would know it, I guess it would be Becca.

"So, we're looking for free *vegetarian* food," she says deliberately. "Hmm. Okay. There's a soup and salad place over there."

"Yeah. Nobody eats there. It's healthy."

"Perfect. Follow me." Again I see her slip into some other personality like it's a coat she's putting on. She suddenly seems older, and she seems, impossibly, taller, and she walks with great purpose toward Green Machine, the only food place in the mall that doesn't have a deep fryer, but instead has a big flat of wheatgrass perched at the end of the salad bar. For those of you not from California, wheatgrass juice is something that is supposed to be really good for you, but it's basically like mowing your lawn, putting the clippings in a blender, and serving with a bendy straw. The vegetarian places usually have squares of it growing in their restaurants so it's fresh, but it looks seriously like somebody stole a piece of a golf course and you expect Tiger Woods to show up and ask to play through while you wait for your tofu wrap.

She approaches the counter, and I nearly collapse and melt into a puddle. Austin Buckley is talking into a silver cell phone while he leans next to the well-manicured wheatgrass.

Austin Buckley: unapproachable senior at Green Pines, the absolute perfect combination of every element that should exist in a guy. He's about five feet nine and has thick straw-blond hair; a tan complexion with perfect skin; broad, muscular shoulders (he's a swimmer); and the highest IQ of anyone at Green Pines. He aced his SAT, and there was a rumor floating around last year that the testing service hired him to help debug their tests. He speaks two languages (other than English) and is a member of Mensa. He's the only guy I've ever seen who turns me into absolute Jell-O, and I've never even talked to him. I feel myself hunching over to cover my killer boobs. I don't want someone like Austin Buckley thinking I'm using my sex appeal to get his attention.

Becca stands at the counter, looking slightly bored, and I desperately pluck at her sleeve, trying to get her to give up whatever plan she has. Austin sees her, ignores her, and turns his back so he can continue his phone conversation. Becca clears her throat, and he sort of half looks at her, then goes back to what he's saying. "I told him that if we didn't get the next Halo game, I was going to totally run away." Becca rolls her eyes, picks up a baby carrot from the salad bar, and flings it with amazing accuracy at Austin's perfect head. I'm tempted to faint, but that would only draw attention to me, and so I decide to remain conscious.

He turns and she flashes him a big smile. "I'll call you back," he says into the phone, clearly annoyed with the distraction. I can't believe we're interrupting Austin Buckley! Very bored, he says, "WelcometoGreenMachinecanItake-yourorder?"

"Hi." Becca studies the menu board above his head. "I'd

like a large Green Garden salad bar, with the potato salad and the Meatless Meatball soup. And my assistant will have—" she glances over at me, motioning for me to get in the game.

"Uh . . . a Green Giant Jumbo Baked Potato with everything, a salad bar, and a cup of Oodles of Noodles soup. Oh, and an iced tea."

"Two," Becca adds.

Austin, who is working alone, sighs heavily as if we have just asked him to donate a kidney. He punches numbers in the cash register, then practically throws two large, waxy cups at us. "Drinks over there." He flops a finger in the general direction of the beverage station as if all his power has been sucked dry from our taxing order. "Uh. That'll be eighteen fifty-eight." He extends his left hand to take our cash, with the right hand poised over the register to open the drawer. Becca doesn't move.

Finally, when no one dumps cash in his hand, he realizes we are going to be more of a pain than he thought. "Is there a problem?"

"Problem? No." Becca squints behind him, then takes a small spiral-bound notebook from her back jeans pocket. To me she says "Pen, please."

I fumble in my purse for a pen, praying it's not covered with gum or a melted Hershey bar or anything. "Pen," I say, handing it to her like a nurse assisting an eminent surgeon.

She clicks the pen decisively. He had begun to prep our

food, but now slows and pays attention to what Becca's doing. She's writing furiously, eyeballing various things behind the counter, clucking now and again, shaking her head in disapproval.

Now he's a bit nervous. "Uh . . . is there a problem?" he asks again. To distract my mind from the awesome presence of Austin Buckley, I imagine that the Green Machine training manual probably only gives workers something like four phrases that are to fit every occasion: (1) Can I take your order? (2) That'll be such and such amount. (3) Is there a problem? and (4) I've caught a body part in the juicer and need medical assistance.

"Go about your business," Becca says authoritatively. Amazingly, Austin does as he's told, but still eyes her warily. He's prepping my jumbo potato without looking, sprinkling cheese, then chives, then Comet cleanser on it. Becca shakes her head, points to the potato, and purses her lips like a teacher who just caught someone cheating.

"Oh, my God!" Austin's deep, dark, rich voice sort of squeaks, which slightly tarnishes his greatness. He fumbles with the potato like it's on fire, then dumps it in a big gray trash can near the door. "I'm so sorry."

"I don't think she ordered scouring powder with her potato," Becca says sweetly as she turns to me. "Did you?"

I shake my head, simultaneously trying to disappear under the counter. Austin has now turned a bright shade of red, and he's kind of hyperventilating. He's moved on to serving soup from the big steaming pots, but he's shaking and it's spilling out of the ladle, most of it missing the bowl. Becca puts the notebook decisively down on the counter. "Listen, Austin is it?"

His eyes widen. "How did you know my name?"

Becca points to his name tag.

"Oh." He relaxes slightly. "Yeah. Right."

"Austin. I have to tell you some bad news. I'm Marian Dent, with the Green Machine quality-control task force. We randomly check all of our franchises to be sure the Green Machine name means quality everywhere. I'm afraid that you've failed miserably by nearly poisoning my assistant with Comet."

"But—but I—"

"Shh, shh." Becca stops him with her hand, which she places gently over his mouth. "Don't speak."

"But—"

"Shh."

"I just—"

"Shh. Austin. It's all right. We understand, don't we, Isabelle? We've all been there. We've all put Comet in someone's potato. Well, no, we haven't, but the point is, we've all made little mistakes like this. Now, I don't want to see you lose your job, Austin."

Austin goes from bright red to pasty tan (he can't achieve pasty white due to his flawless skin) in seconds.

"In fact, I'll make you a deal. Let's just forget this ever happened. Let's start over. Why don't we just forget about that potato, and you make us something else? We'll just wait over there. You just bring it over when you're ready. No rush."

Austin is falling over himself with gratefulness. "I—thank you. Thank you." He bustles around the kitchen area, all industrious and saved from minimum-wage destruction. Becca waves to him benevolently, and we take a seat at a nearby table.

"Wow." That's all I can say. I cannot imagine anyone cooler than Becca Gallagher. My huge crush on Austin Buckley has magically vanished. And, just for the record, there was no Comet in my new baked potato.

4

TWINKIES AND SYMPATHY

(or Fat Food for Fashionistas)

When you're a vegetarian at a public high school, your food choices are limited. You can have salad or you can eat the jalapeño chilies from the cheese sauce on the nachos. Because of this, lunch is usually not my best meal of the day.

After a month of hanging out together, Becca and I have formed a habit of sitting in the same spot every day for lunch: It's under a tree near the panther sculpture outside the English building. If you aren't familiar with high school etiquette as it applies to lunch, here it is: Everybody has a Place. If you stray from your Place, it throws off the whole balance of the universe, resulting in potential disaster and possible physical violence. If, for example, we stray from our designated tree and decide instead to sit on the stone bench near the big asphalt black circle, several girls in the Kick Your Ass clique will live up to their name and explain, in no uncertain terms, why we should find another place to sit.

Becca and I sit under our tree from noon to twelve-thirty every day, picking at salads or, if we are lucky enough to bring something edible from home, we eat that. One Wednesday in March, Becca says, between bites of egg salad sandwich on bulgur wheat bread, "We need to find others of our kind."

"Huh?"

"We need to find others of our kind," she repeats. "I mean, there's got to be other girls here who aren't like the bench sitters and the cheerleaders. Aren't most of the kids more like us?"

"I kind of doubt it." I am still excavating a salad that has unidentifiable vegetables hiding in the iceberg lettuce. "If they were more like us, I probably would've had friends before you showed up."

"Well, you date."

After the initial lesbian rumor (which died down after a couple of weeks), my dating life returned to pretty much normal, except that if Becca and I wanted to do something, I always picked her over the date. Guys are no substitute for friends; most of the time they can't even talk to you, and either they're afraid to touch you or they're all hands. Sometimes I wonder why I even do it, but then I remember: They smell nice and make my tummy buzz. I can't explain hormones, even if my dad is a scientist.

Becca picks a blade of grass from the lawn and holds it up. "Here's you." She picks another and puts it next to the first blade. "Here's us." She blows on the pieces of grass and they go scattering, blending into the lawn. "Two of us, we can't do much. But if we had more like us, we could do great things."

"Why do you want to do great things? I've been having a lot of fun, just the two of us."

"Sure," she says. "Me too. But don't you think we have a higher calling?"

Hmmm. When Becca starts to talk like this, I feel kind of out of control, to be honest. I've gone along all my school career just keeping to myself pretty much; I always felt, although I didn't consciously know this, that if I just kept to myself and stayed out of the way, I'd get through high school with minimal damage. But lately, she's started talking like this more and more, about how we need a network of people like us to "do great things." To be honest, it kind of scares me.

"Explain to me what you think is our 'higher calling,'" I ask as I stab at my salad. "And maybe while you're at it, you can figure out why the cafeteria only buys wilted lettuce."

"Shelby, our higher calling is to gather all of the weirdos together, to combine our weirdness into a force of nature."

"Hmm. Sounds pretty exciting." I don't sound excited, by the way.

"Look." She leans in so her face is only inches away, and those green eyes, wide with enthusiasm or insanity, drill into mine. "What I'm saying is, if all the geeks got together, what a wonderful world this would be!"

I look away. "Yeah, safety in numbers and all that. But—"

"Safety! Who's talking safety?" She stands up now, spreads her arms wide, and twirls, which causes most of the Bench People to turn and sneer in our direction. "I'm talking *strength* in numbers. I'm talking about being a force for change. I'm talking about uniting all the geeks who right now huddle in their little dark corners afraid of the jocks and the cheerleaders and the preppies. I'm talking about—"

"Could you talk about it sitting down?" I've shaded my eyes from the sun that blazes behind her, illuminating her bleached hair like a halo on a crazy saint. "People are staring."

"Let them stare!" she yells, but she sits down with a flop, like a puppet whose strings have been cut. She sighs and beams at me, and then her face lights up like a Christmas candle. "I've got it!"

"Yeah, I've noticed. Maybe you can get some medication." I'm mostly kidding. I totally love Becca's energy and enthusiasm, but I'll tell you a secret: The whole "notice me" thing is kind of scary. I've always been the kind of geek who doesn't so much care what people think, but I also don't make it a point to irritate them with my uniqueness. In the social order of a high school, there's an unwritten law: Those who are strange find their place and keep their weirdness to themselves, so it does not infect other, more cool people; the cool people keep to themselves so the less cool people don't feel bad or inadequate. They rarely mix, except on occasion when dating, and that has its own set of rules. But over the weeks I've gotten to know Becca, it's become clear to me that her vision of geek isn't necessarily one of hiding her light under a bushel and blending in.

"You don't sound very thrilled with my idea." She cocks her head to one side, waiting for me to answer.

"Well, I don't know how I feel about it. The fact is, most people on this campus don't want to be different. They want to wear the same clothes, eat the same food, listen to the same music as everybody else. If we try and bring all the people together who *are* different, won't that make them all the same?"

She shakes her head in bewilderment. "Huh? You lost me on that twist of logic, Alice."

"Alice?"

"Alice in Wonderland. She never fit in, never knew what people expected of her. Until she stood up for herself, she got kicked around, got smaller, got taller, and nearly got her head chopped off."

"That's because she kept making a big deal about things. She kept complaining and trying to change stuff, and that's why she got in trouble."

"Oh, so if she'd just done what the Mad Hatter said, she'd have been fine?"

"Why are we arguing about Alice in Wonderland?"

"We're not. We're arguing about the Red Queen." The lunch bell rings, and I feel less full than when we started eating. There's a hollow place in my stomach, and I'm worried that Becca has decided to ditch me in favor of some braver geek. Of course, I don't say this to her.

She cleans up her lunch stuff, grabs her backpack, and gives me an unexpected hug. "Listen, Shelby, whatever we do, we'll be friends. Don't worry about that. But," she says with a twinkle in her eye, "think about the Red Queen. What does she want most from Alice?"

"I don't know," I moan hopelessly. "This feels disgustingly like English class."

"Think about it. I'll see you after school?" She's already flying away, tromping over the green grass in her hightop sneakers, shedding unseen waves of weirdness after her.

"Where should we meet?" I call after her.

"Library," I hear faintly over the roar of the hordes going off to class for fifth period.

Our library is unlike most other school libraries. One difference is that we have a two-sided fireplace; the other is that the people who go there don't usually go to read. Okay, well, maybe all the school libraries are like that last one, but I know they don't have fireplaces.

It's more of a social hub after school than at any other time. Kids go there to work on reports and to wait for rides, but you also see a ton of them on cell phones, or text-messaging people, or even making out in the reference room. One time when I was working on a report about

STDs, I found an unused condom in one of the reference books, which meant that either the publisher was pretty progressive or the person reading the book before me hadn't read closely enough.

Becca is sitting at a table near the window, with a bunch of magazines spread out in front of her. "Hey," she says. "Sit."

"What are you working on?"

"My plan for global domination," she answers casually. I wait for her to say she's kidding.

"Okay. Really, what are you working on?"

"Here." She shoves a *Cosmo Girl* magazine in front of me. "Look at the ads."

I thumb through the glossy pages, seeing photo after photo of waifish supermodels who look like they just got off a bad heroin binge. "Yeah. And?"

"This is the way we find Our People." She grabs the *Cosmo Girl* from me and opens it to a particularly icky ad for bras where the model looks like a rack of baby back ribs with a side of silk. "We need to start a campaign."

"For what?"

"Just hear me out. I know you aren't exactly the activist type—"

"Hey! I *am* a vegetarian!" I remind her.

"Okay, you're not an activist except for when it comes to cows. But here's how we find others like us. We start a campaign that will unite all the girl geeks, bring them out of hiding, as it were."

"What does this have to do with fashion models?"

"Okay, here it is," she says in hushed, reverent tones. "Campaign for Calories."

"And . . . ?"

"Oh, Shelby! C'mon! Do I have to spell it out?"

"I guess so, because I have no idea what you're talking about, Becca!"

She hangs her head in discouragement. "All right. We introduce a movement called Campaign for Calories. We collect really fattening food to send to supermodels to help them get fatter."

"They don't want to get fatter. That's the point."

"I know that!" she practically yells at me. "It's not really about the Campaign for Calories! It's about finding people who think like we do!"

"So, by collecting gross snack food, we will be able to find others who don't fit in, and then we can form a group, and then they can fit in with us?"

"Precisely."

"And what happens to all the Twinkies?" I think this is an important point, because everyone who has read anything about nutrition knows that Twinkies could be the one food that will survive a nuclear blast. No one should eat them. Not even fashion models.

"Who cares!" Becca's green eyes shine maniacally. "By that point, we've found our girls. We've found Our People!"

"And then what?"

"Exactly." She scoops up the fashion magazines triumphantly. "Our first step is to find a place to meet."

"How about the benches in front of the telecom building? I don't think those are usually taken." Remember the bench etiquette thing: Only empty benches can be used for activities that are not usually scheduled.

"Yeah. That'll work. You put in a bulletin announcement for a meeting next week at lunch. Wednesday's a good day."

"Oh, but I have to have some kind of club name to give it if we want it in the bulletin. They won't just let random students put things in there. So, is it the Campaign for Calories Club?"

"Remember Alice in Wonderland? How about something from that?" We both ponder and reject all the various possibilities from the book: Jabberwocky Club (easily confused for linguistics), the Walrus and the Carpenter Club (but that sounds too much like something the Christian Club would do, or a Beatles fan club), Cheshire Cat Club (could be mistaken for an orthodontia support group) and Mad Hatters (a bunch of angry people wearing baseball caps).

"How about the Queen?" I finally ask. "Remember, you were talking about the Red Queen at lunch?"

Becca smacks herself on the forehead. "Duh! Of course I was. I wanted to tell you that the Queen is the one who is crazy, but she's in charge. Alice is the only sane one, but she stands out because she's not like all the others, and the Queen tries to have her killed. So, I think it should be something to do with queens."

"Okay," I say slowly. "What about Queen Bees?"

"No. Sounds like a quilting club." Becca squints in concentration.

"Speed Queens?"

"We'd get suspended for using drug terminology. It would probably attract the wrong crowd too."

"Queen Geeks?"

The name resonates with both of us, like a bolt of lightning electrifying the otherwise drab library. I am surprised the *Cosmo Girl* doesn't catch fire. "Queen Geeks!" Becca says the name quietly at first, then it keeps getting louder each time she repeats it. "Queen Geeks. Queen Geeks! QUEEN GEEKS!"

The librarian is frowning in our general direction, trying to decide if we're dangerous or simply teenagers. She apparently decides we're benign, because she turns her back after shooting us one purse-lipped look of disapproval.

Becca extends her hand. "Congratulations. You've just witnessed the birth of greatness."

"Okay." I shake her hand and wait for her to stop pumping my fist. "Queen Geeks, huh? And I'm supposed to write what in the announcements?"

"Wait." She rips out a piece of loose-leaf paper and scrawls across it hastily. She hands me the paper, and it reads: *ATTENTION ALL FEMALES: Are you tired of clothes that don't fit, friends who don't care, and boys who don't get it? Are you tired of stick-thin fashion models and magazines that say you must look exactly like them?*

Then come to the first meeting of the Queen Geek Social Club and join our cause, Campaign for Calories, designed to fatten up those skinny models and put the fun back in fashion! Wednesday lunch, in front of the telecom building."

"Okay," I tell her. "I'll submit it. I don't know what will happen, but I'll give it a try."

"That's great." Becca puts an arm around my shoulder. "This is going to be the best spring ever."

At home that afternoon, I find Dad actually sitting on our porch, reading the newspaper like a normal human being. I half expect him to be smoking a pipe with a golden retriever at his feet. Or, perhaps, smoking a golden retriever and stepping on the pipe. "Hey, Shelby." He waves as I dash up the steps. "How was school?"

"Oh, kind of weird." I sit on the old green swing, my favorite thing on the whole porch. It creaks, like it always does. "Becca wants us to start a club."

"Hmm. What kind? Chess or something?"

"I don't even play chess anymore, Daddy."

"Yeah. You're too busy. So, what's the club?"

I tell him the whole story, complete with my fear of Twinkie accumulation, and he nods and smiles the whole time. "Queen Geek Social Club, huh? Well, it sounds like it could be fun. Why don't you want to do it?"

"I don't know, to tell you the truth." I keep swinging, trying not to let my feet hit the white banister that lines the outside like a row of soldiers guarding our house. "I don't know."

"Don't you?" He folds the paper up and drops it to the floor.

"What? You think I do know? And why, by the way, are you just sitting out here? Why aren't you out back?"

"I finished the project and I'm taking some time off." He sighs and stretches, puts his hands behind his head. "I need to relax a little."

"Well, I've been saying that for months. Not that you listen to me."

"So, back to the club. What are you afraid of?"

"Afraid? I'm not afraid!" But even as I say it, I realize that I am. "I'm hungry. I think I'll go in and get something to eat. You want anything?"

"Nope, I'm fine." He picks up the paper again, and sighs contentedly. "If you figure out what you're afraid of, that's half the battle, you know."

"Thanks, Obi-Wan." I lean over and kiss him on the forehead. "I'll remember that."

Euphoria is in the kitchen chopping tomatoes for spaghetti sauce. "Hey, Shelby," she buzzes. "How was your day?"

"Oh, I don't want to talk about it. Do we have any chocolate?"

"Supper's gonna be ready in about half an hour, so don't be fillin' up on sweets." She has turned on the stove and is throwing onions and mushrooms into a big skillet. "Super Spaghetti tonight. Is Becca coming over for dinner?"

"No," I say sort of defensively. "She doesn't live here, you know."

"Sorry, Miss Uptight. No need to get your widgets in a knot."

I grab a few chocolate cookies from a jar on the counter in defiance of Euphoria's command. "Ha!" I mutter as I savagely bite into one and head to my room.

"Why does everything have to be so complicated?" I say to no one in particular as I flop down on my bed. Staring at the ceiling is one of the best ways I've found of clearing one's mind. It also allows you to give the appearance of deep thought without the commitment of actually doing it. But even though I try to think of stupid, unimportant things like Twinkies, that thought brings me back to Becca, and to what my dad said about me being afraid. What does *that* mean?

Okay, so here's the reason I don't want to have some dumb club. If Becca and I find "others of our kind" then that would mean that we're not best friends anymore, right? Maybe that's what I'm afraid of. Or maybe what she said about the Red Queen is true: Maybe I don't really want to be Alice, standing out from everyone else because I'm different. This is a shocking thought to me, really, because I've always been someone who didn't mind being different. Maybe there's a difference between being different and pointing it out to everyone, though.

Thursday morning, I put in the bulletin notice with minimal argument, although the receptionist does quiz me quite a bit about the club, asking me if it's "official" and if we have a staff sponsor, and could I spell my name, please. I give her Ms. Napoli's name as our faculty person, which could be a potential problem since she doesn't know anything about it, but I'm a risk taker. So, the next day while I'm listening to announcements in Mrs. Pettinger's third period algebra, I hear the thing that Becca wrote and I turned in, apparently read by someone with dyslexia and cataracts, and a cold chill goes up my spine. "ATTENTION ALL FEMALES: Are you tired of clothes that fit, friends who don't care about boys who can't get it? Are you tired of sticking fashion models and magazines and looking like them? Then come to the first meeting of the Queen Geeks and joint claws, Campaign for Calories, designed to flatten up those skinny models and put the bun fack in fashion! Wednesday lunch, in front of the telecom building."

I sink into my desk, trying very hard to disappear. The only good thing about this is that no one knows who put the bulletin announcement in, I guess, so—

"See Shelby Chapelle for additional details." Somehow, the dyslexic near-blind announcement reader got *that* part right.

All eyes in the class turn to me. Mrs. Pettinger arches her eyebrows and motions toward me with a very dramatic wave. "So, Shelby. What's that all about?"

"Uh," is all I manage to say. The class sort of giggles, especially the pretty girls. Pretty girls can be mean. I will not be Red Queened by the pretty girls. I sit up straight and clear my throat. "It's a new club, Queen Geeks, and it's for girls who want to do something besides shop, talk about boys, and worry about hair extensions."

"Well, that describes me," says Spencer, the class clown. "Can't I join, even if I'm not a girl?"

"You're still a queen," somebody in the back of the room says loud enough to be heard but not loud enough to be identified.

"Well, it sounds pretty interesting," Mrs. Pettinger says. "Now, let's talk about probabilities."

Unfortunately, the only probability I become aware of all day is the one where, as unlikely as it seems, someone in every one of my classes has heard the stupid announcement. What are the odds of that? I'm sure if I'd been able to concentrate in math class, I might know the answer, but I was too busy trying to will the earth to swallow me whole. That doesn't work, by the way.

The lunch bell finally rings. Becca is already under our tree devouring another egg salad sandwich and a huge jug of iced tea. "Hey," she says through a mouthful of bread. "Did you hear our announcement?"

"Oh yes. And I kept hearing about it all morning." I flop down onto the ground, dejected.

"What? All publicity is good publicity! It's great that people are talking about it. It's creating buzz." She tosses a banana to me. "Eat something."

"Becca, maybe this isn't such a great idea. I mean, what if

a bunch of people show up and they just want to be disruptive and stupid, and—"

She puts her hand up in front her to stop me from speaking. "Wait, wait. Go back. Let's try that once more from the top, without the negativity."

"Is that what Buddhists do? Just make everything okay, no matter what?" I angrily peel the innocent banana.

"Yeah, pretty much. But look, this could really turn into something great. The meeting's next week, so we should figure out what we want to do."

"It's your idea. What do you want to do?"

"I told you. Campaign for Calories first. World domination later. Then maybe a nice pool party."

This is the first time I've had this thought: I sort of miss the old days before Becca, when my world revolved around school, dating, and my dad. It was a small world, after all, but I knew what was going on. I never felt out of control like I do now. As I watch Becca chow down on the rest of her sandwich, I wonder if I've made a huge mistake befriending a giant with a dragon tattoo.

The week ends, the weekend ends, and since Becca's driven up to L.A. to help her mom with some "movie work" (she won't specify what), I'm on my own except for a Saturday night date with Spencer, the class clown I mentioned from math class. We decide to see a movie, and when he tells me he has tickets to a kung fu marathon at the old Ken Theatre, I nearly decide to kill myself with popcorn and Jujubes. It would take too long, though, so I figure I'll just sit through the karate movies and think. Spencer is so into watching the feet and fists fly that he doesn't even notice when my answer to every question is "Absolutely, Oprah."

As I munch on my second Godzilla-sized tub of real popcorn in real butter (with real artery-clogging cholesterol for no extra charge!) and watch the flickering giants of martial arts, I realize how nervous I am about Wednesday's meeting. Why? At worst, it'll just be a bunch of strange kids getting together to hang out at lunch, right? At best, we might actually come up with something cool to do, and I might meet some other interesting people from my school. So why the anxiety? I can't figure it out so I go to the bathroom.

As I'm reapplying lipstick in the silvery old mirror, Jasmine Jesperson comes into the bathroom. Jasmine is probably the prettiest senior girl on campus, and why she would be at a kung fu movie marathon is a bit of a mystery, but stranger things have happened, I suppose. She stops next to me and takes a brush from her purse, and then runs it through her long golden hair. "Hey," she says, glancing over at me in the mirror. "Aren't you Shelby Chapelle?"

"Guilty."

"Are you the one starting that geek thing?" She turns toward me, gesturing with the hairbrush. "I heard the announcement, and I was like, what's the deal? Why are you bagging on models?" Her brown eyes drill into me maliciously.

"We weren't trying to offend any models—"

"Oh, really. By saying we're all skinny and we need to eat or something? I think that's kind of insulting, like we don't know how to do it and you're going to help us. That's insulting. I'm perfectly capable of eating by myself. I don't need help."

"Of course you don't," I say as sympathetically as I can. The white thought bubble above my head reads *PLEASE GET OUT OF THE GENE POOL!* "So, Jasmine, nice to see you. Good luck with that eating thing."

I walk out of the bathroom, leaving Jasmine in a cloud of confusion and vanilla body spray. Maybe the Queen Geeks thing isn't such a bad idea after all.

5

QUEEN GEEK SOCIAL CLUB

(or Chocolate Should Be Its Own Food Group)

Becca comes over on Tuesday night, the eve of the Queen Geeks, and we strategize for our meeting over a plate of fudge pecan brownies. I do my best thinking when chocolate is involved.

"Okay. So, the first thing is, we need to get e-mail and cell phone info on everybody. Can you be in charge of that?" She hands me a bright periwinkle-purple clipboard with neatly printed sheets of paper attached.

"Wow. You're organized." I flip through the pages. "Are you expecting hundreds?"

"It just looks better if we have papers." Then she hands me another paper, a flier she's created. "What do you think of that?"

The flier is well done; Becca knows her computer graphics. It has a picture of a '50s-type housewife on it with an expression of utter horror; she's wearing a crown. Next to her is a pile of fashion magazines that comes up to her waist, and she's holding one open to a page with an ad from the current *Seventeen* magazine, the one with movie star–pop slut Dallas Benton and her teeny-tiny boy body wrapped in what they call "boy shorts" and a teeny-tiny bandeau bra that barely covers anything because she has no breasts to speak of. Her ribs stick out, she arches her back as if she's having a chiropractic adjustment, and the look on her face is either *Please do me* or *I shouldn't have had the bean burrito for lunch*. In big purple letters, it says *STOP THE MADNESS! LET'S GET THIS GIRL SOME TWINKIES!* Below that, it says *Queen Geek Social Club. Every Wednesday at lunch, telecom benches. Be there, be square, and let's feed those supermodels with our Campaign for Calories!*

"This is awesome." I pin the flier to my wall, right next to the big photo of Johnny Depp (from his *Chocolat* period, not the time between *Pirates of the Caribbean* and that creepy *Secret Window* movie where he wears unwashed clothes and weird glasses). From across the room, the flier is eye-catching. "Once we put these up on campus, people will be going nuts!"

"So, you like it?" Becca grabs another brownie from the plate and takes a huge chunk out of it. "I think it's pretty cool."

"Definitely. Now, once we get people to the meeting, what do we do?" Brownies are calling to me, so I eat another. Never argue with baked goods.

"I figure we won't have a ton of people tomorrow, since the fliers aren't up. All they have to go on is the announcement, which probably confused people."

"Yeah. I submitted it and even *I* didn't know what it was about. It's too bad they don't teach kids how to read in school anymore." I take the flier off the wall and give it back to Becca. "So, you gonna copy these? I think lavender paper, if you're going to Kinko's."

"Could your dad take us tonight? I'd love to pass these out tomorrow to the girls who do show up."

I shrug. "Supposedly he's relaxing, so I guess that would be okay. Let's see if we can find him."

We go through the house looking for Dad, but instead we find Euphoria scrubbing the sink with a long-handled scrubber brush. "Hey, have you seen Dad?"

She snorts, which for her sounds a little like a garbage disposal trying to eat a metal spoon. "Last I saw of your father, he was on the back patio 'relaxing.' If you ask me, he's just bein' lazy. Expectin' me to scrub the sink. I rust, for goodness' sake. That man ain't gonna rust if he picks up a scrub brush, ya know. It'd probably take his mind off things."

Euphoria is still grumbling as we head for the patio. The glowing red light from the fire pit throws patterns against the latticework, and I see Dad in silhouette, sitting absolutely still, something I rarely see him do, but now I've seen two days in a row. "Daddy?"

"Right here."

We pick our way over flagstones, brushing jasmine flowers as we pass the fence. "I love that smell," Becca murmurs.

"Dad, could you drive us to Kinko's?"

Shifting in his chair, Dad reaches over and grabs a stick, pokes at the fire pit, and doesn't answer.

"Dad?"

"Hmm?"

"Could you drive us to Kinko's?"

"Oh. Sure." He stretches, sighs, and puts some sand on the fire to put it out. "Let me just get my keys."

He seems old at that moment, and he slowly walks toward the house. "Is something wrong with him?" Becca whispers.

"I don't know."

In the Volvo, Dad plays some really weepy old music and doesn't say anything, which is totally unlike him. Becca and I sit in the backseat and chatter the whole way, and he doesn't even try to interject comments like he usually does. We get into the copy place, get the lavender paper, and Dad just sort of trails along like a bewildered puppy.

"Dad. Check it out. Look what Becca made!"

"Well," she interrupts hastily, "we made it together."

He takes the flier and examines it, frowning. "Hmm. Funny," he says and gives it back.

"O-kay." I feel his forehead. "You feeling all right?"

Waving my hand away, he says "Fine, fine."

Becca and I find an empty copy machine, load the lavender paper, and begin copying our masterpiece. "What is with your dad?" she asks. He's leaning against the counter, looking at greeting cards, but not really reading them. In fact, the one in his hands is upside down.

"Honestly, I have no idea. Maybe it's male menopause or something."

"Yuck."

The Xerox machine is spitting out lavender papers and I must admit they look fantastic! "I cannot wait to put these up at school," I tell Becca. She gives me a wide-eyed, crazy nod, and after we print a hundred, we stop.

"Okay, Dad. Ready. Can you pay for them? Please?" I sidle up to him and give him the puppy-dog eyes that always work when I want something.

"Hmm." He pulls his wallet out of his back pocket, takes the papers to the clerk, and gives her the cash without saying anything to me.

"Whoa. Did you get a bad report card, or barbecue your dog or something?" Becca frowns as Dad gets his change from the clerk.

"I don't have a dog. And I usually get straight As, so I don't think that's it." Dad walks right by us and out the door, and says nothing. We just follow him, exchanging puzzled glances. Parents. They are so moody.

When we get home, Dad gets out of the car and barely acknowledges that we're in the backseat at all. He's clutching my lavender posters against his chest. "Umm. Dad? Can we have the fliers?"

"What? Oh." He realizes he's got them, and chuckles a little. "Here you go. Sorry about that. I'm not with it tonight."

"Is something wrong?"

Becca, who's always nervous around my dad anyway, bolts like she got hit with a jolt of lightning. "Gotta use your bathroom!" she shouts as she scurries toward the front door.

Dad says nothing. He looks up at the stars, sighs, and puts an arm around my shoulder. "Sorry, Beebee."

He hasn't called me Beebee for a very long time. I barely remember it at all, but once he says it, I get this rush of heat and sadness rolling through my middle like a tidal wave. I start crying, and I don't even know why. "Sorry, Dad," I mumble, wiping away a couple of tears dampening my face. "I don't even know why I'm crying. Isn't that weird? Must be hormones or something."

"Night. Love you." He hugs me, then goes into the house, leaving me looking up at the stars with wet cheeks.

In my room, Becca is organizing our materials for tomorrow. She's chirpier than usual, probably because of my dad's weird state. "So, we have our posters, we have our clipboard. Now we just have to figure out the plan of action for Campaign for Calories. Should we designate certain types of food to collect, or specific foods, like Twinkies?"

I'm happy to forget the thing with my dad and to just sink into the excitement of the Queen Geeks. "What are we going to do with all this crap once we get it? Are you seriously going to send it to some supermodel agency?"

"Of course. That's the point. But it's only the beginning." Eyes shining, Becca grabs my wrists and guides me to the floor, where we both sit cross-legged. "We get the food, we identify some agency to send it to. We send it. But here's where things start to work: We advertise what we're doing, we let people know, like newspapers and television stations."

"Why do we do that?"

"It's all about public relations. If we want to be accepted, I mean really accepted, which means envied, then we have to get people to notice."

"Envied?" I shake my head. "No. I don't care about being envied."

"Please. What about Jasmine what's-her-name in the bathroom at the movies? You don't want her to envy you? Just a little?"

"No. I don't care what she thinks. *If* she thinks." To be honest, though, that's not quite true. In the back of my mind, way back between the insecurities and the phobias and the memorized Trivial Pursuit answers, there is a tiny part of me that would love for Jasmine Jesperson to envy me, just a little. But I cannot admit it to anyone, even to Becca, because then—well, there must be some reason I can't admit it, but I can't think of it at the moment.

"So. Food. General snack or specific?" Becca has clicked a pen and is poised to write in her notebook, which is color-coordinated to the periwinkle clipboard.

"I say specific. Much easier, and more control of product." Becca scribbles furiously. "I am in favor of Twinkies, pork rinds, Ding Dongs, and Scooter Pies."

"Do they still make Scooter Pies?"

"Don't know. I just like to say it. Scooter Pie."

"Scooter Pie. Scooter Pie!" We both start yelling "Scooter Pie" as loud as we can. This is probably an indication that it's time to go to sleep. Instead, Euphoria rolls into my room, tsking and whirring her disapproval.

"Miss Shelby, I believe it is time for you to be catchin' your forty winks, and time for Miz Becca to head on home."

"Becca's sleeping over, right, Becca?" I give her the conspiratorial look to communicate that she should act like the plan is already a given.

"Oh. Sure. I'm sleeping over." She pantomimes that she needs to call her house.

"I ain't blind. I can see what you're doing." Euphoria sighs (which sounds sort of like letting the air out of a compressor). "Just call your mama right now so she don't worry. It's time for bed, though, so I don't want you two hens stayin' up all night squawkin' about whatever you're doing. Is this a school project you're working on?"

"You could say that." I nod. Becca picks up my phone and keys in her number. Euphoria sighs again and rolls back into the hallway.

"Hey, Euphoria," I call after her.

"Hmm?"

"What's up with Dad tonight? He was really weird." I follow her down the hall toward the kitchen, which is scrubbed clean and lit by just a tiny light over the stove.

"Don't you remember?" she asks softly.

"Remember what?"

"What day this is?" Her green lights blink judgmentally, I think.

I try and remember what it might be. Father's Day? Dad's birthday? Guy Fawkes Day? I have no idea. "I give up. Is it some new national holiday?"

She rolls away from me. "Not exactly. It's the anniversary of your mother's passing."

Becca can't figure out why I am crying, and I can't tell her. Her mother says she can't stay, and it's ten o'clock, so she's driving over in her purple Jeep to get her, and I wish I were dead.

"Sweetie, can't you tell me what it is?" She has her arm around me as I'm sobbing on my bedroom floor.

"I can't. I can't." We're sort of rocking like a mama and baby, and that makes me cry even more. How could I forget something like that? I must be the most self-centered, spoiled, stupid, forgetful person on the earth! Who forgets the day their mother died? Nobody. Not even Hitler, I bet. I mean, that makes me worse than Hitler, and he was like, the devil. Which makes me what? Devil spit?

I hear the Jeep's nasal honk outside. I am suddenly really angry at Becca's mom for being alive. I've never even met her, and she doesn't seem to care at all what Becca does, which seems really unfair since my mom cared a lot and she's not here. "I want . . . to . . . meet . . . your mom," I stutter in between sobs.

"Uh, I don't think that's a great idea." Becca kisses my forehead and springs up from the floor. Standing above me, she looks even taller than usual, like Alice after the *EAT ME* cake. "She's really cranky when it's late. I'll see you tomorrow. Do you want to postpone our meeting?"

"No, no." I wipe the tears from my red eyes. "I'll probably look like a lobster instead of a geek, but we should go ahead. I'll be okay tomorrow."

"Okay. Well." Awkwardly, she grabs her stuff and opens my bedroom door. Her mom honks again, and her Jeep sounds pissed off, if that's possible. "See you tomorrow. Lunch. Don't forget the fliers. Should I take them?"

"Yeah, that would be better." I stand up and hand her the stack of lavender paper. "Sorry. I'll be okay. Don't worry."

She nods, smiles sort of halfheartedly and bolts for the door. I get my flannel pajamas on, crawl into bed without washing my face or brushing my teeth, and leave the door open for Euphoria to come in. As I start to drift off, I hear her mechanical wheels whirring on the carpet, and hear her roll into my room humming some old lullaby that makes me feel better and worse all at the same time.

* * *

When I wake up the next day, I have a splitting headache and I immediately feel that I'm being punished for something awful. So I do what I always do when something is unpleasant: I pretend it does not exist. To accomplish this, I get dressed and leave the house without eating or saying good-bye.

That morning at school is torturous; Becca and I have to sit through first period English and yet more disgusting decay in *Lord of the Flies*, all on an empty stomach; then I go on to other equally uninteresting subject matter just waiting for lunch to happen so we can have our meeting. Finally, the bell rings, and I dash out of fourth period Life Management (where I endured Mrs. Johnston's laughable comparison between premarital sex and an undercooked Thanksgiving turkey—and in order not to ruin future holidays for you, I won't go into the details of how stuffing and cranberry sauce factor into this disgusting analogy). Becca is already at the telecom benches, and she's setting up her periwinkle clipboard and she's taped the fliers all around the benches so there are multiple images of the mad housewife in lavender. I am very disturbed to see that she has also changed out of her jeans and is wearing a lavender dress with a matching apron, pearls, and heels. Even her little hair spikes match.

"Are you excited?" she whispers as I set my books down. "I hope we get a lot of people."

"Don't expect too much." I scan the grassy commons area for potential Queen Geeks. "Nobody at this school wants to stand out. They all want to be just like everybody else. Which is totally hilarious because they all think they're totally original. Speaking of, did June Cleaver drop acid and throw up on you or what?"

"Wow. Somebody got a visit from the negative fairy." She continues to flit around the papers as the army of lavender housewives flutters in the breeze. "Let's be optimistic."

"Hi. Is this where the meeting is?" a dark-haired girl with braces asks timidly.

"Queen Geeks? Yes! Take a flyer and put your name on the clipboard." Becca practically swallows the girl. "What's your name?"

"Elisa Crunch." She waits, I guess for somebody to tease her. "Okay. So, no jokes about the name. I've already heard all of them."

Two more girls walk up to the table, chatting happily to each other. Eventually, we have a total of six, in addition to Becca and me, and other kids nearby glance over, curious, but then go back to eating their lunches.

"Okay, well, let's get started." Becca's violet apron flutters in the breeze as she absently smoothes her blond-violet spikes. "Welcome to the first meeting of the Queen Geek Social Club. I'm Becca Gallagher, and this is our co-founder, Shelby Chapelle." She motions graciously to me and I smile, sort of. "If you could all look at the mission statement . . ."

Huh? Mission statement? I don't remember doing a

mission statement . . . but looking down, I see it on a white piece of paper, the mission statement of the Queen Geek Social Club:

To gather and empower all the Queen Geeks
in the immediate area
To accomplish tasks that only Queen Geeks can
(and want to) do
To recruit new young Queen Geeks
To take back the rightful leadership role of the geek
in high school society
Pranks, bowling, and other social causes

"Let's introduce ourselves quickly, and then tell why we're here. I'll go first. Becca, freshman, and I'm here because I'm tired of feeling like the only person on campus who's like me." She beams at the other girls, who nod knowingly. "Let's go right. Elisa, wasn't it?"

Elisa Crunch recounts her unfortunate name and the fact that she wants a community of people who won't look at her as simply an opportunity to compare her to a candy bar.

A girl with long black hair that hangs in her face speaks next. "Amber Fellerman, sophomore. I'm here because I write poetry and everyone thinks I'm weird."

Two tall, rangy black girls with cornrowed hair look awkwardly at each other, then the taller one says, "I'm Claudette and this is my sister, Caroline, both sophomores. We're here because the announcement was funny."

A very tiny girl with thick glasses who barely speaks above a whisper says, "Cheryl Abbott, freshman." She pushes her glasses up on her nose nervously and looks around. "I got kicked out of Chess Club because I beat everybody else."

The last person was a girl I would never have guessed would be interested in anything labeled "geek." She is athletic, tanned, and blond, and has perfect teeth. I can't understand why she's here until she says, "I'm Samantha Singer, senior. I thought it said Queen *Greeks*, and that it was, like, a group talking about sororities or something. Sorry. Do you want me to leave?"

"You can stay if you want," Becca offers. "Okay, and this is Shelby Chapelle. Why are you here, Shelby?"

Many answers compete in my head and fight to get past my lips. *I'm here because I'm really an undercover cool person trying to bust you all for excessive lameness!* Or *Becca is paying me to be her friend.* Or *My dad said that if I didn't join a club he'd sign me up for tango lessons.* Instead, what comes out is, "It's Becca's idea. I'm just helping."

She looks at me sort of shocked, but it doesn't rock her pearls-and-heels composure.

"Now. Our first task, as you know, is the Campaign for Calories. I'd like Shelby to fill you in on just how this campaign will run."

"Oh, you go ahead, Becca. I'm sure you know all the details." I sound much more mean than I intend. But it sort of feels good.

Again, she flinches slightly as if I've slapped her, but she doesn't lose her cool. She only has about twenty minutes left to hook these girls, so she has to make it count. "Okay, Campaign for Calories. We want to start a movement where we collect specific snack foods and then send them to a modeling agency famous for its starving, anorexic-looking meat puppets."

"Meat puppets?" Samantha asks, surprised. "Is that some demeaning term for women? I think that's offensive."

"No, it's a term for fashion models," Becca answers.

"Oh, then I guess that's okay." Samantha smiles. "Go on."

Becca continues. "Okay. Anyway, Shelby and I have narrowed the focus of our foods to those on this list." She hands out a half-sheet of paper with the items in bold. "And we have a two-week window in which to collect them. In the meantime, we'll do some research about the absolutely most offensive modeling agency, and get their address so we know where to send the stuff we collect. I'll also be asking you to put up fliers in your classrooms and to make announcements to your classes personally about this."

Mousy Cheryl Abbott raises her hand and Becca points to her. "We have to get up in front of people and talk?" She sounds terrified.

"Well, that's the idea. Of course, if you're not comfortable with that—"

"I get a really bad rash," Cheryl says, her voice quavering.

There is murmuring among the other girls, which Becca, a slight glimmer of panic in her eyes, tries to squelch with a perky, "Okay, ladies. Hang on." They all stop and look at her, anticipating. "Listen. I know that most of you don't like the spotlight, right?" They all nod. "You don't have to be in the spotlight. That's why I'm here. I'll be the face of the Queen Geeks, you just do the work that makes it happen. I'll be doing an announcement on Panther TV to let people know about our campaign, but you'll do the actual collecting. And remember—we're in this to show everybody that it's Chic to be Geek!"

"Sheik? Like in Arab?" Samantha Singer pipes up. She just sits there, fascinated, with the look of intense concentration on her face that kids have when they get their first ant farm.

"No," Elisa Crunch snaps. "*Chic, c-h-i-c*, it's French for 'in style.' Don't your people read?"

"No," Samantha snaps back. "You guys are weird." She jumps up from the bench and wiggles off into the thick of the lunchtime crowd.

"Okay, so are you all in or not?"

Everybody kind of nods, confused, and Becca passes around the clipboard and pen, then reaches into her carpet-bag and passes out Twinkies to everyone. Elisa pulls an electronic organizer out of her backpack and waves the stylus at Becca. "Okay. So, if I'm going to be committed to this cause, I'll need to know schedules." She furiously taps on the surface of the device. "Meeting times? Dates? Locations? Events?"

"Uh." Becca stalls in the face of such organization. "We're sort of working out all the details, Elisa. But by next week, we'll know more."

"So, I should just schedule you in for lunch on Wednesday? Location to be announced." She nods and taps with passionate efficiency. "Excellent. I'll see you then."

The lunch bell rings a few minutes later, and all the fledgling Queen Geeks take their Twinkies and disperse, leaving me and Becca alone. "So, how do you think it went?" she asks.

"Great." I scoop up my books and pointedly put my Twinkie back in the box.

"That's it? Great?" She puts a hand on my shoulder, and I shrug it off. "Why are you mad?"

"Well, it just sort of seems like this is all your idea. Like I don't have much to do with it."

She stammers, "Well, it is sort of my idea, isn't it? You didn't even really want to do it!"

"Right. But I thought if we're friends, we do things together, as a team. You just did all this stuff without even telling me—"

"That mission statement? That just happened last night. I thought of it when I got home, and I knew you weren't feeling good, so I didn't want to bother you. Sorry." Her shoulders drop a bit, and her face softens. "I don't want you to be mad, Shelby. I'm sorry. Do you want to just cancel the whole thing?"

"Yes."

She just stares at me. "Huh?"

"Yes. I want to just cancel the whole thing. I don't like those girls, and I don't think you like them either, and this whole Twinkie thing is just weird."

"Fine." She looks like she's going to cry as she scoops her stuff into the carpetbag. "I have to go to class. Bye." She leaves the lavender housewives waving in the breeze as she marches away. I can see her brush a tear from her face.

I feel awful. Maybe I should just be frozen until I'm thirty or something, and maybe by then I'll have learned how to figure out what people want me to do. I think they did that to Walt Disney's head . . . when he died, they just took his whole head and put it in a liquid nitrogen tank to preserve it, but of course, I have no way of knowing if you come out the same when they thaw you out, or if your brain can get freezer burn. I should ask my dad.

Either way, I'm totally stupid and I have to find Becca after school.

6

JUNE CLEAVER VERSUS SUPER MODEL

(or The Cream Filling Has to Be Good for Something)

I ask my sixth-period French teacher if I can leave a few minutes early for a personal emergency, and she says, *"Bien sur,"* which means "of course" in French. I run over to the Social Science building, where Becca has sixth period with Mrs. Yung, a class called Life Management, which only teaches you stuff that will not really help you manage your life in any way. They never talk about how to handle friends who get mad at you, or how to talk to your dad after your mom dies, or how to deal with a surly robot. Nothing helpful at all. Just sex and stuff.

The bell rings, and kids pour out of the room. Becca is talking to that girl Elisa Crunch, and I immediately feel like

I could punch Elisa in the face, which is highly unusual for me. As a vegetarian, I'm very against violence, so punching anybody is kind of against my principles. But I still want to belt Elisa Crunch. Hard.

"Hey," Becca nods to me. To Elisa she says, "Okay, well, I'll see you on Friday. You've got my number." Elisa waves and, looking much less depressed than earlier in the day, she goes on her way.

"What's Friday?" I fall into step beside Becca.

"We're going bowling." Becca seems really aloof.

"Hmm. Hey, stop a minute." She stops, says nothing. "I'm sorry about lunch. About the meeting."

"Why is that?" She's not even looking at me.

"Hey." I touch her shoulder, which seems to break down this invisible wall that's between us. "I'm sorry I was weird. I don't even know why I was like that. Really. I do want to help with the club and all. Anyway, I'm just sorry."

She turns to me, all smiles, as if a cloud had passed from in front of the sun. "Okay," she says brightly. "Wanna go bowling on Friday?"

"Sure." I really stink at bowling, of course. But I suppose it's not really about bowling at all; it's about geek solidarity.

"On to more pressing matters," Becca says. "We need to make our ad for Panther TV."

"I'm guessing you have an idea already."

"Of course. But I want to use Euphoria to videotape us and edit the film, so it can come out really professional."

"Euphoria doesn't have movie-editing software. Besides, it's not a good idea to use her for anything. She's way too judgmental."

"She's a robot. How can she be judgmental? Isn't she supposed to do your bidding and stuff?"

"Tell *her* that." I struggle to keep up with Becca's long strides as we walk to my house, which is only about three blocks away. "Are you sure a Panther TV thing is the best idea? I mean, it will make us targets, won't it?"

"Targets?" Becca slows down just a bit, but I still have trouble keeping up. "You're afraid that people will know we're geeks and do something to us because of it?"

"Well . . . yeah, I guess."

"That's extremely paranoid." She walks faster. "We have nothing to fear but fear itself, you know. So, here's my idea . . ."

The whole way home my mind is revving even though Becca is babbling on and on about our first meeting and the TV spot. I'm thinking about what I'm going to do when Becca decides she needs a braver geek sidekick than me. It's like she's the geek Wonder Woman, and I'm—well, Wonder Woman didn't even *have* a sidekick. I think she had a secretary, or maybe a dog walker. But whoever it was didn't get a costume or the keys to the invisible jet.

The Volvo's gone when we get to my house, so we have Euphoria to ourselves; she's in rest mode in her corner of my room. Once I walk in, she turns on and beeps a few times, does a self-diagnostic, and flashes green eye-lights in greeting. "Hey, Shelby. Welcome home from school. Hello, Becca."

"Hey, Euphoria," Becca says, all perky. "We need a favor."

"Hmm. Is that so?" She beeps and clicks and whirs while Becca and I get comfortable on the edge of the bed. My friend looks at me with big eyes, nudging me to ask Euphoria about the Great Geek Cinema Event.

"Uh, Euphoria," I begin. "Could you bring us a snack?"

"Is that all? Of course I'd be happy to get you a snack. Any preference?"

"I'd like something sweet," Becca sighs as she lies back on the bed, her hands behind her head. "Preferably chocolate."

"Yeah," I say. "And coffee if we have it."

"Oh, we always have coffee," she says as she rolls toward the door. "I'll be back in a minute."

Her clicks and whirs get fainter as she makes her way down the hall, and when we can't hear her anymore, Becca turns to me, frantic. "Okay, Shelby, you've got to talk her into helping us. Does she have to do anything you say?"

"I guess. What do you want her to do?"

"I want her to film us and then I want you to plug her into your computer and have her edit the film so it looks professional."

"I don't know if I can even do that!" I protest. "I mean, I know she can hold the camera and all, but as for the editing, I don't know if that's possible. I don't think her system is compatible with the laptop."

"Well, let's play it by ear. Let's just start with shooting the footage first."

When Euphoria returns with chocolate cookies on a plate and two steaming mugs of coffee, I admit that I'm more focused on eating than filming. "Shelby, be careful you don't take off a couple of fingers while you're chewing on those cookies," Euphoria snaps as I devour more. "We will be having supper, you know."

Becca has taken the last cookie and is giving me that scrunchy-eyebrow, purse-lipped look of insistence, so I ask: "Euphoria, do you think you could hold our digital video camera while we do a project for school? Could you film us?"

"I suppose."

Becca jumps in. "And is there any way you can interface with the laptop computer so you could edit the film into a movie?"

Euphoria's red lights start flashing in a disturbing sequence, and a high-pitched mechanical whine threatens to inflict permanent hearing damage. "Whoa, whoa. What's that all about?" I ask.

The whine eases like a downshifted motor; the red lights blink more slowly, and then go out. Finally, she speaks. "You expect me to just *interface* with any old computer? Even one I've never spoken to?"

Becca looks at me, puzzled. "Uh, Euphoria, is that, like, against the robot code or something? We didn't know it would be offensive or weird or anything."

"How would you like it if I told you to go interface with some strange human boy you might meet at the mall? Wouldn't that bother you?"

"Well, it would depend on what he looks like—" Becca's eyes twinkle wickedly.

"Okay, okay," I stand up between them. "I mean interface, like talk, communicate. We just want you to use the movie software on the laptop. Is that too weird?"

"Yeah, is that, like, robot sex?"

I do that thing they do in cartoons where you clamp your hand over your eyes in utter pain and disgust at the sheer stupidity of what you witness. "Becca, please."

Euphoria has started whir-whining again, and this time the pitch is even higher, and I'm afraid she might blow a gasket or something. Also, there's some kind of dark gray smoke starting to leak out from her undercarriage, and it smells a little bit like burnt dead hamsters, something I've smelled only one other time and was hoping I'd never smell again. Don't ask.

"Euphoria, calm down. You don't have to interface with the laptop, okay? We'll figure it out on our own." I pat her silvery sides, even though I know she doesn't feel it. She does seem to chill out; the smoke clears, although I have a hunch I'm stuck with the hamster-kebab smell for a while. "Do you think you can hold the camera? Hmm?"

"Yes," she says meekly. "Sorry, Shelby. I just haven't . . . been with another computer since your father made me.

It's something that's always made me nervous. I just over-reacted."

"Hey, it's only natural," Becca says without thinking. "Uh, anyway. Here's my idea for the Panther TV spot."

Becca proceeds to detail the concept: an old-fashioned science fiction movie featuring the Queen Geeks (us) as the larger-than-life heroes who save the world from the evil monster, Super Model. "Who plays Super Model?" I ask.

"Yeah, that's kind of a problem. We need somebody who's almost perfect, and who's willing to totally humiliate herself. Do we know anyone like that?"

Euphoria whirs and buzzes. "What about Briley?"

I groan. "Bad idea."

"Who's Briley?" Becca asks. "C'mon. We need to get this done. If she's someone who'd be willing to do it, and she's nearby—"

"She lives next door," Euphoria offers. "I can call her—"

"No. Absolutely not."

I suppose I have to now explain about Briley Princeton, the girl next door. She lived there when my dad and I moved in three years ago. My first encounter with Briley was actually at my elementary school, where she was in my sixth-grade class. On the very first day of sixth grade, Briley and I were seated next to each other. As she brushed her long blond tresses and scattered the rogue hairs to my side of the table, the teacher was asking if we had done anything interesting over the summer. She raised her hand, gestured to me, and said "This girl, Shelby, and her dad just moved into my neighborhood this summer. I think it's interesting because she doesn't have a mom."

I remember going all numb in my seat, that first day of sixth grade at a new school, in a new place, in a new life. And Briley Princeton had, without knowing it, found the one thing to say that would cut my heart in two like a sharp axe cutting soft butter.

I had run crying from the classroom, with the teacher, bewildered, following me. Briley's voice behind me sounded baffled: "What? I just thought maybe they kept her locked up or something interesting . . ."

She hadn't meant to ruin my first day of school, but to me, Briley is the symbol of all emotional pain and anguish. Therefore, I avoid her whenever possible. I certainly don't go to her house and initiate contact. And I absolutely don't call her to be part of my promotional videos, not that I've ever done any.

"So? Can we call her?" Becca stares anxiously at me. "C'mon! We need to get this done soon!"

"Sure. I'll call her." Euphoria dials the number and I pick up the house phone receiver. I faintly hear the phone ring next door.

"Hello?" Same dumb-blond voice. "Hello?"

"Briley?"

"Speaking." So very perky. She's picked up perky points every year. If she keeps on this way, she might actually perk out of existence.

"Hey. This is Shelby, from next door."

"Oh. Hi." She apparently doesn't want to talk to me any more than I want to talk to her. Swell.

"Listen, this is a weird request, I know, but—"

Becca grabs the phone from me, nearly knocking me off the bed. "Hey, Briley? It's Becca Gallagher, from school? Listen, I know you have no idea who I am, but I have a favor to ask. We're doing this video project for school, and we need another person in it. Would you be willing to do it for us?" She nods and smiles, then frowns. "Oh. Sure. Well, I understand. It's just that I'm new in town, so when I asked Shelby who we could get to play a model in the video, she immediately thought of you, but said you are so *incredibly* busy she doubted we could get you. I mean, we need someone who can look, well, *glamorous*, and so many girls just can't pull that off. Oh well." Becca sighs heavily. "Guess we'll just keep—huh? Oh." She jumps frantically, waves her hands, and does a little jig that I think means either good news or the sudden onset of stomach cramps. "I guess you could put it on a résumé. Sure. So, what we need is for you to come over in about an hour, as glammed up as you can get, big hair . . . oh, and try to look as skinny as possible. Okay. Thanks!" Triumphantly Becca hangs up the phone.

"What have you done?"

"I have made our video a raging success."

"There is no video yet." I peek between the slats of my blinds. "I can't believe you asked her to come over here."

"Okay, okay. Let's just focus on what we're doing, and it'll all be over really quickly. Here's the plan." Becca proceeds to tell me how we're going to do this supercool sci-fi video with no script, no props, and no scenery. "Can we use your dad's lab?"

"Oh, I don't know—"

Euphoria pipes up. "Your father would not want you girls pokin' around in his work area. I know that for a fact." She has picked up the video camera and is fiddling with the controls, the zoom, and the artistic effects. "I wonder how this would look if we filmed it all in black and white?"

"Great idea!" Becca screams. "Then it'll look especially old. Let me see the camera." She gently takes it from Euphoria's claws and squints into the viewfinder, pressing buttons madly. "Okay, yeah, you have that black-and-white grainy effect on here. Perfect. Let's find costumes."

"Costumes? Do you think I just have superhero costumes sitting around in a drawer somewhere?"

"Doesn't everyone?" Becca slaps my arm, a little too enthusiastically. "Don't worry. All we need are geek clothes. You have lots of those."

"Thanks." We rummage through my closet and come up with, I must admit, some interesting combinations. We settle on a plaid mini and black Oingo Boingo T-shirt for me, with knee socks and loafers, but for Becca, we're kind of stumped. She's so tall that nothing in my closet fits her.

"Okay, what about your dad's clothes?" she asks. "Maybe I could turn something of his into a costume."

A thought occurs to me, and I immediately bat it away. My mom had some of these very June Cleaver '50s dresses, you know, the housewife ones, but on her they looked retro and cool. I think I know where they are: Dad put all her stuff in big plastic bins and shoved them into the back of the garage three years ago when we moved in. He hasn't taken them out since. I don't know if I'm brave enough to get them out.

"What? You have an idea. I can see it. Tell," Becca demands.

"Never mind." I shove shirts and skirts back and forth on the rod in my closet, hoping something will appear that will spare me from digging through Mom's old clothes. I don't find anything. "I was just thinking that you could maybe wear some of my mom's old clothes."

"Oh."

We haven't really talked about this. It's like over time, the death of someone important doesn't go away, it just sort of hovers over your shoulder, always there but kind of quiet until you acknowledge it. I know for both of us, this hovering thing that is my mom's absence hangs there all the time, but we don't talk about it, just like my dad and I don't talk about Mom. In a way, we don't have to. But digging out Mom's clothes might wake it up, and I'm afraid. So is Becca, I can tell.

"Should we look?" I ask.

"Can you?"

"I think so." I turn to Euphoria. "Could you get us some aluminum foil and Christmas lights from the utility room? Bring them out to Dad's work space. We're filming there."

"Oh, but Shelby, your dad won't—"

"It's fine," I say. "We'll be careful."

Becca follows me out to the garage, and with each step, something heavy seems to drag at my feet. As we get closer to the orderly stack of bins on the back shelves, I feel that angel or demon or whatever it is hovering off my shoulder coming closer, whispering in my ear, trying to get me to feel something. I've gotten so good at not feeling anything.

Becca puts an arm around my shoulder. "We don't have to—"

"No. Might as well."

Everybody thinks that big moments in life happen when you plan them, and that they announce themselves, but I don't think that's true all the time. Like, this night when I take the bin with my mom's dresses off the shelf, and I open it, I'm hit with a wave of incredible sadness, but also this amazing swell of relief and joy, because it smells like her, like the combination of jasmine and lavender powder that she always wore. And I also laugh, because lying on top of the neatly folded dresses is a huge, gaudy tiara.

"Oh," Becca whispers, lifting the crown from the plastic box. "Look. It's like your mom knew what we were going to do." I feel the lump of tears forming, bite it back.

I don't know how long we stand there like that; a few minutes, forever. Euphoria presses the intercom button that connects every room in the house, which brings us back to reality. "Are you girls ready yet? I've got all the tinfoil I could find in here."

I wipe my face on my sleeve and lift a starchy sleeveless pink dress from the bin. It has a tab collar and buttons down the front, and it poofs out at the skirt because of a stiff crinoline underneath.

"Perfection," Becca says reverently. She turns to me and says, "I think we should both wear the June Cleaver dresses. You're just as much the queen as I am. Here." She pulls a satiny mint-green dress from the box. "This one will look great on you. Even in black and white. And you can wear the crown."

"Oh, I don't have to—"

"No," she says, smiling. "I insist."

We place the bin back in its resting place, take the dresses and the crown, and meet Euphoria in the lab. We both shimmy out of our clothes and into the dresses, which are a little big, but fit otherwise. "How do I look?" Becca asks.

"Very queenlike. What about me?"

"Looks like you should be baking some cookies. Here. Let's put your crown on." She nestles the tiara in my hair. "Lovely."

"Now, what do we actually do on this video, and where does Briley come in?"

We spend the next forty-five minutes figuring this out, and when the doorbell rings, we're ready for our villainous Super Model. "I'll go get her," Becca offers.

Euphoria plays with the video camera, pushing buttons and zooming the lens in and out. "That was your mother's dress," she says.

"I know."

"Are you all right?"

"I guess." There are no mirrors in the lab, but I do catch a reflection of myself in the window. "I wonder if I look like she did." Euphoria doesn't respond. After all, she never knew my mom.

Briley is the perfect Super Model; she comes in wearing a silver sequined minidress, silver high heels, too much makeup, and really crappy jewelry she bought at a cart in the mall. Her hair is in a bubble so large it should have its own orbital path. We shoot her footage first so we can get rid of her. We prop her up on a stool next to my dad's microscope, poof her hair out even more than it's already poofed, and tell her to read her lines.

"But, like, I don't understand how this is going to even look good on video," she whines. "I mean, it's dark in here, and you've got some vending machine running the camera."

"Excuse me?" Euphoria's red lights blink threateningly. Briley makes the I-smell-something-bad face and rolls her eyes, which Euphoria catches on video, thankfully.

"Okay, now Briley, just say your lines as menacingly as possible," Becca says from over Euphoria's shoulder.

"Menacingly?"

"Uh, like you're really mad and evil."

"I thought I was supposed to be glamorous!" she pouts.

"Yes," Becca says, gritting her teeth. "Glamorous and mad and evil."

"Fine." Briley grumbles as she adjusts her big bubble hair and crosses her Super Model legs. Then she studies the paper we've scrawled her lines on. "So I say 'Ha ha, Queen Geeks, you'll never get me to eat that Twinkie!' That's my line? What does that mean?"

"It's artistic," Becca sniffs. "You'll see how it all fits later. Let's go! Rolling!"

The camera whirs on and Briley turns on the charm, smooching her lips at the lens as if she's trying to French-kiss it, or at least give it a good hickey. "Ha ha ha, Queen Geeks, you'll never get me to Twink that Eatie!" She giggles. "Oops. Sorry. Let's try again."

We do this like eight more times. I'm about ready to set her hair on fire (and, by the way, I know this would be spectacular because I can smell the amazing amount of Aqua Net she's used, and I happen to know from previous science experiments that of all hair sprays, Aqua Net is the only one that is guaranteed, when lit, to burn all the hair off your head). We finally get her to say the one line correctly.

"Now, Briley," Becca says sweetly, putting her arm around our villain. "We have to do something a little unorthodox—"

"Un-what?"

"A little weird. We're not going to tell you what it is,

because we want your honest, raw reaction on film. You're such an amazing natural actress that we want to get those spontaneous reactions, and if we tell you what we're going to do, it'll spoil everything. Okay?"

Briley frowns at her. "I don't know—"

"Go!" Becca and I run out of the frame, leaving Briley looking bewildered. "Look mad and evil, Briley! C'mon, give it everything you've got!"

Briley snarls and arches her back like Catwoman if Catwoman had had some kind of nerve disorder. "Now!" Becca yells.

We both rush into the frame with hands full of Twinkies, and we smash the cream-filled yumminess into her perfectly perky face. She squeals and flaps at us like an overwrought chicken, and then Becca yells, "Cut!"

"Oh!" Briley shrieks as she wipes the cream filling from her face. "What's wrong with you? Why did you do that?"

"Your reaction was perfect!" Becca hugs her. "That was so honest. Thank you so much!"

"You're welcome!" Briley stands up, teetering on her silver heels, scrapes the Twinkie goo from her face, and smooshes it, two-fisted, onto Becca's cheeks and into her hair. "You two are even weirder than I'd heard." She stomps off, bangs on the swooshy door, and can't get out. "And you don't even have a doorknob! You're freaks!"

"Okay, thanks. We'll call you," Becca sings after her as

she leaves through the swooshy door that I've opened. We both collapse in a heap, laughing.

"You've never looked lovelier." I grab a paper towel and wipe the snack cake off her face. "I wonder if that's good for your skin."

"Lots of preservatives. Maybe I won't age." After most of the sticky goop is wiped off, Becca checks her watch. "Whoa, it's almost eight-thirty! I suppose I should call home. Will my cell work in here?"

"No, probably not. Just go right outside and it should be okay. Are we still going to try and do the rest tonight?"

"I hope so. If not, we'll do it tomorrow? Well, let me call first. Maybe I can stay over."

As she leaves, I take the camera from Euphoria. "Thanks for helping. That was great."

"Hmm. Very interesting project. I suppose you're hungry?"

"Yes," I say, somewhat surprised because I am, actually, really hungry. "Where's Dad, by the way?"

"He said he was going to a meeting or something. Told me he wouldn't be here for dinner, and that he'd be home late."

"A meeting? This late?"

Becca comes back in. "Whew. She's in a good mood for a change. Said I could stay. I am famished. What about you?"

We eat leftovers (and chocolate, of course) and finish filming our part of the video. The highlight of this is when we are standing in Dad's lab, with all the weird blue and green neon lights glaring up at us in our froofy dresses and pearls and Euphoria shooting from the floor so we look extra tall. We stand with hands on our hips in the classic superhero stance, and Becca says her line: "The Queen Geeks: making models fatter, one Twinkie at a time."

7

BOWLING FOR BOYS

(or You Always Hurt the Ones You Love)

The week goes quickly, and by the time Friday rolls around, we're looking forward to taking the weekend to edit our masterpiece. I try to talk Becca into going to her house for a change; I mean, I've never been over there. I've never even met her mom, and I am starting to wonder if maybe she's hiding some deep, dark secret, like her mom's a gun runner or a Jehovah's Witness or something.

"It's just not a good idea," Becca says as we walk to our last class of the day.

"Why not?"

She pauses uneasily, then turns a sunny smile toward me. "I'll have you over in a couple of weeks, okay? We're still unpacking, and the house is a mess, and my mom's a little bit uptight. She can't stand having people come over if things aren't absolutely perfect."

"I wouldn't care—"

She puts a finger to my lips. "Just wait. Believe me, you don't want to come over right at the moment." And with that, she disappears into her classroom, leaving me wondering what the big mystery is. Well, I guess it's going to have to go on the back burner for the moment, because I have other more pressing problems on deck for this evening.

There's the issue of bowling with Elisa Crunch.

I am still not thrilled by the idea of spending my Friday night in someone else's musty shoes with a big spherical piece of plastic wedged onto my hand. While I'm not exactly a germ freak, I don't think sharing things like shoes and balls is hygienic. Call me crazy.

But bowling we do go. Dad, who for some reason has become friendlier than usual, volunteers to drive me, pick up Becca (who insists we pick her up at school), and deliver us to the Finger Bowl and Restaurant, one of the few places around that still thinks arterial clog is a selling point for its cheeseburgers. The front of this place looks like God's jigsaw puzzle, and God, apparently, likes to leave his playthings lying around. The main entrance is plaster cast in geometric shapes that slope on a diagonal into the ground, giving it the appearance of having been swallowed by a huge chasm in the earth. Combined with the dog-pee yellow and deep violet paint job, the Finger Bowl's architecture has earned it a place in Ripley's Believe It or Not as one of the ugliest places that still charges less than two bucks for a Coke.

Dad waves to us and agrees to pick us up at eleven, which astonishes me even more. As I watch him drive away, Becca shakes her head and laughs. "What?" I ask.

"Your dad. He cracks me up." She yanks open the frosted-glass-and-chrome door and we walk into the refrigerated air of the Finger Bowl. "I mean, can't you figure out what's going on here?"

"Huh?"

We walk past knots of people in various stages of bowling. The hollow sound of pins striking polished wood alleys rings in my ears. Becca gets to the shoe counter and stops. "Size nine, please. Try to get me something that isn't smelly." She turns to me again. "Have you noticed that your dad is extremely cheerful lately?"

"Yes. I don't see why that's a problem. I like it. Six and a half for me, please."

The clerk brings Becca's shoes; she sniffs them, wrinkles her nose, and pays her five dollars. "You should be paying me to wear these," she says to the clerk, who shrugs and gets me my shoes. Turning to me, she smiles patronizingly. "Sweetie, your dad is dating."

Sound rushes out of my ears like the calm suck of the tide before a tsunami. My mouth gets dry, my hands go numb, and I am torn between wanting to cry, wanting to hit Becca, and wanting to set my bowling shoes on fire.

"Did you hear me?" she asks, waving her hand in front of my face. I slap it away. "Whoa. Sorry. Should we find Elisa?"

"Why don't you find Elisa, and I'll just go—go do something else. Maybe *she* should be your best friend." I take the shoes the clerk has set down for me and throw them viciously against the racks of other shoes waiting to infect strangers' feet. I walk away, then start to run blindly, looking for the bathroom. Why can you never find a bathroom when you're crying or have diarrhea?

I end up at the farthest end of the Finger Bowl, squatting down next to a gigantic gumball machine crammed with multicolored plastic balls. The carpet smells of old French fries, floor wax, and foot powder, which is something I can guarantee you don't ever want to smell, but especially not when you're having an emotional crisis. I feel like puking.

Becca huffs up next to me. "Do you have to run so fast?" She wheezes. "I mean, I really try not to participate in PE, so my endurance is pretty crappy. Why did you throw your shoes at the nice attendant?"

"What do you mean, my dad is dating? How could you say something so awful?" Now tears are flowing freely, mingling with all the other unidentified fluids that have set up a colony in this bacterial Club Med of a carpet.

Becca squats down next to me. "Gosh, I'm so sorry, Shelby. I—I guess I didn't think. I'm really sorry." She gently touches my shoulder. "C'mon. Let's go get a drink or something. I'll buy."

"It's just such a mean thing to say." I wipe my face with the edge of my sleeve. It smells, inexplicably, like Corn Nuts. I think I'll have to burn it.

"Why is it mean?"

I turn and look in her eyes, unbelieving. "What if I said your mom or dad was dating? Wouldn't that piss you off?"

"Yeah, but my parents are divorced. And my dad was already dating even before that, which is a whole other story." Becca frowns at me, puzzled. "Your dad isn't divorced, though—oh. Oh."

She puts her arm around me, and doesn't say any more. We sit there, hugging, for a long time, and finally I stop hiccupping, and the waterworks slow to a trickle. "Let's just go bowling," I say finally.

"Okay. Whatever you want." She gets up, pulling me with her. "We should look for Elisa, though. She's probably thinking we stood her up."

Elisa is parked on lane twelve with a quart bottle of Mountain Dew, which is nearly empty. She vibrates at a higher frequency than others around her, due to the excessive sugar and caffeine. "Hey guys!" She jumps up like she's just landed on an electrified whoopee cushion. "Wow, I'mgladyou'rehere. SeemslikeI'vebeenwaitingforhours!" She rushes to the cool aluminum ball-spit-out thing (I know it probably has a real name, but I don't know it) and grabs her green custom-made Lady Ball. "Lucille and I have been waiting to kick some ash!" She laughs as if she's just made the funniest joke in the history of comedy. "Kick some ash!

Get it? The bowling lanes are made of ash wood! Isn't that fantastic?"

"Did you drink all that Mountain Dew by yourself?" Becca asks as she looks on a shelf for a ball the right size.

"Yep." Elisa's eye twitches. "I don't even drink coffee. Whatarush!"

As we go about the business of bowling (or pretending to bowl, in my case), I can't stop thinking about what Becca said. My dad, dating? I guess there have been times when the car has been gone . . . and he has seemed a little bit happier lately. But I couldn't believe he'd actually go out on a date. He is my dad, after all. How gross. I decide to tuck the whole concept away in the back of my mind, in my mental broom closet where I keep elementary school embarrassments, bathroom mishaps, and inappropriate fantasies.

After about a half hour of bowling, Elisa crashes from her caffeine high and becomes more normal, at least for her. "So, tell me about the video." She is marking my score in the little squares that light up on a tote board above our heads. I have a disgustingly low score. "It sounds like a hoot."

"Yeah," Becca says as she takes a swig of Diet Pepsi from a can. "If you could've seen Briley's face when we smashed her with the Twinkies . . . priceless!"

"Ooh." Elisa turns and starts primping her hair. "Hottie at three o'clock."

"Huh?" Becca turns to look at the open area behind us. "Where?"

"Over there." Elisa grabs her head and turns it so she's staring out past the main doors.

"Yeah, no one is going to notice you staring if you twist her head off," I remark as I search for my ball, the gold one with the swirly things on it.

"Oh, wow."

"Um-hmmm."

"Helllooooo."

"Geez, you guys sound like, well . . . guys." As I am about to send the ball down the lane and into the gutter (at least I'm consistent), I turn instead and see the most gorgeous guy ever created since time began. You may think I'm exaggerating, and maybe I am, but at that moment, with the sunlight bouncing off the chrome door of the Finger Bowl and lighting him like a saint with a halo, he seems to me to be Adonis, or Hercules, or that other guy with the golden fleece.

"He's with Tim Lilly and Brian Cambridge." Elisa whispers in Becca's ear. "No, don't look. Pretend you don't care."

"I don't know either of those guys," Becca whines. "How can I meet him?"

"I know them. They're both in my Honors Chemistry class." Elisa rubs her hands together. "Fresh meat, ladies. I'll be back."

Watching her walk away, I feel as if I may actually follow the little bowling ball down the lane and disappear into the pin changer. Elisa Crunch is not only stealing my best friend, but she's now trying to cozy up to the one guy that has really interested me since, well, forever. Could life get worse?

"She's bringing him over here," Becca whispers. "The guys are all coming over here!"

"No." I know I look like crap because I've been crying; those of us of Irish background don't do well with tears. If I were darker-skinned, maybe then I'd just look intriguing, but instead I always look like somebody left my face in the oven too long and everything melted into everything else and then burned. "I've got to get to the—" Before I can even speak it, let alone get to the bathroom, Elisa is dragging the new recruit and the two other guys into our bowling cubby.

"Becca Gallagher and Shelly—"

"Shelby." I am trying to hide my face with my hair. I probably only succeed in looking wasted.

"Right. Shelby Chapelle. This is Tim, Brian, and *Anders.* He's from Norway."

"He's an exchange student," Tim offers. "He's staying at my house."

I barely register Tim or Brian; I think they are wearing jeans and shirts and they definitely have hair. This is because I focus all my essence and energy on Anders, the Nordic god. He is as tall as Becca and has neck-length sandy-blond hair. His eyes are ice blue, with long silky lashes, and his complexion is fair, but with ruddy cheeks. He's wearing a cream sweater, which sets off his eyes as well as his perfect Cupid's-bow lips. I can't stop looking at the lips.

"Hello," he says in a deep, gently accented voice. When he speaks, it sort of vibrates all through me, like bass drums in a marching band at a parade. "I'm Anders Sorensen. Pleased to meet you." He shakes Becca's hand, then turns to me. I extend my hand, the one with the gold bowling ball wedged to it.

"Oh. Sorry." I giggle in a disgusting girly way and try to dislodge the ball from my fingers, but apparently excessive lust has made them swell. "I guess I'm sort of, uh, stuck. Hi." I give him my other hand. He laughs gently, presses the ball-less hand to his lips, and kisses it. I feel very dizzy. I guess the blood rushing to my head makes my fingers smaller, because the gold bowling ball suddenly falls off my hand and onto Anders's gorgeous Norwegian foot.

Howling in pain, he dances on one foot like a great Viking flamingo. Running into the pin changer to hide is looking better and better.

"I'm so sorry." I dive for the ball, which has rolled off on its own toward lane thirteen. I guess it's embarrassed too.

"Here, *Anders*, sit down," Elisa purrs, grabbing his arm and leading him to a chair next to hers. "You poor thing. Here, let me take off your shoe before your foot swells. Shelly, could you get some ice?"

"Shelby," I mutter as I dash for the concession stand. Becca scampers after me.

"Oh my God! I can't believe you did that." She is giggling uncontrollably. "That has got to be one of the funniest things I've ever seen."

"I'm glad my misfortune amuses you." I ask the lady behind the counter for a bag of ice. She looks at me as if I just crawled out from behind the pin changer. I wish. "The universe hates me."

Becca is still shaking with laughter, wiping tears from her eyes. "Seriously, Shelby, that was so priceless."

"Yeah, I get it." I grab the baggie of ice and stomp back to the cubby. "Here you go." I throw the ice at Elisa, who dodges it and mutters something indignant.

Tim and Brian have decided to team up with us, so Elisa has made the executive decision to start the game over. Anders is on the long plastic bench with his foot up, the ice bag draped over it. "How's your foot?" Becca asks, barely able to keep from bursting out laughing all over again.

"It's okay, I think." Anders checks the swelling; the foot does look red and puffy. Fantastic. Now I've started an international incident. "I don't think I'll bowl, though."

"Do they bowl in Norway, Anders?" Elisa oozes what she supposes to be charm. I wish I'd dropped the ball on *her* foot.

"Umm, yes. But we don't usually throw the balls at other people." Everybody busts up laughing. I shoot a look at Anders, who is staring straight at me with this absolutely heart-stopping twinkly smile and he winks—winks!—at me.

So we bowl, but all I can think about is that smile. I don't even know if I hit any pins or not. We're there for almost forty-five minutes, and I keep trying not to look at him, but my eyes are magnetically drawn in that direction. I try to pass it off like I'm looking at the clock or checking the front door, or monitoring how many people buy Slushies at the concession stand. But every time I look back, Anders is looking at me with that sexy smile. I feel him watching me, and it makes my tummy churn, not in a too-much-cotton-candy-and-nacho way, but in the could-this-be-love way.

While Elisa is bowling, Anders says, "Shelby, could I ask a favor?"

"Anything." I stand up, hoping my legs don't collapse.

"Come here."

Walk, legs, walk. Please be team players. "Sure." I walk over to him, conscious of every clunky move of every part of my body, which now feels like a Macy's Thanksgiving parade float.

When I'm within a foot of him, I smell this clean soap scent mingled with sandalwood. I want to put him in a bottle and dab him behind my ears. It is all I can do not to dive into his cream-colored sweater and roll around like a puppy.

"I wonder, could you perhaps get some food for me?" He reaches into a pocket and pulls out a wallet. "Something not too greasy. Also, I'm a vegetarian."

Thank you, thank you, thank you.

"Shelby's a vegetarian too," Becca pipes up.

"Really?" Anders smiles at me again, his perfect white teeth lined up against his perfect lips. "Well, then you know what I want." I check his eyes to see if that was a flirting line or if I'm just taking it wrong. His eyes, those ice-blue eyes, are crinkling at the edges as he teases me.

"I might be able to figure it out." I boldly put my hand over his when he tries to take money out of the wallet. *Zing!* "But let me take care of it. My treat. It's the least I can do since I crippled you. Drink?"

"Just water, thanks." As I brush past him, he touches my arm lightly; I feel as if I've been shocked by a million-volt lightning bolt.

"I'll help you," Becca yells and scrambles up the steps after me. We quickstep to the concession stand. "Oh my God. He's flirting with you, isn't he?"

"I think so."

"You're all red!" She turns me so she can look at my face, then puts her hand to my forehead. "I think you have a fever!"

I shake her hand off as the counter person comes over. "No I don't. Oh, hi, could I have a medium veggie pizza and two bottles of water, please?"

"Pizza? You can't eat pizza in front of him."

"Why not?"

"It's messy, first of all. Second of all, it's full of cheese. You'll start farting."

"Thanks for that helpful dating tip. Let me write that down: 'Don't fart in front of cute guy.' I wouldn't have thought of that."

She ignores me. "Seriously. He is absolutely amazing, Shelby. And he definitely has the hots for you. Elisa is so jealous!"

"Can I help it if the Norwegian people have good taste?" I look over toward our bowling area, and Anders is watching me over the edge of the plastic bench. "Oh God. He's staring at me."

"Yeah. He's been doing that since you dropped the ball on his foot. What a cute story to tell your kids."

I slap her arm. "Shut up!"

"Do you think he'll ask you out?"

"I don't know. Maybe in Norway they do things differently. Maybe there's some mating ritual that involves whale blubber and icicles." He's still watching me. I am terrified to walk back there. Knowing me, I'll fall face first into the pizza and burn my features beyond all recognition. I'm not sure my dating life can recover from that.

"Here's your pizza and water," the clerk says. "Ten ninety-eight. Napkins and utensils on the cart over there." I pay her and grab the cardboard box.

"Could you get napkins and grab the water?" I ask Becca. She does, and I make my way back toward Anders, hoping against hope that I don't look too much like a drunk baboon as I walk.

"Here we go," I say, gracefully lowering myself to the bench next to him. I put the box between us as Becca hands him a bottle of water and a stack of napkins. "Hope you like pizza."

"Do they have pizza in Norway, *Anders*?" Elisa is still desperately trying, but I think she senses it's pointless.

"Oh, yes." He turns toward me, edging his foot off the bench and onto the floor. He flexes it. Even his foot looks sexy. "I think I'm going to walk again."

"That's great. So you're not going to sue me?" I use a little plastic knife to cut the pizza into slices.

"I do think I'll need some kind of compensation," he says in a very quiet voice that only I am meant to hear. "And just so I can be sure you're not some government agent trying to poison me, I think you should take the first bite. Here."

He picks up a goopy piece of pizza and aims the pointy end toward my mouth. Our eyes lock, and as I take the first bite, I wonder if any pizza has ever tasted this good.

We finally end the bowling after another forty-five minutes. I've come in last, but I couldn't care less. "Okay, well, I'd better call my dad," I say. "He's picking us up. You all have a ride, I guess?"

"Yeah, my brother's in the parking lot waiting," Tim says as he takes a last swig from his soda cup.

"He just sat there the whole time?" Elisa asks. "Why didn't he come in?"

"He didn't want to be bored," Tim answers, then shrugs. "His friend Fletcher is out there too. I think they're playing PlayStation. That's pretty much all they do, except football."

I walk up the stairs again so I can get cell reception. "Dad? Hey. We're ready to go. Can you come get us?"

"Sure, honey." I hear a woman's voice giggling in the background.

"Where are you?" The Conversation suddenly slams back into my head.

"Finishing dinner. We're—I'm finished, though. Just waiting for you to call."

"Who's with you?"

"What?"

"Dad, who are you having dinner with?" I can hear the anger edging my voice.

There is an awkward pause, and then Dad says, "Listen, honey, I can't hear you very well, you're breaking up. I'll be there in about ten minutes, okay? Meet you outside." The call cuts off.

I stomp back to the group; the glow of meeting Anders has evaporated like mist in strong sun. My heart is beating so hard I'm afraid it might break through my ribs, and Anders is studying my face, trying to figure out if he has done something wrong, I suppose.

"Is everything okay?" Becca asks gently.

"Sure. He'll be here in about ten minutes." I angrily throw my stuff into my purse, grab my street shoes, and yank the laces of the bowling shoes apart.

Tim and Brian say good-bye and help Anders stand up. "I think it's fine," he says, testing the swollen foot. It supports his weight, but still looks puffy. To Tim and Brian, he says, "Could you guys meet me at the car? I'll be right out."

"Sure," Tim says. "Think you can walk?"

"I'll make Shelby help me if I can't." He smiles at me again.

"Elisa, come on. Let's return the bowling shoes." Becca grabs Elisa's arm and pulls her from her chair as she protests.

"So. You had a bad phone call, or just realized you don't really like blonds?" He leans on the bench for support.

"No." I stare at the floor, willing tears to stay put. The last thing I need is for this guy to see me as an emotional basket case. Even if I am one, I don't want him to know it. "It's my dad. We . . . he's just doing some stuff that I don't like."

Anders nods, but says nothing. "Come here." He puts his arms out and folds me into his cream-colored sweater. Something that must be pure joy rushes through my veins and zooms from my head to my toes like a high-speed roller coaster, makes my eyeballs burn, and makes my legs all rubbery. I am swimming in the cloud of sandalwood-soap smell, stronger now that my head is resting so perfectly against his neck. He's the absolute perfect height for slow dancing too. I lean into him, let him support me even though he's the one with the injured foot.

He breaks the hug, puts his hands on my shoulders, then looks deeply into my eyes. "I'd like to see you again. What do you think?"

"I think so." I can't help but smile, even after the weird conversation with my dad. It's like Anders is a feel-good drug and when I'm around him, all the bad things sort of fade.

"Good. Can I call you?"

"Oh. Yeah, that'd be great." I rummage in my purse for paper and pen, then scribble my numbers on it for him. "If you hear kind of a weird mechanical voice answer the phone, don't get freaked out. It's my robot."

"Your robot?" He searches my face to see if I'm teasing him.

"Seriously. My dad's a scientist. He builds stuff like that. I just want to warn you ahead of time."

"I think science is fascinating. Do you like science fiction movies?"

I feel a glow burning in my tummy again.

We walk outside, and Tim's brother has already pulled his old Cutlass up to the curb and it's rattling so loud I think it might break the chrome-glass bowling-alley doors. It's dark now, so the car is lit from within by the glow of video games and the yellowish streetlights. The friend of the brother is leaning out of the front seat window. "Hey," he calls to me. "Be careful of this guy. He's a player, you know."

Anders grimaces and climbs into the backseat next to Tim and Brian. The kid in the front seat keeps needling him by talking to me. "Did he tell you about his recent adventure with the Norwegian naked volleyball team? I'm just saying, make sure you have all your shots."

I blush violently and give this kid, a red-haired guy who looks older than us, a dirty look. "I'm sure if you had a date, she'd need shots too," I say lamely.

"Ooo. Feisty. I like that. I'm Fletcher, by the way."

"Not so nice to meet you," I reply to the jerk. The guy grins at me, a lopsided, slightly off-center smile that's kind of cute, but maddening since he's being such a jerk. Jerks shouldn't have nice smiles. I turn my attention to the back-seat, and our eyes meet. I feel that golden glow of pure yum-miness melt down through my legs and into my toes, totally eliminating any jerk residue. Anders waves to me as the Cutlass rattles away, trailing clouds of loud metal music.

"So?" Becca squeals. "What happened?"

"Yes. Do tell us," Elisa says dryly.

"He wants to go out." I still feel doped. "I gave him my number."

"Wow!" Becca jumps up and down. "That is so cool! He is so gorgeous. Is he as nice to talk to? What happened in there?"

"He saw I was upset after talking to my dad, so he asked me why, and I didn't tell him, and then he hugged me."

Both girls squeal. "He hugged you?"

Becca asks, "Is he a good hugger?"

How to describe it? "It was like being sucked up into a cloud in heaven and then being petted by an angel who smells like soap."

"Oh," they both sigh.

"Can you guys give me a ride home?" Elisa asks, break-ing the mood.

"I guess." I see my dad pulling into the parking lot. "Here he is now. Don't say anything, you promise?"

"No way," Becca says. Elisa stays silent. "Elisa?"

"Oh, all right. Don't you talk to your dad about dating?"

"Do you?" I ask as he pulls the Volvo up to the curb.

"If I were dating somebody like Anders, I'd tell everybody I see!" Elisa yanks open the car door. "Hey, Mr. Chapelle. Elisa Crunch. Mind giving me a ride home?"

Becca rolls her eyes and climbs into the backseat next to her.

"Did you girls have a good time?" Dad asks cheerfully.

"We sure did," Elisa chirps as she snaps her seat belt into place. "Bowling is a lot of fun."

Becca interrupts, I guess to cut Elisa off in case she decides to rat me out to my dad. "Are you a bowler, Mr. Chapelle?"

"Not so much," he answers, steering the car smoothly out of the lot. "I used to golf when I was younger, but it's a damn boring game. Not quick enough. I have the same problem with bowling too. It's too slow."

"Sometimes it's pretty fast," Elisa mutters under her breath. Becca jabs her sharply with an elbow. "Ow."

"Want to work on the video?" Becca asks.

"Oh, can I help?" Elisa pipes up.

"What video?" Dad asks.

"We're shooting a promotional video for our club," Becca explains. "It's going to revolutionize high school society."

"Oh, nothing too ambitious, then," Dad turns to look at me. "Shelby, are you feeling okay? You look sort of feverish."

The two girls both giggle. So do I, I can't help it. "No, Dad, I'm fine."

"It was just kind of warm in the bowling alley," Elisa says teasingly.

"Really? I remember those places as being like meat lockers. Maybe they're cutting back on the air conditioning for cost purposes." He keeps his eyes on the road, but once we get to a stoplight, he focuses on me again. "So, it's just the climate, huh? Nothing wrong?"

"Nope." Right now, I decide, I don't want to talk about my dad dating at all. I am going to pretend I know nothing about it. Instead, I am going to think over and over again about that beautiful sweatery hug, and about how Anders smelled, and about how he asked for my phone number and fed me pizza and likes me even if I did drop a bowling ball on his foot.

8

PLAYING TELEPHONE

(or Love Between the Lines)

We finish filming our promotional video over the weekend; although I try not to, I keep jumping every time the phone rings, hoping it's Anders.

Dad is gone most of the time, and in the back of my mind I keep remembering what Becca said: that he's dating. Sunday night I'm alone, and I curl up on the big couch with *The Day the Earth Stood Still.* If you've never seen it, it's about a spaceman who comes to earth to have a friendly conversation, but instead the military practically disintegrates him. He has this robot, Gort, who looks like a guy wrapped tightly in tinfoil (with the dull side up). Gort never speaks, but he does walk around looking menacing. Euphoria actually watches this film with me; I think she has the hots for Gort.

"So you don't have any idea where Dad is?" I ask Euphoria for, like, the tenth time. I glance at the digital readout on the stereo: eight-thirty p.m. "Isn't it kind of late for him to be out?"

"Well, he *is* over twenty-one," she answers. "I wouldn't worry about him."

"That's easy for you to say. He's not your father. Of course, you don't have a father, so that makes it even less likely that any of this would bother you anyway."

"Any of what?" She whirs and blinks wildly. "Oh, wait a minute. I love this part." Gort has stalked out of the spaceship in all his Reynolds Wrap glory, and his face visor is flickering with some obscure message that only Euphoria could find exciting. "What a great actor," she sighs.

The front door opens and closes quietly. I am struck by the oddity of the situation: My father is trying to sneak into the house without me noticing. As a teenager, isn't that *my* job? I pause the movie. "Hi, Dad."

"Oh, Shelby." He pokes his head into the family room. "I didn't know if you'd be up."

"It's only eight-thirty." I stare at him, drilling into him with my x-ray vision. Unfortunately, it appears to be malfunctioning. "Where've you been?"

"Hmmm?" He sits down on the sofa next to me. "What are you watching?"

"Where've you been, Dad?"

Euphoria buzzes and rolls to the kitchen. "That's my cue to exit stage left. Are you hungry, Mr. Chapelle?"

"No, thanks, Euphoria. I had dinner."

"I bet you did," I mumble as I start the movie again.

"Excuse me?" Dad arches his eyebrows at me in that *Don't sass me, I'm your father* way.

"I just figured you already had dinner." I turn the volume up on the television.

Dad gets up and turns off the set, leaving just the two of us and ringing silence. "Can we talk?"

"It's a free country." I cannot believe how snotty I sound. Wow. If I were my kid, I'd slap me.

"Obviously something is bothering you. Let's get it out in the open."

I click the TV back on. "I'd rather not."

"Well, I would." He clicks it off.

I turn and glare at him. "I suppose your personal life is your business, isn't it? I mean, if you were, say, dating somebody, you'd probably not feel the need to discuss it with your only daughter, because after all, this is *your* life. It has nothing to do with me. So, since we have that out in the open, let me get back to my movie."

Before I can grab the remote, he has his hand over it, and then snags my hand too. "Shelby."

"What?" I stare straight ahead at the blank television screen.

He lets go of my hand and sighs. "Honey, I'm not dating anybody."

"Then where were you?" I turn to glare at him again, but he has this really sad look on his face that makes me crank down the snottiness. "I was worried, that's all."

"I understand." He is studying the carpet, which, by the way, is all silver-gray and not at all interesting. "Do you want the truth?"

No one ever really asks me that question. Being a teenager, I notice that most adults usually just tell you the truth whether you want it or not, or they make up some convenient lie along the lines of Santa Claus and the Tooth Fairy. They don't give you a choice. Somehow, in this moment, I find that much safer. Being given the choice implies that maybe I don't want to hear the truth. But now it's too late.

"Okay. Shoot."

Dad leans into the couch and throws his hands up in a gesture of defeat. "You got me. I did go eat dinner. I ate dinner with another person. The other person was a woman. Kill me now and get it over with."

"Dad!" Tears well up at the corners of my eyes. "How could you do that?"

"Eat dinner?"

"Dammit!" I throw a big purple pillow at his head. He catches it. "No! The eating with a woman part!"

"Women eat too. You should know that," he points out.

"But how can you—I mean, what about—Oh, forget it!" I jump up and throw him a supremely vicious look. "I'm going to bed."

"You mean how can I eat dinner with someone other than your mother?"

There. He said it. With the words unleashed, I cry, an angry, violent, wild sobbing that makes me feel out of control and very small. I pound my fist on the doorjamb, over and over again, and I don't even feel it. Dad comes over, grabs me, holds me, hugs me, envelops me. He pets my hair, then turns me around so he's covering me in a big bear hug, the way he used to do when I was little.

"Shelby, I'm not dating. I'm not getting serious. I'm simply having dinner with a woman." He rocks me gently as we stand. "Oh, honey, I know it's hard. Believe me, I've stayed up nights crying about it too." Now my dad is crying too, which makes it even worse. Nobody is supposed to see their own dad cry. There must be some code somewhere that prohibits that, right? Dads are strong, unbreakable, superhuman. But mine is sniffling, holding me as tightly as I'm holding him.

After what seems like a day, a night, a year, he breaks the hug. His eyes are red, and mine are too, I suppose; he wipes the wetness from my cheeks and smiles at me. "Beebee, you were the most beautiful baby. We were so happy to have you. Your mom—" his voice catches there, "she couldn't stop looking at you when you were born. She kept asking me if it was bad to kiss a baby so much."

"I know. That's why I can't understand how you could just . . . just . . . go out with somebody. I mean, that's what teenagers do, Dad. Not people with wives."

I focus on the hazel-green eyes, those intense eyes that I guess my mom must have fallen in love with when she met him. For just a second, I can see something that scares me: My dad is a person. He's not just a dad. Somebody else might look at him and think, "Hey, there's a good-looking man."

What I say is, "I'm not ready for you to be somebody else besides my dad. And her husband."

He sighs again, and smiles at me. "Okay. But am I still allowed to eat dinner?"

I can only nod. "I'll see you tomorrow."

"Good night, Beebee." He kisses me on the forehead.

"Dad?"

"Hmm?"

"Do me a favor. Don't call me that anymore." I run to my room as fast as I can.

Another day goes by. Anders doesn't call me.

Now, I'm not one of those girls who lives for a phone call from a guy. I don't sit around watching the phone, willing it to ring, going to bed each night in despair because another twenty-four hours has passed without any communication from Him. No. I don't do that. At least, I didn't do that until Anders.

Every day at school seems gray and blurry, as if someone dumped dirty dishwater on it. Becca can tell something is wrong, but I won't tell her what; she just keeps trailing along behind me in my gray, dishwatery wake, giving me Queen Geek updates, chattering about the video and the upcoming Wednesday meeting.

"So, I've had about ten different girls ask me about the club," she says, all bubbly, as we come out of the cafeteria on Tuesday and head for our regular spot under the tree. "I mean, this thing is really taking off. And we haven't even aired our video yet!"

"Hmmm." I plop down in the grass, which seems unusually rough and unfriendly.

Becca eases to the ground and pulls a paper bag from her backpack. "Aren't you eating?"

"No." I lean against the scratchy bark of the tree, willing it to swallow me, to make me part of its sap, to consume me and melt me into the earth—

"Could you please snap out of it!" Becca is in my face, shaking me by the shoulders as if I am a rag doll. "What is with this tragic teenager crap? Have you lost it?"

"Maybe I have." *Oh, earth, please find me and make me part of your dirty . . . dirt. Envelop me, snuggle me, and help me disappear like the elements into—*

"Helllooooo!" She's practically screaming in my ear. "Earth to Shelby. Could you please return the human Shelby to us and take back the sickly, depressed, and boring Shelby that has been sitting here for two days?"

"What is *your* problem?" I sit up, square my shoulders, and glare at her. "Why can't I be depressed once in a while? Is there some law, like Shelby Chapelle must always be cheerful, kind, and thrifty, and help old ladies across the street, and never be a bother to her friends, and—"

"Okay! Thanks! I get it!" Becca rolls her eyes at me

and shakes her head. "God, Shelby, is this all about Anders? He hasn't called you, and that's the end of life as we know it?"

"Well—"

"Well nothing! Yes, he was cute. Yes, he smelled great. And? We have bigger and better things to do than worry about some Swedish—"

"Norwegian."

"*Norwegian* Ken doll who gets your panties all in a knot!"

I laugh in spite of myself. "Keep my panties out of this. He never got that far."

Now we're both giggling, then it breaks into full-on laughter, and suddenly, with the tension gone, I'm laughing so hard I'm crying, and I roll over face first into the grass, not caring who sees me.

"Umm. What's in the frozen yogurt today?" Elisa Crunch is hovering above us like an oversized troll doll.

"Nothing." Becca wipes her eyes on her sleeves. "Sit. We're just talking about Shelby's panties." This makes us howl all over again. Elisa looks puzzled, and somewhat disturbed.

"Right. Okay, well, I wanted to talk to you about tomorrow's meeting. We really need to have it in a classroom, so we can watch the video."

"Hmm." Becca has calmed enough to hungrily bite into her egg salad sandwich. "What about McLachlan? Would she let us use her room?"

"I have her this afternoon. I'll ask." Elisa takes out her Palm Pilot and efficiently jots down a note. "So, how does it look?"

"The video? We're finishing it up this afternoon. But it looks great so far. I can't wait to show everybody." Becca glances at me. "And tomorrow, we have to plan for our Twinkie collecting, give somebody the task of researching modeling agencies for the one with the skinniest models, and then I want to talk about our next project."

"Which is?" Elisa sits poised to jot.

"Yeah, which is?" I ask.

"National Invisible Boy Day." Becca smiles, nods knowingly. "It's a great idea."

"What is it?" I ask. I have a feeling I know where this idea has come from.

"Well, it's where all the girls who want to do it sign a pledge and wear, like, some sort of badge or bracelet or something—"

"Like those little plastic bracelets for cancer and other diseases!" Elisa's leg vibrates excitedly.

"Boys aren't a disease," I remind them.

Becca snorts and gives one of her donkey-honk laughs. "Yeah, right. They're the worst kind of disease. You can never be truly rid of them. Unless you move to Antarctica. And then you have boy penguins, so I suppose that could be just as bad—"

"Okay, so now we've moved from problems with panties to flightless-aquatic-bird obsessions." Elisa purses her lips and shakes her head. "I'm not sure I like the direction things are taking."

"Have a little faith. Remember, when Alice jumped down the rabbit hole, she had no idea where she was going to land." Becca stands, then pulls me up and dusts the grass off my jeans.

"But once she got there, it turned out everybody was crazy." Elisa tucks her PDA back into her backpack. "So, in a way, it's really similar to you guys."

"See ya," Becca calls to me. "I'll meet you after school. Library?"

"Okay." I feel marginally better after all the laughing. After all, who cares if the only guy I've ever been truly interested in has totally blown me off after I dropped a bowling ball on his foot and totally embarrassed myself by thinking he liked me? In the grand scheme of things, is it really that important?

Um, yeah. Yeah, it is. But for now, I'll just focus on something else.

We meet after school and walk to my house. "Okay, so I know you're depressed about this Anders thing," Becca begins. I put a hand up to stop her.

"Wait. I've decided to totally ignore my feelings on this and simply become a cog in the machine for your global domination."

"Cool." We walk in silence for a while. "Just so I know, are you mad that he hasn't called you? Or did he call and—"

"Okay, this is not helping me ignore the whole thing."

"Sorry." Becca awkwardly matches my steps, even though she's so much taller. It makes her look like a greyhound racing a Chihuahua. "Okay, so let's focus on our video. What do we still need to do?"

"We need to put in music, captions, fades, and stuff. All the clips are pretty much in the right order. We also need to record the voice-over part that goes with the whole thing."

By the time we get to my house, I've curiously forgotten about Anders, at least consciously. I'm so wrapped up in the details of our video that, for the moment, I'm sort of happy. We sit down with my laptop and record the music from *The Day the Earth Stood Still*, that wobbly high-pitched music used in all the old horror flicks. Then we record Becca's voice reading our script. After a lot of screwups, we finally get something useable. By the time we edit everything into a final product and dump it onto a videotape, it's almost midnight.

"Guess I'm staying over tonight," Becca says.

"Why hasn't your mom called or something? Isn't she worried about where you are?"

Becca is rummaging through the freezer. "Got any ice cream?"

"Yeah. In the back. Hey, won't your mom be—"

"I'm going to have some. Got any chocolate syrup?" She's grabbing a big dish from our cupboard.

"Hey. Could you get your face out of my freezer for a minute and answer my question?"

"My mom doesn't care where I am." She grabs a gallon of Cookies and Cream and thumps it onto the counter, rips the lid off, and then proceeds to dig into it with fury no frozen treat deserves.

"Uh . . . okay. Want to call her, at least?"

"Not really." Becca licks the spoon, rolling her eyes in ecstasy. She continues to scoop more ice cream from the container. "Seriously. She won't care where I am. She knows I'm here, and if she does get a sudden attack of motherly instinct, she can call. She'd only be mad if she had to come out and get me. If I stay here, she'll be totally fine with it. So quit worrying."

I let it go for the moment, but I know something is weird with Becca and her mom, mostly because I've still never met her. We've been friends for a while and I've never been invited to her house, never even seen her mom except when she picks her up or drops her off. Next time, I vow, I will run out to that purple Jeep and force a meeting.

"Okay. So are you ready to view the masterpiece?"

"It's really late. Maybe we should just go to bed."

She throws the dirty dish and spoon into the sink, stretches, and yawns. "Yeah. I'm suddenly really wiped. Must've been all that hard work."

"Or all the ice cream."

"Funny. C'mon." She leads the way to my room, where Euphoria has already inflated an airbed and made it up with fuzzy flannel sheets and a quilt. "Aw, Euphoria. You do care!" Becca tries to hug my robot, but it's a little hard to cuddle something made of a metal alloy, no matter how nice the thing might be.

We get ready, dive into our beds (which, by now, are looking really good), and Euphoria douses the lights. "Tomorrow!" Becca whispers as she studies my fluorescent ceiling stars. "Tomorrow, the Queen Geeks ascend to power!"

"Long live the Queens!" I whisper back.

"You two go to sleep, for Pete's sake," Euphoria whirs, disgusted. "I sleep more than you do, and I don't even need it! Not another word!"

We get to school the next day on adrenaline. Exhausted, we both throw on whatever clothes are clean (Becca can wear some of my less height-specific clothes, but she doesn't like them because she says they are from my "I Love the '80s" period) and we eat breakfast because Euphoria won't let us leave without it. No sign of Dad; again, I remember to forget all about that situation and to simply concentrate on other, less important things. To be honest, I am kind of excited about our video; I think it's going to be quite a hit at school.

"See you at lunch?" I call as we leave first period English. "Did we get McLachlan's room?"

"Don't know. Let's meet at the benches and then we can go there if Elisa did get the room." Becca hoists her backpack onto her shoulder.

I count the minutes until lunch, totally ignoring my classes, my teachers, my fellow students (even Dustin, who has decided I'm no longer a lesbian and might still be worth dating.) The lunch bell rings, and I dart out of my class and practically run to the telecom benches, where Becca, Elisa, and two other girls are already sitting, engaged in full-tilt babbling.

"Shelby! Listen, this is Amitha Bargout and her friend Sherrie Johnson." Amitha is dark-skinned with shiny black hair, and Sherrie has a caramel-colored complexion and long, wavy brown-blond hair. "Amitha is Pakistani, and she wants to be a doctor. And get this: Sherrie has actually memorized part of the dictionary!"

"A through K." Sherrie looks modestly at the ground. "The letter I took a long time. Lots of Latin roots."

While we are talking, people from the first meeting drift in: the two black girls, Claudette and her sister Caroline; the tragic poetess, Amber Fellerman of the long black stringy hair; and Chess Club reject Cheryl Abbott, the short girl with thick glasses. All together, we have nine people.

Becca waves excitedly. "Okay. We're moving to Ms. McLachlan's room to watch our promotional video!"

Elisa falls into step with me as we walk. "So the video came out well?"

"I think so." I walk faster to keep up with Becca, who is racewalking her way to the English building. "We actually haven't watched it. We were up till midnight finishing it. I hope it makes sense."

"Have you heard from *Anders*?" She snickers in a very nasty way that makes me think she got into his pockets and disposed of my phone number.

"As a matter of fact, I've been so busy that I haven't even checked my voice mail." She looks disappointed, which is what I was going for.

Becca gets everyone situated in the classroom, and we all introduce ourselves again. She motions for me to stand up front with her. "Okay, so welcome to the second official meeting of the Queen Geek Social Club," she says. "As you know, we're here to make a significant impact on the way high schools view geeks, and we want to make a social change in the way geeks are viewed all over the world."

"Wow, and I just came for the Twinkies," mutters Amber. Everybody laughs. Imagine, a whole room full of people who get the jokes!

"First, we want to show you the promotional video that will air Friday on Panther TV. This is something Shelby and I put together, with help from Elisa, and it will kick off our Campaign for Calories. Elisa, do we have a designated modeling agency yet?"

Elisa is scrolling through her PDA. "I think I've narrowed it down to two. I still want to do a body-fat-to-height ratio analysis before I absolutely pin it down."

"Okay, so without further discussion, let's see the video!"

My phone rings as Becca is messing with the VCR. It's my dad, which is kind of unusual. He doesn't call me at school unless it's an emergency, so I step outside to take the call, just in case it's something that will make me cry.

"Hi, Dad."

"Shelby?"

"Uh, yeah. Nobody else answers my cell phone." A pack of punk kids walks by, and one throws a cardboard boat of half-eaten nachos to the ground. I have to skip to avoid being splashed with liquid cheese.

"It's lunchtime, right?" Dad sounds nervous, I think. It's kind of hard to tell since the campus at lunchtime most closely resembles a shark feeding frenzy with a soundtrack of flushing toilets and heavy metal.

"Yeah, it's lunchtime. And I'm in the middle of a meeting, so what's up?"

"Oh, sorry. Well." He clears his throat and says, "What?"

"I didn't say anything! What is wrong with you?"

"Oh, never mind," he mutters. "I'll just talk to you at home."

"Wait, Dad." I switch the phone to my other ear to shut out the sound of two freshman boys fighting over a hot game of cards near the bathroom. "You must have something you need to say if you called during school. What is it? Did something happen?"

There is a pause that stabs at my heart. It reminds me of

the way he told me about my mom three years ago. "No, nothing happened." He doesn't sound too sure.

"Well, then, spit it out!" I peer through the window of the classroom, and see that the video is running. The girls are laughing, which is good.

"Okay. Well, I want to be sure you're home for dinner tonight."

"Well, I usually *am* home for dinner. *You* aren't." I see Becca rewind the tape, and there is general chatter in the room. I missed the whole thing! "Why does it matter? Are you cooking?"

"No." He clears his throat again. "We're having a dinner guest. Somebody I want you to meet."

I do something I've never done to my dad. I hang up on him. Calmly, quietly, I just shut the flip phone, set it to vibrate, and slip it into my pocket.

Inside, everybody is chattering. "Well, I think in a way it's good that it's sort of strange," Cheryl Abbott is saying as she pushes her glasses up. "It will sort of act as a filter. Only the sort of intelligent people will get it. And isn't that, sort of, who we want in the club?"

"I really like the science fiction element," Amber says. "Especially the clips from the old movies."

"And the cream-filling assault on that girl!" somebody shouts. Everybody hoots at that; girls like Briley are universally disliked by girl geeks, and I guess seeing her embarrassed by cheap snack food has high entertainment value.

"Okay, okay." Becca tries to calm down the noisy chattering of the club. "Now, remember, this is funny, but we're really trying to make a statement. We want other geeks to find us, and together, we can change the way things are done at school."

"Yeah, no small order," Caroline mutters.

"What?" Becca asks. "Go on, say it out loud. I know that somebody is going to disagree with me."

"Well, I just think that we should keep to ourselves," Caroline says as her sister, Claudette, nods in agreement. "Why do we need to force ourselves on everybody? I mean, I'm happy with who I am. I don't care if all the cheerleaders and football players like me or not. So why this big need to make us so big on campus?"

"I get what you're saying." Becca nods and paces in front of the crowd as if she's rehearsed it a million times, which I know she actually has because I've seen her. "All throughout time, geeks have kept to themselves. It's a survival strategy, really, kind of like what animals do when bigger animals come out hunting. You just keep your head down and hope nobody will notice you, or hope that if a big old tiger comes along, he eats the kid next to you."

"You're mixing your metaphors," Amber points out.

Becca ignores her. "But we're not little bunny rabbits, are we? Aren't we smarter and stronger and more on top of stuff than most of the other people on campus?" A couple of the girls are nodding. "So if that's true, why aren't *we* making decisions about stuff like student government and dances and fashion and trends?"

"Because we don't care?" Elisa mutters snottily.

"No!" Becca wheels on her, eyes ablaze. "We don't get involved because we're still operating on the bully-taking-the-lunch-money mentality!"

"Huh?" Amitha frowns, puzzled.

"You mean like when they trick you into dropping your purse and then take all the change that falls out, and you can't tell on them because they'll come after you?" Cheryl squeaks. "Is that what you're talking about?"

"Exactly!" Becca shouts. "And—"

"Or when they come after you with chloroform on a towel in the bathroom—" Cheryl goes on. "Or when they take tire irons out of their cars and—"

"Oh brother." Elisa covers her head in her hands. "This is all sounding much too dangerous."

"Wait!" Becca yells. "Listen to me! If we just keep letting ourselves be invisible, where does that leave us?"

"The emergency room?" Sherrie says. Everyone chuckles.

"No. It leaves us as victims. Is that who we want to be?"

"Well, at least I'm used to it," Cheryl says. "I mean, if I never make waves nobody bothers me. I mean, most of the time."

"Is that good enough?" Becca puts an arm around my shoulder. "Shelby and I don't think so. We want to be the hunters instead of the prey."

"Okay, all these analogies are making my brain hurt," Amber says, shaking her head. "Can we just focus on what we're doing and leave the philosophy for a coffeehouse? We only have about ten minutes left."

"Exactly." Becca fishes translucent mini-clipboards from her carpetbag, each fitted with several sheets of paper and a matching pen. "Here is your assignment for next week. I want you to talk to as many girls as you can. Ask them the three questions on the first sheet, and record their answers. If they answer yes to all three questions, get their name, grade, and advisory class."

The other seven girls are reading the survey. I haven't even seen it, so I grab one and read it out loud. "One: Do you think that writers should make more money than football players?"

"Two," Becca continues. "Do you think that boys should be more interested in your IQ than your bra size?"

"I can't say 'bra' to a complete stranger!" Cheryl mutters.

"Three: Do you believe in extraterrestrial life?"

"What will this prove?" Claudette asks.

"It will filter, like Cheryl was saying. Only people who answer yes will be the kind of people we want in the club."

I decide to put in my two cents. "Okay, being devil's advocate, what if someone answers no, but they have a good reason?"

"Like?"

"Like writers shouldn't make more than football players

because football generates more money than book sales," Amitha pipes up. "That's a good answer."

"Okay," Becca sighs. "Use your judgment. If the person answers well, you can put their name on the list. Then we'll invite all of them to our event." Everybody starts talking all at once, and then the bell rings for fifth period. Becca raises her hands again to get everybody quiet. "Okay, we'll talk more about that next time. For now, if you could all just get names on the clipboard, as many as you can, that would be awesome. And Elisa, can you check and see if we can meet here every week?"

"I'll ask."

"Great." All the girls gather their things to leave. Becca, a tornado of activity, shoves all of her stuff into her carpetbag, and then swoops the video out of Ms. McLachlan's VCR. "Wasn't that a great meeting?"

"Yeah."

We move out into the human freeway of kids going to class and try not to get broadsided as we dive into the flow of traffic. "Are you okay?" Becca asks as she dodges somebody's rolling backpack.

"Sure." I feel Becca squinting at me sideways, trying to figure out what's wrong even as she navigates the hyper waves of the sugar-fueled postlunch crowd.

"Okay, well, want to meet after school?"

"I have to go home."

She pauses. We're at the junction where we usually split

off and I go to PE and she goes to math. "Yeah, I sort of figured you were going home. What's the deal?"

"Dad's having a dinner guest over tonight."

I don't even have to explain that comment. This is why
it's so great to have a friend, especially if you're a geek. With
most people, I'd have to go into some long explanation
about why this dinner is a big deal, and why this means that
my dad is bringing some stupid woman to our house, and
why that is such an incredible insult to me and to my mom.
But with Becca, I just have to say "dinner guest over
tonight" and she totally gets it. Which is good, because if
I had to explain the whole thing, I'd be crying all through
PE, and not only is that embarrassing, it's also poten-
tially hazardous, especially if you're trying to dodge a soft-
ball.

Becca pulls me out of the stream of kids, and we're sort
of flat against the wall of the Foreign Languages building.
"He is *not*."

I nod. I am trying really hard to blink back those tears
that are now rushing to jump out of my eyes like rats off a
sinking ship. That thought makes me laugh, though, so
Becca squints at me, confused. "What's funny?"

"Never mind."

She hugs me, which makes a couple of kids give us that
dirty look and snicker that says *ooh, two girls hugging, they
must be gay* because as everyone knows, touching someone
of the same sex in any way (other than in sports) means you
are absolutely and positively on the lavender end of the

rainbow. "Listen. I'm coming with you. You shouldn't have to face it alone."

"Oh, yeah, that would go over great." I'm wiping at my eyes, trying to pretend it's a contact lens problem.

"Seriously. If he can bring people into your life without consulting you—"

"Well, he did sort of consult me—"

"—and just expects you to deal, then you deserve every possible support. I promise, I'll be good. I won't throw onion dip in her hair, or spill Kool-Aid on her white linen pantsuit."

"Nobody wears white linen pantsuits."

"This woman is dating your dad. We have no idea if she even shares our DNA, let alone what her fashion sense is. We must be prepared for anything. Library. After school. Be there."

At least I go to PE laughing instead of crying.

We walk home after school again, and Becca is coaching me for The Dinner. "So, what is your ultimate goal with this dinner? Do you want to scare her away, or make her mad, or commit a felony?"

"Well, I think the felony thing is out. One more and I go to jail, you know."

She chuckles, then stops walking, turns to me, and fixes me with this really serious expression. "This is the hard question. Do you want your dad to stay single forever?"

"Huh?"

"What I mean is, unless you want your dad to stay single forever, this date thing is going to come up. So you have to decide where you stand on it. Do you want him to be single forever, or do you think he, at some point, could or should find another woman besides your mom?"

"Geez, Dr. Phil. Why don't you just say what you mean?" For some reason, this whole line of discussion is making me very angry.

"Okay," she says, and continues walking. "Maybe you're just not ready to think about it. But I guess your dad is, so you better get ready."

The rest of the walk to my house, I say nothing. I'm ridiculously mad at Becca, and want to hit her. There is some part of me that realizes this is some weird psychological twist, but I still want to hit her.

Euphoria is buzzing around the house vacuuming when we get home. "Oh, Shelby!" she squeals in excitement. And by the way, if you've never heard a robot squeal in excitement, it's something. It's kind of like the sound of a diesel semi hitting an asthmatic duck. "We're having a dinner guest! Isn't that exciting?"

"Yeah," I say as apathetically as possible.

"You don't sound excited," Euphoria says, puzzled. "Why not?"

"Listen, Shelby is just experiencing some technical difficulties with this whole dinner thing," Becca says. "Could you leave her alone for a little bit? She's processing."

Euphoria harrumphs (again, a sound that has no natural equivalent) and rolls off to the kitchen to continue preparations for her gourmet meal. I wonder how Dad's date will respond when she finds out her dinner was cooked by R2-D2.

"C'mon." Becca nods toward my room, and I follow her. "Let's take your mind off this subject. Let's talk about the club."

"Whatever." I flop belly down onto my bed.

"I will ignore that poopy attitude and continue." She sits on the floor so she's eye level with me. "We need to make some posters for the Twinkie collection. I'd like them to look like the video, so I want you to do that because you're so good on computers. Then, the next thing is our National Invisible Boy Day."

"Yeah, I wanted to talk to you about that. Where did that come from?"

"Well," Becca looks down demurely at the floor, innocently tracing her finger in a pattern on the rug. "I did it for you. You are obsessed about this Anders guy, and it's not healthy."

"Right." I sit up and hug my pillow. "Did you ever think that maybe I *like* thinking about Anders?"

"Even if it's making you miserable?"

"That's what boys are for."

She groans, exasperated. "No, no, no! You're missing the whole point! The Queen Geeks are to help us forget about all these other dumb distractions that take away our time and energy. If you keep focusing on boys, where are you?"

"Hopefully at some expensive restaurant?"

"You are hopeless. If you weren't my best friend, I would totally wash my hands of you." Becca jumps up, grabs my hand, and yanks me off the bed. "Okay. I wanted to save this for later, but I can see that you are in dire need of distraction. Come with me."

She grabs her backpack and rummages through the folders and binders until she finds a green piece of paper. "Here you go," she says proudly, shoving it toward me.

At the top of the paper, the heading reads *Green Pines Freshman Dance Committee*. "This is supposed to cheer me up?"

"Keep reading." She is practically bouncing with anticipation.

"Okay." I scan the description of the committee's function: to meet and discuss, plan, and implement the spring freshman dance. "Big deal. I probably won't even go."

"Do I have to do everything?" She grabs the paper and points to the bottom, where our two names are the last in a list of people.

"Why are our names on this paper?"

"We are on the dance committee!" She grabs my hands and starts whirling me around. "Isn't that great?"

"Whoa, whoa." I stop the dizzy spinning. "*We* are on the dance committee? Did it occur to you to ask me?"

She looks hurt. "Well, I just figured that if I wanted to do it, you would too. Don't be mad." She takes the paper from me and puts her finger on the names at the top of the list. "Look who's on here. It's all the class officers, the real movers and shakers. We can get on here and really make a change. No more stupid DJs or crappy papier-mâché decorations. We can make this a dance to remember!"

"Really? And you think people like Briley and her crew are really going to let us just take over and change their precious event into something geeky?"

"Ah, that's the beauty." Becca's eyes have that maniacal gleam that tells me it's already too late to back down. "We will make them think it's *their* idea. That's how all great leaders fool people."

"Okay, well, this has definitely cheered me up."

The phone rings. I freeze, and my heart starts to thump in my chest like a jackhammer plowing through titanium. "Shelby, can you get that? My claws are full," Euphoria calls from the kitchen.

It rings again. Becca silently motions me toward the phone, so I pick it up. "Hello?"

"Shelby?"

A male voice. With an accent. I think I will have a heart attack and die a virgin. Not fair, universe! I clear my throat and try to sound sophisticated. "Yes?"

"Oh," the voice sounds relieved. "I'm so glad. I've been trying for days to get to you."

"And you are . . ."

"Oh! Sorry. Anders. From the bowling alley."

"Oh. Hi, Anders." Becca silently screams and jumps up and down, then hops onto my bed and jumps up and down, pumping her fists in the air in victory. "How are you?"

"My foot's much better." He chuckles with that husky Norwegian laugh that melts my toes.

"Yeah, sorry about that."

"Oh, it was worth it." He pauses for a moment as I feel my way toward the edge of the bed so I don't fall to the floor and faint from sheer ecstasy. "Anyway, I wanted to know if you'd like to go out. I'm so sorry I haven't called earlier—Tim's mom washed my pants and I couldn't read your number, so I've been trying all the possible combinations of numbers that look like yours."

"You should've tried the phone book." I slap myself on the forehead. Duh! The guy tells me he's been desperately trying to call me and I insult him! No wonder I'm single!

But he's laughing! "You're right. Oh, well. At least I finally found you. So what do you say? A bunch of us are going to see a movie on Friday. Want to go?"

I wave at Becca. "Do I want to go to a movie on Friday? Wow. I have to check my book. Hang on."

She's nodding violently. "Yes!" she whispers. "You have to go!"

I hiss back at her. "Why don't you come too? With Tim?"

She sneers. "I'm not good at dating."

I go back to the phone. "Hey, Anders, I have an idea. Listen, I made plans with Becca for Friday, but maybe Tim could come too and we could have a foursome. What do you think?"

"Sure, I think we have room. What's that saying, 'the more, the merrier'? But let me ask Tim. Hang on."

While he's gone, I talk to Becca again. "He's asking Tim."

"Eww! I don't want a charity date!"

"It's not a charity date, you dork. It's a double date. You're not marrying him. We're just going to a movie!"

"But he didn't ask me. That makes it a charity date." Becca rolls her eyes and flops, dejected, onto the bed. I realize we flop a lot, but it's a very satisfying way of sitting down, really.

"Hey, Shelby?" Anders and his smooth soapy sandalwood voice are back on the phone. "Tim says that would be great. He thinks Becca's cute, actually."

"He thinks Becca's cute?" I say it loudly so she pays attention. She turns over and buries her head in my pillow. "That's really cool. What movie are we going to see?"

"We kind of wanted to see *Star Wars* again. Are you into sci-fi?"

I pray silently, thanking gods, goddesses, the Great Spirit, Buddha, and the almighty Wal-Mart for this amazing gift. A cute Norwegian guy who likes me and enjoys science fiction? Pinch me. Pinch me hard.

"Yeah, we love sci-fi. Want us to meet you at the theater?"

"Sure. How about the seven-fifteen show?" he asks.

"Great. We'll be there at six-thirty. See you then."

"Okay. Hey, Shelby, I'm really glad we met."

"Me too." I can barely contain my squeals of delight. I feel as if they will burst right out of my tummy like the bugs in *Aliens*, except that instead of killing me, they will fill the room with bubbles and butterflies and puppy dogs. Even as I think this, I realize how utterly gross and disgusting it is. I feel doomed to be a sappy romantic, even if I know better. Hormones suck.

"Bye."

"Bye. See you Friday." I hang up the phone, and we both scream so loud I think the roof will blow off my house. Euphoria calls from the intercom: "Are you girls all right? What's going on in there?"

"Everything is fan-freakin-tastic!" Becca screams.

"Well, I guess that's good," she answers. "Try not to break anything."

9

SHERLOCK HOMES

(or If You Lived Here, You'd Be Rich by Now)

In my extreme joy about the Anders situation, I forget totally about The Dinner, so when I hear the front door open, my dad's keys jangling in the lock, and then a female voice, I freeze and get a stabbing feeling in the pit of my stomach.

Becca puts a hand on my shoulder. "It will be fine." She puts up one finger, the universal signal for "wait a minute," and silently opens my bedroom door, sneaks into the hall, and peeks around the corner. She scurries back within minutes with a report.

"Okay." She sighs heavily, then leads me to the edge of the bed. "You might want to sit down."

"Oh no." I park on the edge and lean over with my head in my hands. I feel like throwing up.

"Yeah, oh no. Good news first: She's not really old, kind of pretty, seems fairly intelligent from what I could see."

"That's the good news?"

"It gets better." She scratches her scalp between the spikes and bites her lower lip, a sure sign that this is a bitter piece of news. I rarely see Becca unable to find the right words. "Brace yourself. It's someone you know."

"What?" I sit bolt upright. "Someone I know? Like who, Briley from next door?"

"Gross. It's not that bad." She pounds an open palm on a closed fist and takes in a loud breath through clenched teeth. "All right, this is like taking a Band-Aid off an old scabby wound. The best way is to do it quickly. Your dad is dating Ms. Clarke."

"Ms. Clarke? Who is—" But then the lightbulb illuminates with a blinding flash, and I suddenly remember who Ms. Clarke is. She's a second-year biology teacher. At my school. She's a *teacher*.

"You've got to be wrong. There's no way Dad would date a teacher from my school and not tell me." This eases my mind for a second; I hope I'm right, but of course, deep down, I know that this is like those morons on the *Titanic* who kept saying the whole thing was a publicity stunt to sell ice cubes.

"Yeah, but what if he doesn't *know* she's a teacher at your school?" Becca is whispering now. "What if he met her somewhere else, and doesn't know about her job?"

"I guess." Great. The best day of my life (the Anders call) is also the worst day of my life (the Dad-dating-a-teacher thing). Why is it that life seems to put those two things together so often? What I say is, "Let's just go get it over with."

"That makes sense, I guess." Becca leads the way, opening the door with a sense of impending doom. We trudge down the hallway into the living room, and there they are, my dad and a teacher, sitting together having a friendly drink. It's enough to make a girl run away from home.

"Oh, hi, honey." He jumps up, totally nervous, and spills a little of his white wine on the carpet before he sets the goblet down. "I'm glad you're home. And Becca's here too, huh?" He looks expectantly at Becca, who doesn't look inclined to grant him any slack.

Neither of us says anything for a very long minute, but finally Ms. Clarke clears her throat and stands up. She does not have a white pantsuit on, but it's almost as bad: She's wearing very tasteful black dress pants and a pink silk top with pearls. Her dark hair is swept up on her head in a sort of bun-thing, and she has on these old-looking pearl earrings. She gives me kind of a sheepish smile, and I notice that her pink lipstick is smudged at the corner. My female tendency is to fix it for her; my daughterly tendency is to chortle with internal glee at the fact that she looks like a badly drawn cartoon. "Hi. I'm Kristin Clarke. I think I've seen you at school." She extends a well-manicured hand.

Courtesy demands that I shake hands with her, of course, and I'm nothing if not polite. So I shake her hand, but I do it with that limp-fish wrist that means *I'm not at all pleased to meet you*. She looks like she's probably a nice lady, really, but because of the situation, I am morally bound by a code of honor to torture her, at least a little. "Hi. Shelby. This is Becca."

Dad is sweating. He loosens his tie and laughs as he comes between us. "Shelby, I think you may know Kristin. She's a teacher at your school, did you know that?"

"Well, I knew she was a teacher at my school, but I had no idea you were going out with her, so I don't really know how to answer your question." I send Ms. Clarke a wan, pale smile and cross regally to the couch, followed by Becca. We sit, leaving the adults looking awkward.

"So how did you two kids meet?" Becca asks, sweetness dripping from every word.

"I used to work with Shelby's dad at Gentech," Ms. Clarke says, then sips her wine. "We met again recently at a . . . meeting."

"You met at a meeting?" I ask.

"Shelby." Dad doesn't even have to say anything else. It's clearly a warning not to grill his new whatever-she-is.

"Dinner's ready," Euphoria chimes from the kitchen.

"Great. I'm starving." Becca hops up and leads the way to the dining room, where the table is set with china, crystal, and good silver. This makes me determined to facilitate some type of disaster that will result in Ms. Clarke's pearls spilling all over the eggplant parmesan. Euphoria rolls in, and I brace for a scream, a squeal, even a slight wince, but Ms. Clarke maintains her composure. Clearly, she's met our cyber servant before, which means she's been to our house before. With that realization, I want to reach over and choke her with the pearls rather than let them spill needlessly.

"You know what? I'm not really hungry." I push back from the table and throw my napkin down."

"Sit down, please," Dad commands.

"I feel kind of nauseous. I think I might throw up." And that's not an exaggeration.

Becca stands too, and follows me out of the dining room. I hear Dad say, "Just give her some time," as I walk down the hall, an impending crying jag tickling my nose.

A kaleidoscope of images flashes against the tears behind my eyes—Dad hugging Mom from behind as she washed the dishes, and how she always wore this silly pink apron, how she smelled like lilac but never seemed old-fashioned. You'd never have caught Mom in a stupid black pantsuit with pearls, hair in a prissy, uptight bun! Dad and his stupid smile introducing that woman, the woman who's now sitting in Mom's chair and eating off Mom's plates and—

"Hey, why don't we get out of the house for a while?" Becca grabs her backpack and takes her cell phone from her jeans pocket. She quick-keys somebody. "Hey, Thea? Can you come over to Shelby's and pick us up? We need to get out of the house. We have a situation."

Fighting the rush of images and memories, I take a deep breath and send Euphoria a text message to tell her that I'm leaving for a few hours, so Dad won't worry, even though he deserves to. Becca phones Elisa, Amber, and Cheryl, calls an emergency meeting of the Queen Geeks, and gives them directions to her house.

"I had to leave Cheryl a message. But Amber and Elisa said they can come over."

We sit on the porch outside waiting for the purple Jeep. I notice I'm rocking back and forth like some crazy person. "Won't your mom care if a bunch of us invade your house? And who's Thea?"

"Thea *is* my mom."

"You call her by her first name?"

Becca rolls her eyes again and flips her phone open angrily. "Thea? Where are you? Okay, cool. Hey, listen, I called a few other people. We're having an emergency meeting for school. We won't bother you." A pause, and Becca sighs, exasperated. "Yeah, I know that you work best in the early evening. We won't bother you, I promise." She flips the phone shut. "God, she's so selfish. Aren't moms supposed to, like, put their kids first? I guess my mom didn't get the memo."

"Neither did my dad." I consider leaving my microchip watch in the mailbox, but decide that it's too cruel.

"Anyway, she'll be here in about five minutes. Do you want to take some stuff so you can stay over?"

"I don't want to go back in. They might be making out on the couch or something."

Becca cringes. "Yuck. Thanks for that visual."

We wait.

Becca's mom pulls up and leaves the motor running on the Jeep. "Hey," she calls as we cram ourselves into the backseat.

"Hi, Thea. This is Shelby."

Becca's mom turns to face us. She's young-looking and has short-cropped black hair. She also has a nose ring. This is not something you usually see on moms. "I'm Thea. Hi." She cranes her neck to check the street as she backs out of the driveway. "Where to, Bonnie and Clyde?"

"Just take us home." Becca groans, shaking her head.

The Jeep is noisy, so I don't get to ask Thea any questions on the drive to Becca's house. It turns out that it's only two freeway exits away, which is weird because I'd always had the impression that it was really far, or really ghetto, and that's why Becca stayed over so much, and why we never went to her place.

When Thea pulls the Jeep into this huge circular driveway, I nearly have a heart attack. Becca's house is a palace. How this place ended up in the middle of suburban San Diego, I don't know, but it has two towering palm trees in front, a stone fountain, two stories, and a third-story porch around the top of the house where deck chairs and umbrellas make it look like some bar in Puerto Vallarta. Not that I've been to a bar in Puerto Vallarta. I just read a lot.

Thea parks the Jeep and we contort ourselves out of the backseat. "Now I can properly shake your hand," she says, extending hers. "Thea Gallagher. It's so nice to finally meet you. Becca has talked about you so much, I feel as if I already know you."

I cannot stop fixating on the nose ring. Becca sort of shuffles her weight from foot to foot next to me, clearly anxious to get rid of her mom. "Nose to finally meet you," I say as politely as possible.

Did I just say "Nose to meet you"?

I can tell by the puzzled look on Thea's face that I did, in fact, commit a major blunder, but I'm passing it off like she just misheard me, and I shake her hand. Becca grabs my arm. "C'mon, Amber and Elisa will be here before you know it. We'll be in the conservatory, so if anybody calls, can you buzz me?"

"Sure." Thea unlocks the front door, and we enter the interior of the mansion. To describe it as palatial would be an insult. The place is the Enchanted Castle, with inlaid wood floors, oriental rugs, recessed lighting, even an inside waterfall cascading over polished granite rocks! "Have fun, girls. Will Shelby be staying over? I can drop both of you at school tomorrow if you want."

"Maybe. See ya later." Becca walks briskly down a long corridor, and I have no choice but to follow her, even though I desperately want to explore her house. She makes a left and opens two gorgeous redwood and brass French doors, and we walk out into the Secret Garden. Ferns taller than I am, another waterfall, flowering shrubs, and even a tree in the middle. Over all of it, a stained-glass dome with patterns of dragonflies and hummingbirds. Soft Chinese flute music is playing from somewhere; Becca leads me to four overstuffed ivory-and-jade-colored chairs around a table.

"Uh, wanna tell me why we never come to your house?" I nestle into one of the chairs, which is big enough for me to curl up on.

"Want coffee?"

"Sure."

Becca pushes a recessed button on the table. "We don't have a robot, but we do have a maid." She plops into one of the chairs opposite me. "Yeah, well, I never bring anyone to my house until I'm sure about them. I've had too many friends who only like me because my parents happen to be extremely rich, so I always wait until I'm totally sure before I invite anybody over."

"Well, I'm glad I passed the test. This is pretty amazing. Makes my house look like the local landfill."

"Oh, please." She taps her foot nervously. "Would you please stop looking at me like that?"

"Like what?"

"Like I'm some sort of freak now that you know where I live?" She is more angry than I think I've ever seen her. The sparkly, bubbly Becca I usually see has been replaced by worried, sullen Becca.

"Look, I don't care where you live. It is spectacular, but

that's not why we're friends." The French doors open, and Elisa walks in, followed closely by Amber, who resembles a largemouth bass on a hook.

"Hello, Richie Rich," Elisa says, gawking at the ceiling. "Is this the Sistine Chapel?"

Amber continues to stare skyward, her mouth agape.

"Okay, now you know." Becca sounds like she's just revealed that she has two heads or something. "I'm sorry I kept it a secret, but I don't like people judging me based on my parents' questionable wealth."

"Oooo. Are they jewel thieves? I've always wanted to be a jewel thief." Elisa fairly drools with envy.

"God, no, you moron." Becca sneers, disgusted. "They're artists. Well, my mom is."

"Artists? And they live like this?" Amber manages to squeak.

Becca nods. "Yes. I swear. No crimes have been committed to bring us this disgusting opulence, unless you count crimes against art."

"What kind of art does your mom do?" Elisa asks. Just at that moment, a dark-haired woman in a black dress comes in and sets a silver tray on the table.

"Hello, Becca," she says with some exotic accent. "Who are your friends?"

"Amber, Shelby, Elisa. This is Meredith. She goes with us everywhere." Becca pours coffee from a carafe into four small china cups. "Don't we have any mugs, Meredith? These little baby cups won't do."

"I don't think so, Miss." Meredith chuckles. "You know how your mother is about stimulants."

Becca grimaces and takes a sip of her coffee. "Yes, I do know. And she's so full of green tea she can't see straight, so I don't care what she says."

"Call if you want anything else." The woman smiles and glides silently back the way she came.

"Wow." Amber watches the woman recede into the distance. "Wow."

"Okay, let's stop ogling Becca's riches." Elisa sips her coffee. "So let's go. Why are we here?"

I had momentarily forgotten about the whole Ms. Clarke episode and the call from Anders. My stomach suddenly feels like a swirling sweet-and-sour stew of emotion. That whole nausea thing starts up again, and the coffee doesn't seem like such a good idea. "Maybe I should have some Sprite or something," I say lamely.

Becca can read my nausea (and that proves a true friend, in my book), so she licks her lips uneasily and says, "Anders called Shelby."

"What?" Elisa blurts. "He actually called you?"

"You don't have to sound so surprised," Becca says stiffly. "He obviously liked her."

Elisa arches her eyebrows slightly, but sensing her disadvantage, she backs off. "Sure," she says between sips of coffee. "Obviously. Well, I hope you two will be very happy together. Maybe he can teach you to make Swedish meatballs."

"He's Norwegian!" Becca and I both yell at the same time.

"As fun as this is," Amber drawls, "I am totally confused. Is there some other reason we're here besides Shelby's amazing dating life?"

"We need to figure out what we want to do about the spring dance." Becca downs the coffee in her fussy china cup and pours more. "Shelby and I are on the committee, and we need some good ideas to make this dance geek-worthy."

Amber throws her legs over one arm of her chair and leans her head over the other. "Dance? Why do we want to get involved in a dance? It's just a bunch of hormones in nice clothes sweating to lame DJ hip-hop tracks."

"And this is why we get involved." Becca glances around as if she expects a squad of cheerleader spies to be hiding in the potted plants. "So we can take something routine, like a dance, and show everybody what it could be, with the proper involvement."

"Remember, Becca's goal is world domination," I say dryly.

Elisa fishes her ever-present PDA from her jeans pocket. "Right. World domination. Do we have a date set for that yet? And when's the dance?"

"The dance is May ninth. The theme is Caribbean Madness."

Amber sits upright. "What does that mean?"

"Everybody dresses up like pirates?" Elisa suggests. "You know, Johnny Depp, *Pirates of . . .*"

"Yeah, if Johnny Depp actually showed up, that might make it worth it," Becca says. "But no, I think what they have in mind is more like the Tiki Room at Disneyland. But we can change all that."

"Do you think the cheerleaders and student government drones are going to let you go in there and screw with their social event of the season?" Elisa snorts. "Fat chance. The ASB kids are there solely to exclude the likes of us."

"That's what I said," I croak, secretly wishing for bubbly beverages and hoping that by pretending to be in this discussion, my stomach will forget about me. "Becca thinks we can make them think it's their idea."

"Think *what's* their idea?" Amber asks, exasperated. "What exactly are we talking about?"

Becca puts two fingers to her lips and blows, creating a high-pitched whistle that threatens to shatter the hummingbird/dragonfly glass overhead. "Hang on! If we start fighting among ourselves, we might as well just give up right now!"

"Okay," Amber mutters. I can't tell if she means *Okay, we'll stop fighting* or *Okay, let's give up*. I'm not real sure how I feel about it either, to be honest.

Elisa is scribbling furiously on her Palm Pilot, taking notes of our entire conversation. "So, what you're asking for is ideas that might fit into the theme of Caribbean Chaos—"

"Madness," Becca corrects her.

"Madness. Ideas that we could contribute to make it more . . . geekish?"

"Exactly." Becca perches on the edge of her armchair, eyes shining, and says, "So? Give me some ideas!"

"What about pirates?" Amber sits up, more into the challenge. "Make it about the pirates of the Caribbean."

"Is that geekworthy?" Elisa says, shaking her head. "I mean, doesn't everybody like Johnny Depp? Not just us. Johnny Depp's hotness is no respecter of race, creed, or geek factor."

"We already did the science fiction thing," I offer. "So I think we should steer clear of that."

"Okay, that's a non-idea then," Becca says, kind of snippy. "How 'bout something we can actually do?"

"Wait, wait . . ." Elisa sits back in her chair, eyes closed, as if she's waiting for a lightning bolt from above to crack her skull and give her a good idea. "I've got it. What's geekier than hula skirts and coconut bras?"

"If you want to volunteer to actually wear a coconut bra, go for it," Amber says, throwing her hands up in disgust. "I, for one, will not be subjecting anyone to my nonexistent boobs encased in the shells of any fruit."

"Is a coconut a fruit or a nut?" Elisa asks.

"Who cares? It still makes a lousy bra." Amber jumps up and starts pacing between the ferns. "I don't know. Let's think about it for a while. Maybe between now and Monday somebody will get a brainstorm."

Becca shrugs. "Okay. Well, the second thing we need to talk about is Friday. The video is airing on Panther TV during third period. We need to be ready to handle questions."

"We?" Amber asks. "Why would we need to handle questions?"

"As members of the club," Becca says. "If anyone asks about what it is after they see the spot." Amber looks uncomfortable with this concept; I'm guessing she's never been a member of anything before, and the idea of evangelizing for the geek cause doesn't appeal to her. To be honest, I'm not sure it appeals to me either. I hate this, but now I wonder: What will Anders think of me being in the club? And then I immediately feel the need to punish myself for feeling that way, because no self-respecting Queen Geek would let a guy shape what she does! It's all too confusing, generally. Maybe I should just take up knitting.

Elisa stands and tucks her PDA back into her pocket. "Okay, so our order of business is to think about ways to hijack the dance with some crazy pirate scheme, and then to make the ASB think they came up with the idea, and then to convince other people that we're not dangerously psychotic so they'll want to join our club. Do I have that right?"

"Well, when you say it like that it sounds so weird," Becca mutters, deflated. "If you guys aren't into this, then say so. I can't do it by myself."

Are we into it? It's a good question. The rest of us just sort of sit there for a minute, looking down at the floor. I'm afraid to look at Becca, because I know she's going to be looking at me to see if I'm standing with her. After what she did for me at my house, with my dad and that dumb

Ms. Clarke, how can I do anything but stand up for her? I raise my head, look her in the eye, and say, "I'm with you."

Her face lights up, and I feel great again.

Elisa and Amber look up too, and both of them smile a little less enthusiastically. "I'm into it," Elisa says, a bit subdued. "I just want to be sure we're not going to look stupid."

"So what if we do?" Becca says. "There are worse things than looking stupid. Sleeping through life is one of them."

Amber laughs softly to herself, then extends a hand to Becca. "Right you are, Queen Geek. Let's do it. Regardless."

"All right!" Becca squeals. "Let's go. I want to show you guys my room. And then we have to talk more about Anders. But it's more fun to talk about it with a surround-sound stereo and a fridge full of Oreos. So come on."

"You have your own fridge?" Elisa squeaks as she follows Becca.

I take the opportunity as we walk to flip out my phone and quick-key my dad. I don't figure he'll answer; after all, he's probably having dessert with his sweetie. Yuck.

Much to my surprise, he does pick up his phone on the third ring. "Shelby?" He sounds worried. Good. "Are you all right?"

"Of course. Are you all right?"

"Where are you? I've been worried." I hear the faint clang of dishes being scrubbed in the sink, but nothing else. Maybe the date went badly. I can only hope.

"I'm at Becca's house. It's not far away at all, really. I think I'll—"

"I can't believe you just left my house without permission." His voice sounds kind of dadlike, but not in the good way. More like those belt-cracking Beaver Cleaver dads who call you "young lady" and stuff like that. Not like my dad at all. Guess that comes of dating.

"I didn't realize I had to ask permission. Is it okay if I breathe *your* air when I'm over at *your* house?"

"Kristin wanted to get to know you!" He takes a breath, and says quietly, "And I was worried about you."

"Well, did it occur to you that maybe *I* don't want to get to know *her*?" I angrily watch Amber's sandaled feet in front of me as we trudge through hallways and up a richly carpeted stairway. "Listen, I didn't call to fight with you. I just wanted to tell you where I am. I'm at Becca's. I'm staying over, and her mom is taking us to school tomorrow. So don't worry."

There is silence. I hear his breathing, which sounds angry, or sad, or both. "Okay. Sorry, honey. I love you." He hangs up before he can hear my reply, which I hadn't decided on anyway. Just as well.

Becca's room is gigantic and gorgeous. It's all done in sage green and ivory with muted gold trim, and she has a huge, beautiful bed, an entertainment system, two luxurious armchairs, and a soft Chinese rug so thick that you sink into it up to your ankles. She also has a computer station with the latest hardware, and her own bathroom that matches the bedroom.

"Wow. Can your parents adopt me?" Elisa asks, taking in every detail.

"I doubt it. They just got divorced." Becca answers as she sits cross-legged on the bed. "But you can come over whenever you want. Now, let's get to talking about more personal matters."

"Like Anders." Elisa practically salivates as she says his name.

"I thought boys weren't supposed to be our focus." I curl up in one of the velvet armchairs.

"Our prime focus, no," Becca lies down and rubs her foot against the soft comforter that probably cost more than my whole bedroom. "However, let's not pretend that boys aren't of some use. I mean, they do serve a purpose."

"And what would that be?" Amber asks as she folds herself into a lotus position on the rug.

"If I need to tell you, then you couldn't possibly understand." Becca turns to me again, and I can tell by the look in her eye that she plans to put me on the spot. "Okay. So, let's discuss Friday night."

"What's happening Friday night?" Elisa asks.

"We are going on a double date. Me and Tim, Shelby and Anders. To a movie."

"Oh, don't tell me," Amber groans. *"Star Wars?"*

"How did you know?" I ask. If she went out with Anders too, I think I will truly be sick. Not that there's anything wrong with Amber, but if he's just shopping for girls who are unusual (all right, weird) and he liked Amber, then that makes me extra weird, because she wasn't weird enough. And if he thinks I'm that weird, then he will be disappointed, because I'm strange, but not exactly weird. "Did you go out with him?"

"God, no." Amber makes a gagging sound. "I hate foreign exchange students. They all smell like fish."

"Well, thanks for contributing to worldwide harmony and understanding." Becca throws a pillow at Amber. "They all smell like fish? What, have you smelled them all personally?"

Amber ignores this comment. Elisa is pursing her lips and squinting at me in a really devious way, and this makes me nervous. "So even though you dropped a bowling ball on his foot, he still asked you out? I'd be careful. Maybe he's plotting revenge."

"Revenge?" Becca shakes her head. "He just likes her. Wasn't it obvious? Even to you?"

"What do you mean, 'even to me'?" Elisa spits.

"I mean, at the bowling alley you were so obviously in lust for Anders that I expected you to pull out a club, knock him on the head, and drag him by the hair to your cave."

"I don't live in a cave, just for the record," Elisa sniffs indignantly. "But he is exceedingly cute. And I don't think he smells like fish. Of course, Shelby would know better, since she got a lot closer than the rest of us. Shelby?" She turns to me, batting her eyelashes.

"Shut up." Girls are the worst when it comes to guys. I mean, if they're your true, best friends, they want you to get a guy who's worth something, and they're not jealous. But if they are second-tier friends, like Elisa and Amber, all bets are off. Second-tier friends see all guys as potential date bait, and if you're dating them, then they are off the market, at least temporarily. It's one thing I've always hated about girls, ever since we all saw that film in the sixth grade about the sperm with the flowers and the egg in a bridal veil. At that moment, all the girls received this unspoken message: Every egg competes for every sperm, and if you want to receive the flowers, you better be a darn attractive egg with a spotless bridal veil, or you just sit there until you rot or turn into celibate egg salad or something.

"Well," Elisa says as she checks her Palm Pilot, "I'd love to stay and chat all day about Anders and your pity date, but we have school tomorrow, and I still have a poem to write for English about compassion. What a waste of time."

"Yeah, I should go too." Amber stretches, catlike, and rises from the rug. "Great house, Becca. Thanks for having us over. See you all on Friday at lunch? So we can talk about our stunning success on Panther TV?"

"It's not a pity date—" I mutter, too late.

"Sure. Lunch." Becca opens her door and leads Amber and Elisa into the hall. I stay put. "Can you guys find your way out?"

"Yeah, I left a trail of bread crumbs," Elisa says as she and Amber wind down the stairway.

"Okay, okay. Shelby? Be back in a sec." With the others gone, I really get the chance to examine this room, and to think about what it means. It mostly means that Becca and her family are loaded. I mean, like Paris Hilton loaded. Except that Becca hasn't been corrupted by the stupidity of wealth, even if she does have nice consumer electronics.

I start to think about our date Friday, savoring the conversation with Anders like a slow-melting piece of candy. Friday, in fact, will be one of the best days of my life. Our video will be on, everyone will know about the Queen Geeks, and I will almost be able to pretend that my father is *not* dating a teacher from my school. Almost.

10

A DATE IS A CHEWY FRUIT

(or The Utter Inconvenience of Boys)

I stay over at Becca's on Wednesday. Thea takes me home on Thursday afternoon to get fresh clothes and makeup, and my special shampoo. Euphoria, despite the fact that she's totally inorganic, seems extremely upset and emotional.

"I can't understand what's happening to our family!" she whines when I am sweeping through the house collecting items to take to Becca's. "First Mr. Chapelle is gone all the time, now you. I don't know what I'm supposed to do here all by myself!"

"I suppose you could catch up on your data processing." Which blouse to wear Friday night? This is a critical decision. The robin's-egg blue with see-through sleeves? Too suggestive. The black short-sleeve turtleneck? Too nunlike. White cotton? Pure. Hmmm. Maybe something more colorful—

"Have you heard a thing I've said, Shelby Chapelle?" Euphoria's lights are blinking furiously, and she has rolled up in between me and the mirror in my room.

"Uh . . . something about how you're alone?" I hold up another shirt, an olive, burnt-out velvet poncho with copper beading. "What about this for a date? Does it say 'available but not cheap'?"

"Well, Miss Shelby, don't expect me to process your homework for you," she sniffs. "I will be occupied with other matters."

"How was the dinner with Ms. Pantsuit?" I carefully fold the olive poncho and put it into my overnight case.

"Oh, the teacher?" Euphoria's tinny laugh fills the room. "I'm sorry you missed it. If you'll pardon my saying so, your father made an absolute fool of himself with that young woman."

"Really?"

"Absolutely. They ate dinner, and I could sense a high level of tension in the air. Most probably because you left, I suppose."

"Oh well." I dig out some underwear and socks, throw those into the bag, and then toss in my perfume too.

"They finally finished eating, and she left. That was it."

"That was it? That's fantastic!" I grab Euphoria's claws and start spinning her around. "She left. She left!"

"Whoa! My servos are jamming!" She stabilizes and shakes her head a bit. "There. That's better. Well, I'm glad you're happy about it. Your father spent the evening crying in the living room."

"What?" Suddenly, all the glee I feel at Dad's dating demise disappears. I feel small, petty, and not very nice. "He was crying?"

"Well, maybe not crying, but he was definitely moping." Euphoria clucks as she zips up my bag for me. "The poor woman was very nice, but she told him she didn't think it was a good idea for them to date if you were so against the idea."

"Oh." I slowly pick up my bag and walk down the hallway.

"Isn't that what you wanted?"

Isn't that what I wanted? I thought it was. I didn't even consider that if Dad bombed out on his date, he might feel bad, or worse, devastated. And it was pretty much my fault. "Where is Dad?"

"Honestly, I don't know. He's not working in the lab, and he's not at the office. His bag is here, though, so I don't think he's skipped town."

"The car's gone, though." I grab my bag and dash out the door, signaling for Becca's mom to wait one more minute. Thea just smiles serenely and goes back to meditating. "I'll call him."

The cell phone rings twice, then three times. He finally picks up. "Yes?"

"Daddy? Are you okay?"

"Of course. Are you okay?" He sounds kind of fuzzy.

"Well, Euphoria was kind of worried about you. You haven't checked in. Could you tell us where you are?"

"I'm in Sri Lanka, I think." He pauses for a moment, and I hear the sounds of people yelling in a foreign language. "Yes, I'm pretty sure it's Sri Lanka."

"Dad! You can't just . . . just go to Sri Lanka whenever you want!"

"Why not?" He chuckles. "Ha! Had you going, huh?"

"That was a joke? *So* not funny, Dad. Where are you, really?"

He sighs heavily, and I can tell that Euphoria wasn't exaggerating: He is depressed. "I'm just downtown in the international market. I stayed in a hotel last night, just to get a different perspective on things. I figured you'd call when you noticed I was missing. Where have *you* been, might I ask?"

"I've been at Becca's. In fact, her mom is waiting for me right now, so I have to go. Are you staying over again tonight?"

"Ummm . . . yes. Yes, I think so."

"Can we talk later? Maybe tomorrow night? I have a date, but maybe after that?"

"Sure. I'll look forward to it. See you tomorrow."

"I love you Daddy." I almost choke on the words. "I'm sorry I was such a jerk about your date."

"I love you too." He hangs up, and I feel like the tiniest dust mite on the smallest flea on the smelliest dog in the nastiest dog pound on earth. "He'll be home tomorrow. So will I, after my date. Can you be sure you have some food for him?"

"I'm not the one who forgets about people," Euphoria sniffs. "Have a nice date."

I climb into the Jeep next to Thea, who comes out of her trance long enough to put the car in reverse and back down our driveway. "So, got everything you need?"

"I think so." How could I have been so selfish? I mean, Dad has been through a lot. He deserves to be happy too, right? And instead, I focus on my own stupid personal problems, and my own needs, and—

"I'd really love to meet your father at some point," Thea says as she pulls out onto the street. "Is he home?"

"Uh, not right now." I wiggle uncomfortably under the seat belt. "He's away on business. But he'll be back tomorrow."

"Hmm. I'm going to an art exhibit, and I'll be gone for the weekend. I was hoping you girls could stay at your house so I wouldn't have to worry about you." Worry about us? She's never even checked on Becca when she's been at my house! How does she know we're not crazy, knife-wielding cannibals, or in some weird sex cult? As we drive, I wonder: Are all parents crazy? Does something happen when you donate your genetic material to a baby that robs you of brain cells? This is not something they told us about in sixth grade, when they showed the sperm and the egg. The two of them looked perfectly happy together, even if they were oddly shaped. What I say: "Sure, we can stay at my house. Dad will be back tomorrow."

"Oh, good," Thea murmurs as she dodges in and out of traffic on the freeway. "I always worry about Becca whenever I leave town."

When we get to the Mansion (what I've started to call their house), Becca is on the phone in the entertainment area. Just for the record, Becca's house doesn't have a living room, or a den. They have this entertainment area, with a TV almost the size of one wall, two gaming consoles, a pool table, and a deluxe stereo system. "Well, I suppose if you pick us up that would be okay," I hear her purring into the phone. "We'll be at my house. So who's going to drive?"

Thea has moved on into her art studio, which we are forbidden to enter because she doesn't want us messing up her *chi*, which is some sort of energy that fuels her art (or, as Becca puts it, the crap that fertilizes her mom's imagination). Becca's nodding into the receiver, which she tucks under her chin as she paints her toenails a deep crimson. "As long as he's legal. Great. Six-thirty. The address is 66708 Arcadia Drive. It's off the 52 West. Just do a MapQuest. 'Kay. See you then." She continues to hold the phone under her chin as she finishes the last artistic strokes on one of her feet. "Ah, there," she sighs, stretching her foot out to admire her work. "They're picking us up tomorrow."

"I talked to my dad." I ease into the chocolate-brown suede sofa. It's like being enveloped by a giant truffle.

"Yeah? And? Is he going to be Mr. Clarke now or what?"

"Euphoria says the date was a disaster." Again, I feel that little stab of guilt. I get rid of it by thinking about being enveloped in a real giant chocolate truffle. With raspberry filling. Mmmm. What a way to go.

"Excellent!" She finishes off the toes, then sits up, fanning them out to dry them. "Isn't that excellent?"

"I guess."

Becca frowns at me, puzzled. "Okay. Well, let's talk about tomorrow. Video airing during third period, and then our double date. I'm not all that excited about Tim, actually, but it will give me a chance to keep an eye on Anders. Swedes are notoriously romantic."

"He's Norwegian, for God's sake!"

"It's all Scandinavia." She opens a cupboard that turns out to be a refrigerator. "Want a Pepsi?"

"Diet." She tosses me a cold one.

"Diet? I hope you're not trying to lose weight to be more appealing to Anders. That totally goes against our Queen Geek principles, you know." If she knew about how I was fantasizing about being eaten by a big piece of chocolate, she probably wouldn't worry.

Friday morning. D-day. D for date. Dates are supposed to be fun. The problem is, this is the first one I've actually cared about. This automatically takes most of the fun part out of it.

I am absolutely worthless in school. I have an English quiz and somehow tell Ms. Napoli that *Lord of the Flies* was written by Hans Christian Andersen. Truly awful.

The video is set to air during third period, which for me is math with Mrs. Pettinger. Crammed into the class with the regular assortment of jocks, preps, and goth punks, I figure that airing the video will probably result in massive teasing, but it might also generate some celebrity status for me and Becca. You never really know how these things are going to play out in high school. Despite knowing better, I am ridiculously concerned about what Anders will think of it.

The closed-circuit newscast starts with the grainy footage of our school's panther sculptures and clips of various popular kids doing popular things, all set to distorted headbanger music. Then it goes to the anchors, usually two really short guys who can barely read, and then it finally goes to our clip. "And now, an announcement from a new club on campus."

The sound fades in: our wibbly-wobbly sci-fi music over a dark background. One word appears in neon pink: *GEEK*. Becca's voice, cleverly altered with waxed paper and a ceiling fan, resonates: "In this school, a movement is starting. It began as an idea, but it has grown and grown" (and as she says this, the screen gets lighter, and goes to completely white) "and now, the Queen Geeks are here to save those least able to save themselves." The music from *2001: A Space Odyssey* thrums as the white screen gradually becomes the scene from Dad's lab where Briley is sitting on her stool in glorious black and white. She mouths something, which was probably obscene, but the caption reads, "You Queen Geeks will never make me gain an ounce!" Then it shows Becca in her '50s dress shaking a finger at Briley and brandishing a Twinkie as if it's an Uzi. Her caption reads, "Listen, Super Model, you are no match for us. We won't let you be a slave to beauty!"

Then the scene shifts to us smushing Twinkies into Briley's face. The class is roaring by this time, and although I can feel myself blush, I am extremely pleased with the reaction. More music accompanies the Twinkie-mashing scene, and then the video fades to the picture of me and Becca towering over the scene in our Doris Day dresses. A voice-over says: "The Queen Geek Social Club: making models fatter, one Twinkie at a time. Join us Wednesdays at lunch on the benches near telecom. Special meeting today at lunch!" It fades out.

There is a heartbeat where no one says anything. Then the whole class explodes in applause. "Was that you?" a girl next to me asks. I nod, trying to remain humble.

"Okay, okay," Mrs. Pettinger says, trying to quiet the chaos that has erupted. "It was a very creative commercial. Shelby, anything you want to say about it?"

Put on the spot, I'm suddenly tongue-tied and nervous, not at all the image I had concocted in my head. "Uh . . . it's a lot of fun. We need Twinkies."

"Yeah, what's the deal with the Twinkies?" a boy in the back of the room pipes up.

"Well, we want to collect them and send them to a modeling agency. Sort of as a protest." I finally made sense! Hurray for me!

"A protest of what?" someone else asks.

I turn to face the class, a sea of faces whose expressions range from amused to confused. "Models are all unrealistically skinny. We think it's wrong to give women the idea that they have to try to be that."

"I don't think it's wrong," a boy mutters. "Except where boobs are concerned. Those shouldn't be skinny."

Mrs. Pettinger doesn't hear him, but I do. And in a move totally unlike myself, I turn around, glare at the anonymous guy, and say, "There is more to a girl than her boobs!"

Mrs. Pettinger hears what I say just fine. "Excuse me?"

Unfortunately, I cannot stop myself. "Girls have more to them than body parts. Some of you don't get that."

"Yeah, there's more than boobs, that's for sure," another guy mutters, low enough for us to hear but not loud enough to be identified. All the boys, and most of the girls, laugh uproariously.

"That's enough." The teacher gives quizzes to each row. "Let's focus on something a little less controversial, but more fun for me." Everyone groans, and the temporary upset is forgotten in a storm of panic.

I am totally unable to concentrate on my quiz. I am absolutely steamed over the remarks the guys made, and the fact that the girls laughed too! The *girls*! What are they thinking? Don't they care about how women are seen? I look around and realize: nope. They just want, in this order, (1) boys and (2) more boys. The way to get them is to have boobs. And to be skinny everywhere else. I stare down at my own chest, and, oddly, feel mad at it.

My phone vibrates. I have to be very careful about slipping it out of my pocket; Mrs. Pettinger is a cell phone Nazi, and if she sees me looking, especially during a quiz, I could be beheaded. Well, more likely given detention, but she does get pretty mad.

It's Becca text messaging me. "DID U C IT?"

With one eye on Pettinger, who is writing on the board, I key her back: "Y. IM PIST!"

Her message: "WHY?"

Me: "TELL U LTR."

I get the phone back in its pocket before the teacher turns around. I try in vain to concentrate on algebra, but all I can think about is how guys are dogs and girls are stupid, except for me and Becca and a few others. Maybe Becca was right: Maybe the only way to get by is to find others of our own kind. Funny, until I met her I hadn't even realized I had my own kind! I guess I was just as guilty of boob promotion as anyone else. In fact, I have a Wonderbra in my drawer! I vow to burn it when I get home.

"Time." Pettinger stands, smiling, in front of the class, waiting patiently for everyone to pass papers to the front. Time? What?! It's only been five minutes! But no, the clock shows that it's been almost forty. My paper is utterly blank. I desperately scrawl my name on it; it looks even more pathetic than it did blank. For a second I consider the "you-lost-my-paper" gambit, but realize I couldn't carry it off if asked in person. I'm a crappy liar.

When we change classes, people point at me as I walk. I feel like a movie star, minus the amazing salary and limo. Lunchtime finally arrives, and I cannot wait to get to our meeting place so I can tell Becca all about my boob revelation.

She's sitting there surrounded by about fifteen girls. I can't even get to her.

"Pull up a bench," Elisa says as she bites into an apple. "Good response, huh? How did your class like it?"

"They didn't get it." Uneasily I watch as Becca chatters with the new recruits and takes their names and e-mails down on her tidy clipboard. "I explained, and the boys thought it was dumb to expect girls to do anything other than look good."

"Yeah, guys are great. Right up there on the food chain with phytoplankton." Elisa's eyes are following Becca as she flits around the new people. "Guess we'll have a lot of help for the campaign, huh?"

I don't reply. Amber sits next to me and leans so close she becomes blurry. "Notice anything?"

"I would if I could see you." She backs off a bit. "Oh. An eyebrow ring. Nice."

The skin around her eyebrow is red and puffy. A small gold circlet sticks out like the brass ring on the merry-go-round. I desperately want to pull at it and make a wish. "I had it done yesterday," she says proudly. "Isn't it great?"

"Did it hurt?" Elisa comes over and squats down in front of Amber, squinting as she examines the ring. "It looks like it would hurt."

"Not really." She self-consciously picks at the skin around the piercing. "Wasn't the video thing great?"

Becca claps her hands and everybody gathers around on the benches. Kids from other areas are watching us; last week, nobody knew or cared who we were. "Hey, everybody, thanks for coming to this special meeting. I'm Becca, and we're really excited that you are all interested in being Queen Geeks."

A few people ask questions, but mostly I tune out. I feel really depressed for some reason. It's totally stupid; I mean, our club is poised to be successful, and the ad was great, and now, finally, geeks are being seen as something other than oddities. So, what's my problem?

"So," Becca says after about fifteen minutes of babble, "let's hear from Elisa Crunch, our vice president in charge of finding a modeling agency to harass."

Everyone claps and Elisa stands up and does a little fake bow. "Thanks, thanks. Well, I've decided that, based on comparing the body-fat ratio of models to their heights, the worst offender of ridiculous thinness is the Brenda Francis Agency in Los Angeles." Elisa flips open her ever-present Palm Pilot, hits a few keys, and continues. "The average height for female models at this agency is five feet, nine inches. The average weight is a hundred and seventeen pounds. Most normal people at that height weigh one-thirty at least. So, I vote we send them all the Twinkies we can get."

All the girls sitting at the benches nod approvingly. "Okay, then, I'm asking all of you to bring at least one box of Twinkies and then to hit up your advisory classes for more. We'll also be putting up posters all over campus and making collection boxes."

"If you put those anywhere near the locker rooms, the Twinkies won't be safe," Caroline, one of the two sisters from previous meetings, says. "Football players love their Twinkies."

"True. Okay, we'll figure that out." Becca beams at the group. "Well, we just wanted to get to know you all, and to get you started on collecting Twinkies and such. We're also going to be working with the school's dance committee, so if you have ideas about this spring's Caribbean Madness Spring Fling, let us know. We meet on Wednesdays, and we're working on getting a room, so keep listening to announcements. Anybody have anything else to say?"

A hand goes up, and Becca nods toward a girl in front. "None of us would go to the dance, though."

"Why not?"

"Uh . . . none of us have dates?" The girl pushes her glasses up on her nose and shyly looks to others for confirmation.

"Well, let's go without dates, then," Elisa says, jumping up. "I say, why mess up a perfectly wonderful evening with guys?" Some people laugh, some scowl, some seem to be considering.

"Let's all get to know each other in the time we have left, and we'll talk again next week," Becca says. "Thanks for coming." She starts to circulate as the meeting breaks up. I watch her as she goes from person to person, asking questions, seeming to care about the answers. And does she? She's gone from being the new girl in school to being the head of this club; at first, it seemed like I was important to her success, but now I'm starting to feel sort of like a misfit among the misfits. So if you're a misfit within a group of misfits, does that mean you're actually popular and normal? I don't feel like either at the moment.

The Date. I suddenly remember that tonight is The Date, and as of right now, I only have six hours left to get ready. I feel my cheeks go red, and at that moment, I don't care about philosophy or fitting in or clubs: All I care about is hugging Anders's sandalwood sweater. I wonder if I'll get to hug it again? Hmm. I mentally go back to the bowling alley, the hug, the feel of his chest under the sweater, the long, smoky looks he gave me, the—

"Earth to Princess Mope." Elisa's annoying face is right in front of me when I open my eyes. "The Death Star wants its mood back."

"I wonder if you could actually have a conversation that doesn't include *Star Wars* in some way." I am angry with

Elisa for messing up a perfectly good fantasy memory, and I'm also kind of annoyed at myself for being unhappy at such an obviously happy moment. But of course, I blame it all on her, and I zero in on the one thing, with her weight, that will zing her where it hurts. "I suppose you'll personally handle all those Twinkies, huh? Wonder if we'll have any to send to the models?"

I can see I've hurt her; she looks startled, backs up a bit, and blushes. I feel a mix of regret and glee that is really a disgusting combination. "No need to be snotty about it," she says, subdued. "Have fun on your date tonight."

As she walks away, I realize that I am lower than dirt. I am lower than the cosmic dirt on the bottom of the septic tank on the Death Star. "Hey," I call after her. She ignores me, so I run after her. "Hey, I'm sorry I said that."

"Really? Are you?" Her eyes are a bit moist. I made her cry! Oh, God. I'm really bad.

"Yes, I really am. That was a really bitchy thing to say."

"It was." She purses her lips angrily and walks away.

Becca sees this exchange, and comes up next to me. "What was that about?"

"Nothing." The bell rings, and the newly initiated Queen Geeks say good-bye to each other and scatter, dashing off to fifth period.

"Ready for tonight?"

"I feel like I'm going to throw up."

"Well," she smiles, and starts off toward her class. "Then it must be love."

* * *

We go to Becca's house, as planned, to get ready for The Date. From the moment we reach her front door, we are in commando mode: no-nonsense, grim, and ready for anything.

"Okay. Showers first. Then we'll tackle hair and makeup. We only have three hours." Becca runs up the stairway to her room, and I follow, barely touching the ground. "Do you want to go first?"

We both scrub up, me first, her second. I take the longest shower I've ever taken, washing everything twice, and shaving every micron of my legs with expert precision. I suspect I used all their hot water when I hear Becca singing "R-E-S-P-E-C—Owww! Hey! HEY!" Oops.

"Well, that cold shower was very stimulating," she says as she towels off. "Thanks. I won't get any impure thoughts about Tim."

I've already started carefully sponging on base makeup, trying to get every pore covered evenly so I don't look blotchy or chalky. As I run the little sponge around the side of my nose, I freeze. I am terrified to turn my head, to investigate my horrendous suspicions. "Becca," I whisper.

"What?"

"I need a favor. Check the side of my nose. The right side." She squats down next to me and squints, and then I see her eyes get really big.

"Oh."

"It's not."

"It is."

A zit. How could I have a zit on the most important date of my entire life? I turn my head to confirm. I see a volcanic mountain of zittiness. It arches up and over the fold behind my nostril. It is so big it has its own geological designation as a toxic waste site.

"Don't cry, whatever you do," Becca says calmly, putting a reassuring hand on my shoulder. "Crying is the worst thing you can do for a zit. Then your whole face gets red and it stands out even more."

"Maybe if my whole face is red, he won't notice the zit!"

"Right."

Faced with this crisis, I am eerily calm. I assess the situation, and decide on a plan of action. "I'll tell him I broke my nose and wear a cast on it."

"They don't put casts on your nose. I know, because my mom had a nose job. But believe me, the bandages make you look ten times worse. And trying to cover it with makeup just makes it stand out even more. No. What we need is a strategy."

She sits on the bed, closes her eyes, and bites her lower lip. After a minute, she jumps up, runs over, and squats down next to me on the side opposite the Land of the Pimple. "Perfect. Here's what we do. You only sit on his right side. That way, he'll never see the zit."

"You can't see it from there?"

"Nope. You look flawless."

"What if he tries to kiss me?"

"Kiss sideways. Anyway, if he's always on your left, he'll kiss you from the left, and by the time you straighten out your face, he'll have his eyes closed."

"What if he's an open-eyed kisser?"

Becca sighs. "Shelby, there are some things we just have to leave to fate."

We finish getting ready, and I try to minimize the volcanic eruption on my nose with exceedingly sexy eye makeup and a push-up bra. It's nearly six-fifteen when we finish the last curl on the last hair, and we approach the moment of truth: the full-length mirror.

Becca goes first: She looks devastating in a black mini, Candies zebra-stripe platforms, and a '70s-style top that's the same color as the violet spikes in her hair. Her makeup is a little over the top, I think, but definitely striking. "Your turn," she says, obviously satisfied.

I start with the shoes. I'm wearing my black lace-up sandals, the ones that look kind of Greek goddess-ish, and Becca has painted my toenails some copper color called Brassy Brass. I'm wearing my olive-velvet poncho thing with the copper beads over a stretchy black lace skirt that's tight to the knees. From the feet up, I look fantastic. Then I see my face.

"No!" I scream.

"What?"

"Look at the zit! It's eating my face!"

"You're exaggerating. C'mon. Look at the eye makeup. It's stunning. He won't even notice the zit. And your outfit is great." She looks at her watch. "Ten minutes. Let's get downstairs."

"Wait. Practice with me."

"Practice what?" She gives me a wary look.

"I know. But just pretend like you're Anders and you try and kiss me. You don't have to, really, just do the face thing so I can tell if he can see the zit. Please?"

She rolls her eyes and then stands up really straight, throws her shoulders back, and talks with a very fake Scandinavian accent that sounds a lot like Arnold Schwarzenegger. "Hello, Shelby. You look fantastic tonight."

"Thanks. Okay, now drop the role play. Just kiss me."

"Geez, don't I even get dinner first?"

The doorbell rings. "Ah! Hurry!"

I keep my face sideways to her for as long as I can as she moves in, trying to act like a swaggering guy. She puts her hands on my shoulders, turns me to her, and then screams a bloodcurdling scream. "Oh my God! Something's eating your face!" I throw a hairbrush at her as she bolts down the stairs.

I take a moment to compose myself, which is barely possible, then follow her. She's already opened the door, and is kissing Tim lightly on the cheek, very European-style. "Hey. How are you guys?"

"We're okay," Tim says, trying to sound old. His voice squeaks a little.

Anders walks in after him, and my heart stops beating.

He has his arm around another girl. A very tall, blond, beautiful girl.

Becca looks back at me, her eyes wide with panic. "Uh, hi. Who's this?"

"Oh, this is my girlfriend, Ilsa. She's staying with another family, but I didn't think you'd mind if she came with us too. Is that all right? Oh, and her English is not so good."

I am choking on my own internal organs at this point. How is it possible that I so misread the signals? How is it possible that Anders called me and forgot to mention that he has a girlfriend named Ilsa? On the upside, the zit suddenly seems pretty unimportant.

"Yeah, we have a couple of other people in the car too," Tim says, avoiding Becca's stare. "My brother's driving, so he and his two friends are coming with us. Let's go see the Sith get their butts kicked!"

Outside, a minivan is parked in the driveway. A scraggly-looking guy is in the driver's seat, rocking out to some heavy metal music. Tim opens the passenger door, and Anders grabs Ilsa by the waist and lifts her into the car as if she were a fine piece of china. He follows, and they take up residence in the backseat. The dark backseat.

Tim bolts around to the front and climbs into the front passenger seat. This leaves Becca, me, and two strange guys in the middle seat. Four people will not fit. I am sure as hell not sitting between Anders and Ilsa.

"Could one of you guys sit in back?" Becca asks politely. The two boys just stare at her. One is kind of small with dark curly hair, and the other is a freckle-faced redhead, kind of muscular, slightly familiar. They look at each other, and do the eyebrow negotiating thing that guys do, then the dark-haired one sighs, gets up, and plops rudely between the Norwegian lovebirds.

I sit carelessly next to the redhead, who I now recognize as the jerk from the bowling alley who was yelling out the car window at me. Great. I am beyond caring about my fate. I don't even buckle my seat belt. Becca sits timidly next to me, and I feel her checking me. I'm on suicide watch.

"Hi," the redhead says, extending a hand. "Remember me? Fletcher?" I stare rudely at his hand. "Well, nice to see you."

"Don't mind her," Becca says. "She's . . . got temporary deaf-mute syndrome."

"I do not." I turn to Fletcher, who has really striking green eyes the color of jade, and I say, "I'm Shelby."

I stick my hand out this time, and he takes it. I squeeze so hard he jumps. I continue pumping his hand until he snatches it back and begins to massage it. "Hey, Shelby. Nice grip. Are you on the wrestling team?"

"Oh, if I wanted to hurt you, believe me, you'd know it." I face front as Tim's brother maneuvers the van out of the driveway.

"What Shelby means is that she's had a lot of martial arts training. She's a black belt in—"

"The only black belt I have holds up my jeans." I turn to Fletcher. "I'm just a little bit emotional, that's all."

"Oh." He nods knowingly. "That time of the month."

That time of the month. Yes, that is the only possible explanation for any female having emotional issues. I look around for something to hit him with, but there is nothing except a San Diego Padres baseball pillow sitting on the floor. I grab it and whack him in the head.

"What was that for?" He grabs the pillow and hits me back.

"Well, what was *that* for?" I hit him again.

"I was just trying to be nice—"

"By making some bonehead remark about 'that time of the month'? I mean, what century are you living in, Cave-boy? Women do have feelings that don't relate in any way to menstruation—"

He covers his ears. "Don't say that word."

"What?" I ask gleefully. "Menstruation? Menstruation. Menstruation! MENSTRUATION!"

"Stop it!" He covers his ears with the Padres pillow.

"Okay, okay." Becca unlatches her seat belt, gets up, and shoves in between us. "Clearly, you two need to be separated. Move over, Shelby."

"Is everything all right?" Anders asks from the backseat.

"Just great," I mutter. Fletcher is looking at me with a mixture of fear and disbelief. I snarl at him, and he immediately turns his attention toward the fascinating scene whirring by outside.

The movie, of course, is a total disaster. If you haven't seen the last *Star Wars* movie, *Revenge of the Sith*, I don't want to spoil it for you, but let's just say that love plays an important part. So every time the actor who plays Anakin/Darth Vader comes on, I think of Anders. Anakin, Anders . . . it's sort of prophetic that he would turn to the Dark Side. I am sitting next to Becca, and I'm on the end of the row, I think mostly because everyone else is afraid to sit next to me. When Fletcher has to get up and use the bathroom, he actually goes the other way to avoid having to step over me. Who knew I had this kind of power?

When the lights come up at the end of the movie, I see that I have shredded a mountain of paper napkins into confetti. Becca just looks at the mound of paper and shakes her head. As we walk out, she whispers, "National Invisible Boy Day. Remember."

11

ANGER MISMANAGEMENT

(or Make Rejection Work for You!)

By the time Tim's brother drops us off at Becca's, I am a knot of anger and frustration. Not to mention the fact that I feel like a total idiot. And Anders seems totally unaware of any problem.

When we come in at about ten, Becca's mom is doing some weird dance in the living room and this Middle Eastern music is blaring throughout the house. "Belly dancing. It's part of my mom's workout regimen." She goes over to the stereo and presses a button, and abruptly the music stops. Thea nearly falls over.

"Well, hi," she says. "How was your date?"

"Don't ask. Hey, could you turn down the music a little?"

"Sure." Thea wipes her forehead with a towel, and sits. "I was almost finished anyway. So, the movie was bad or what?"

"Anders brought a date." Becca plops down on the couch.

"He brought a date on your date?" Thea looks at me, wide-eyed. "Whoa. That is bad."

"We're going upstairs to mourn," Becca tell her. "We will be eating chocolate, just so you know."

"That's an avoidance behavior."

"Yes, I know. We need to avoid at the moment." To me, she says, "C'mon."

In Becca's room, she opens a cupboard and pulls out a huge, and I do mean huge, satin box of candy.

"Dig in while we plan our revenge." She peels off her skirt and shoes and sits cross-legged on the floor, then picks out a candy and bites into it. "So good."

"Where did you get this?" I indicate the house-sized candy box.

She swallows a huge wad of chocolate. "My dad. He feels guilty about the divorce, so he sends me stuff. Go on, dig in."

"Why not? I guess I don't have to watch my figure now, huh?" As I reach for a piece of cocoa heaven, she grabs my hand. "What? You said I could have some!"

"Yes, but listen to what you just said. You said it doesn't matter what you look like because Anders has rejected you."

"I'm not sure he even rejected me. I don't think I was even in the running. Not against *Ilsa*." I say her name with the same oily nastiness that Elisa Crunch uses to say Anders's name. Then I bite into a particularly huge butterscotch square and chew it savagely to extract all the chocolate goodness.

"Okay. That was one of the crappiest moves I've ever

seen, I agree. Maybe in Norway they do things differently."
She picks up her phone. "Should we call and ask him?"

"No!"

"Fine." Exchanging the phone for more candy, she stuffs
two pieces into her mouth and works her jaw around them.
As she licks a dribble of butterscotch that has escaped, her
phone rings. "Hello?" Her jaw drops, and as she listens,
her eyes grow bigger and bigger. "Sure. Yeah. I don't know.
Let me ask her." She covers the receiver with a teddy bear.
It looks like the toy is trying to make out with the phone,
but that's probably just because of my state of mind. "It's
Fletcher."

"Who?" I reach for more candy.

"The guy from the car. With the pillow."

"The guy I hit?"

"Yeah."

"What does he want?"

She puts the phone to her ear. "What do you want?" She
listens, nods, and then shakes her head. "Why don't you tell
her yourself?"

She hands the receiver to me, and I stuff two more
squares into my mouth before I talk. "Mmmfllfp?" I say.

"Uh . . . Shelby?"

"Yfff." I keep chewing.

"Yeah, this is Fletcher. From the car? The guy you hit
with the pillow?"

"Hmmm. Yfffp."

Silence. Then he clears his throat and seems to be searching for something to say. I wonder if he called to tell me his dad's a lawyer and he's suing me for assault with a deadly cushion. "Tim told me what happened, why you were upset. I . . . I guess I just wanted to call and say—uh—"

"That guys suck?" Motioning to Becca, I say, "More chocolate."

"No, that's not what I was going to say." He sighs heavily, then says, "I just think it was a lame thing for him to do, and I wanted to tell you that I felt bad for you."

"Oh, so are you calling to offer to comfort me?"

"No, not really. I just wanted to—"

"Thinking maybe since I've been brutally rejected I'll be an easy target?"

"Hey, now, that's not fair—"

"Thanks for your concern."

I hand the phone back to Becca. She fumbles with it, then stutters, "Uh . . . uh, Fletcher? Yeah. Thanks for calling. Bye." To me, she says, "Wow. I've never seen you like this."

"Like?"

"Mean."

Because the universe likes to really push people's buttons, my cell phone rings at just this moment. It is, of course, my dad. "Yes?" I say frostily.

"Hi, honey. Are you coming home? It's getting late." Dad yawns. "I'm really tired. If you're staying over at Becca's, I think I'll just go to sleep and see you tomorrow. Is that okay?"

"Sure. I'll just stay over here so you can have a little private love fest, teacher's pet."

"Shelby, what happened? Are you okay?"

"All I got out of this date was greasy fingers from stale popcorn and a bruise on my ego."

"Oh." He sighs and says quietly, "Okay. We'll talk tomorrow. Good night."

All of a sudden, just as I hang up the phone, I feel the need to break something. As I've said, I'm not one of those girls who gets all upset over everything any guy does. Why this whole incident is so disturbing is because I'm doing stuff I've never done before. I'm obsessing over a guy, and that's not something I do. I actually cared about him, which is not something I do. And I let him hurt me, which is not something I do. But here I am anyway. There is not enough chocolate on the planet to heal this wound.

Becca can tell I'm at rock bottom. "It's gonna be okay," she croons. "Believe me, in a few weeks you won't even remember Anders or his dumb girlfriend."

Fat chance, I think. Literally. I've plowed through one whole layer in the satin candy box. Those pounds are going to stay on.

Somehow, I sleep through the night and wake up Saturday morning on Becca's floor. She has a huge air mattress that's actually more comfortable than my real bed, so I don't mind at all. What's weird is that it's really early, and Becca is up already, typing on her computer.

"What are you doing up before noon?"

"Hey." She keeps tapping demonically on the keyboard.

"So? What are you doing?"

She finishes up a word and then turns to me, wearing her rectangular black reading glasses. "After last night, I was inspired to really kick things into high gear."

"What does that mean, exactly?" I peer over her shoulder and see a huge chunk of text. "Are you writing a research paper or something?"

"No, I'm writing a press release." She turns back to the bluish glow of the screen, pushes up her glasses, and returns to her document.

"A what?"

"Press release. My parents used to do them all the time on their independent projects. It's so the newspapers and TV stations can do stories on what we're doing."

"What are we doing?"

She sighs impatiently, closes her document, and swivels around in her chair. "Let's go have coffee. I'll fill you in."

We trudge downstairs (okay, I trudge, she sort of skips) and Meredith has already laid out two mugs and two place settings in their breakfast nook, which is bigger than my kitchen and dining room combined. In the center of the table there are fresh-cut flowers, purple and lavender and blue, in a crystal vase the size of my head. Actually, it's like my head in more ways than one. Transparent, full of water, fragile—

"Have some coffee." Meredith pours me some, and I decline the cream and sugar. "You girls have fun last night?"

"Can't say it was fun, exactly," Becca answers as the woman pours her some of the rich, dark brew. "But it was instructional."

Becca is, to be honest, sort of scary this morning, and I don't think it's just me. She always seems a little manic, a little crazed, but today she has taken manic and crazed to a whole new level; it's as if she's supersized her weirdness. Or maybe it's just the glasses.

After a few sips of coffee, I feel I can join the land of the talking. "All right. So what got you up so early?"

"I am inspired." She leans forward, nearly knocking over her cup. "After your date disaster yesterday, I've really gotten excited about Queen Geeks. I see this as a way to change dating forever."

"Wow. Glad you're not trying to do anything too difficult." I drain the coffee from my cup and reach for the black thermos Meredith left on the table. "Changing dating as we know it. Yeah, start small."

She ignores my amazingly funny sarcasm. "National Invisible Boy Day. It needs to be what it says: national."

"Okay, so if you're talking about national as in the whole country, that isn't starting small."

"I know," she says impatiently. "But what kind of impact will we make if it's just at our school?"

"But how do you expect to get a whole country to do something if you can't even get the whole school to do it?"

I'm thinking about when I first met Becca and joked with her about wanting global domination. Now I think maybe it wasn't a joke.

"I know, I know. But listen. My parents have done all kinds of stuff to get attention for their art. I know how to do this. We start at school, and that has to be really big, but then we get the local TV stations to cover it, and then get other schools to do it too. It's not that hard."

"And you think you'll still have time for homework?"

She rolls her eyes. "Let's get to work."

After swigging the rest of my coffee, I follow the whirl-wind that is Becca to her room, and by the time I get there she's already saddled up at the computer and typing furiously. "Check this out. Here's my press release to the local media. I'll read it." She clears her throat and her voice changes so she sounds like one of those plastic anchor-woman news clones. "'Dateline: April 24. San Diego. Head-line: Teen Girls Vow to Ignore Boys! An upstart new club, the Queen Geek Social Club, has started a movement that is growing all over the country.'"

"That's not true!" I sputter. "You can't just lie!"

"It's not lying. It's public relations." She continues. "'The movement, called National Invisible Boy Day, encourages girls everywhere to take one designated day—'" Here she stops and looks at me. "I haven't figured out the date yet— 'one designated day, May the whatever, to totally ignore all boys. When asked why this is the focus of the club, spokes-person Shelby Chapelle said—'"

"Hey! What do you mean, spokesperson Shelby Chapelle?"

Becca sighs, exasperated, and looks up at the ceiling. "I can't do everything! You're much better to be a spokesperson. Of all of us, you seem the most normal."

"Well, thanks a lot!"

"Anyway, here's your quote, and we can change it if you want. 'It's not that we don't like boys, we just want girls to be able to really focus on what they want without thinking of boys.' Okay. Don't you think that's great? And then I just put in stuff about our school and where they can reach us to do interviews."

I say nothing; I stare at Becca in what I hope is stony, disapproving silence.

"What? You want to change the quote?"

"Do you know what will happen to me if this gets out? I'll never go on a date again!"

"And is that a big loss? Think about the Anders incident!"

I have to admit that she's got a point. All in all, when I look at my dating life from the bigger perspective, it pretty much sucks. If it were a bar graph, and each guy were a different colored bar, and the side of the graph measured things like stupidity, lack of consideration, and overpowering lust, the colored bars of all of the guys I've dated would crash through the top of the graph and rocket skyward like a testosterone-fueled rainbow. Not to mention that many of them (not Anders) smelled bad.

"Shelby?" Becca waves a hand in front of my face. "Are you still with us?"

"Yeah. Sorry. Okay, I'll be your spokesmodel."

"Spokesperson."

"Spokesgeek?"

She smiles from ear to ear, turns to the computer and types frantically.

We work on our campaign all morning, surfacing only for sandwiches and more coffee, and for the occasional bathroom break. By noon, we have the press release finished, a logo and T-shirt design (groovy clip art of a '50s housewife with a book and a crown), and a plan of action for school. This includes posters, announcements, and fliers passed out at lunch to inform everyone of N.I.B.D. (National Invisible Boy Day).

"How do you think the boys will take it?" I ask Becca as we wait for her printer to spit out a hundred posters on cherry-pink paper.

"If I were a guy, I'd be flattered. I mean, if they weren't important, why would we have to make a special day just to ignore them?"

"Yeah." I remember that I absolutely have to see my dad today, not that I want to. If he tries to swap date details with me, I will surely lose my lunch. "Hey, so I have to go home at some point today, to talk to my dad. Want to come with me?"

She makes a face that tells me she doesn't really want to (and who would, with a house like this?), but she agrees.

She finds her mom (who is in the art studio breaking cheap dishes to use in a ceramic mosaic of vegetables commissioned by some farm bureau) and she reluctantly agrees to give us a ride to my house. "I need to get on the road. Remember, I'm going to L.A. tonight for the gallery opening. But the eggplant is really speaking to me right now," she says. "I need to get back before I lose the inspiration."

"Never get between a woman and her vegetables," Becca mutters as we climb into the Jeep.

When Thea drives up to our house, I notice there are about a dozen big cardboard boxes parked out front. My first thought is that Ms. Clarke has moved in while I've been away. Or that Dad has moved me out.

Thea waves to us and speeds away, in a big hurry to get back to her eggplant. "What's with the boxes?" Becca asks as I unlock the front door.

"Guess I'll find out."

Inside, I hear Euphoria's tinny voice humming some Rolling Stones song (Dad programmed her for oldies) and I find her in the kitchen chopping lettuce. "Well, well, if it isn't the prodigal daughter!" She whirls around, lights blinking merrily. "I missed you! What's going on?"

"Going on bad dates, hating boys, eating chocolate," I say, grabbing a shiny red apple from a bowl on the counter. "Where's Dad?"

"Garage." She lines up a tomato and slices it perfectly. "He's been cleaning stuff out all day."

Becca's eyes meet mine, and I know we're thinking the

exact same thing. Without a word, I rush out the back door and dash around to the garage with her right behind me. Dad is there in a grungy pair of jeans and a T-shirt, perspiring as he hoists a huge cardboard box from a high shelf.

These are the boxes that hold most of the stuff that belonged to my mom. This is why I'm so freaked out. "What are you doing?" I yell as I slap his hand from the box he's holding.

He looks surprised, and I'm surprised too. "Just cleaning up," he says, confused.

"Your idea of cleaning up is to just throw out Mom's stuff? Like she never existed?"

"What?" He glances over at the spilled box that is leaking papers, photos, and brown bags full of who-knows-what. "You think I'm throwing out Mom's things?"

"Aren't you? So your teacher friend can just move right in and take her place?" I'm beyond making any sense now. I've passed into some realm where the part of me that actually sometimes makes sense has been locked in a closet in the back of my mind. I hear myself babbling on, and even though I hate myself for saying the things I'm saying, I can't seem to stop.

"Am I next?" I scream. "Will you just kick me out to the curb like yesterday's trash, and wait for somebody to pick me up so you can clear some personal space in your life?"

"Shelby—"

"I guess I thought maybe Mom meant more to you than

that." Now I'm out of control again, and I have to tell you, I'm really getting sick of it. Becca puts a hand on my shoulder, and I shrug it off.

Dad turns away from me, puts a hand on his forehead, and kicks the box on the floor. "I'd never throw out your mom's personal stuff," he says finally. "These things are just papers, bank records, and office stuff from where she worked. She wasn't about records and papers. She wasn't that kind of person. So I think I can get rid of these things without it being an insult to who she was, or to you."

"Uh . . . I think I'll go see if Euphoria needs a tune-up or something," Becca mumbles, then ducks out of the garage.

"Shelby, I know losing your mother was hard for you." Dad's eyes are half-closed, like he's trying not to look at me. "But I lost my wife too. Don't forget that." He finally looks at me directly. "I could never replace her. Never. I don't want to."

Why am I such a jerk? I'm thinking about myself, how I feel, and my dad is suffering just as much as I am, if not more. Is that just a teenager thing, or am I just an exceptionally awful person? All I say is "I'm sorry, Dad."

He smiles then, breaking the tension, and grabs me in a big, tight hug. "I love you, sweetheart. And even if I do occasionally have a date, I'll never be able to replace your mom. She was one of a kind. And to be honest," he pulls back and kisses my forehead, "I'm not ready yet either. I realized that the other night."

"Dad, I don't want you to go through your life all by yourself. I mean, except for me, but I mean without a . . . a . . . companion." That sounds so stupid, but I have no idea how to express to him that I understand his need for female company. It's just not something a teenager should have to do: counsel a parent on his or her love life. It totally goes against the laws of nature. But this is our situation, so I guess I'd better adapt. "I mean . . . what I mean to say is . . ."

"I think I get it." He mercifully turns back to the cardboard boxes. "Now, you want to help me sort through this old box of books? We brought them from the other house and I have no idea what's in there."

"Well, actually, Becca's here, and we were going to do something a little more normal, like go to the mall. Is that okay? And can you drive us?"

He laughs, and shakes his head, which I guess is a good sign. "I can't blame you there. Clean out the garage or go shopping? Hmm. Yeah, go get me my keys."

Dad drops us at the mall; Becca doesn't say anything until he's already pulling away from the curb. "So? What was up?"

"He was just cleaning out old junk. Not my mom's stuff, just papers and tools and books. I just freaked out for nothing."

As we walk through the massive glass doors to the Temple of Stupid Spending, Becca says "Oh, I called Amber and Elisa too. They're coming over in about half an hour."

"I hope we're not just going to talk about club stuff. I'd like to do something purely fun for a change."

"Then let's go to GameRage." GameRage is the store for people who like challenges of all kinds: trading cards, board games, video games, everything. So far, my excitement has been limited mostly to the board games, but I could easily see myself getting addicted to some of the RPG (role-playing game) stuff.

"Where are they meeting us?"

"GameRage."

"Of course."

Since it's Saturday, the mall is crammed with kids. I wonder, what did teenagers do before malls? I guess there were shops and stuff, but they were all spread out, so where did they all go to hang out in the days before shopping became a national pastime? Maybe they just sat on porches and drank lemonade or something, like in the movies, but I have a feeling they must have been bored to death. Or maybe they just walked around and traded their old stuff to other people for new stuff. That's almost like shopping, I guess.

GameRage is, of course, packed. Almost every kid I know plays some sort of game, whether it's on a handheld or a home gaming system or a computer, and the select bunch of supergeeks who play chess and RPG mingle with the kids who learn about how to carjack a Cadillac and pick up prostitutes in the comfort of their living rooms. It's kind of a strange mix, like one of those suicide sodas you make from putting every drink from the beverage bar into one cup.

"Hey, check this out!" Becca excitedly waves me over to the board game part of the store. She's holding up this retro-looking box. "Mystery Date! My mom told me about this. She used to play it when she was a kid."

I read the back of the box. "So the idea is you just open this plastic door and get a date with whoever is on the other side? Where's the strategy in that?"

"It's just for fun." She puts the box back on the shelf, disappointed at my lack of enthusiasm. "Well, what about this one? *Star Wars* Monopoly."

"What do you buy for properties?"

"Planets." She's reading the sleek black packaging. "And I think if you land on Chance, Yoda tells your fortune or something."

"That's okay. After last night, I've had enough *Star Wars* to last me for quite a while."

"Shelby?" It's a guy's voice, vaguely familiar, but when I hear it I get this stabbing pain behind my right eye. "Hey, Shelby!"

I turn and it's Fletcher, the guy I assaulted with the Padres pillow. What a coincidence. It's like the universe is making sure I don't forget the excruciating humiliation of my date with Anders. Nice job, universe. "Hi, Fletcher."

"How's it going?" Becca has seen him, and she's ducked over into the next aisle, the coward.

"Oh, okay I guess." I am trying very hard to ignore this guy without being rude, which is really a science all by itself. "Just hanging out."

"Yeah." He acts like he's reading the games on the shelves. "Oooh. *Star Wars* Monopoly. That would be cool."

Please, I think for what must be now be the tenth time, *please let the earth open up and swallow me whole.* As usual, the earth does not comply.

"Uh, Shelby. I was wondering. Are you going to the spring dance?"

"I'm on the dance committee."

"Oh." He isn't sure if that's a signal to go ahead or to get lost. It's my own fault. If I just had the guts to say something compassionate but direct, like *Leave me alone, moron*, then I would get much better results.

However, I am unable to be this cruel, having recently been the victim of cruelty myself. So, instead, I say, "Dance committee members aren't allowed to have dates." Lying is always preferable to uncomfortable truth, right?

"That's stupid." He's squinting at me, all the freckles on his nose lining up in such a way that I want to grab a pen and connect them to see if a pattern will form.

"Yeah, it is kind of dumb," I agree. "Of course, since we have so many responsibilities, it kind of makes sense. We have to be free to fix any problems, you know."

"Problems with what?" Becca chirps over my shoulder.

"Oh, Shelby was just telling me about the dance committee thing." Fletcher brushes his unruly Ronald McDonald hair out of his eyes. "You know, how you all can't have dates?"

"What? I never heard—" I'm staring daggers at her at that moment, and sending brainwaves toward her at light speed: *agree, agree, agree.* She finally gets it, pauses and then says, unconvincingly, "Oh, yeah. Well, maybe we can get the rule changed." Oh well. Close enough.

"Maybe. I was just asking Shelby to go with me. But," he smiles, green eyes twinkling, "since I'm on the dance committee too, maybe they'll let us go together."

"You're . . . you're . . ."

"Yeah. I saw you were on it, so I volunteered too." He leans against the shelving, with his arms crossed, an insufferably smug look on his face. "So, guess we'd better get together. To do some planning."

"I wish I'd brought a pillow, so I could whack you again," is all I say as I storm past him. Becca follows me, trying really hard not to laugh. I jog-walk out of that store, out into the stream of humanity flowing through the mall, and I try to get lost. But it's never that easy.

"Oh my God! That was awesome!" she squeals as she prances next to me. "Can you believe that? He's as smart as we are!"

"Yeah, great. I just made a total fool of myself."

She calms down and I finally stop jogging when we get to the opposite end of the shopping center. I feel flushed and out of breath.

"Want to sit for a while? I don't think he'll follow you," she says as she slides onto a worn park bench. "Okay, but you have to give him credit. That was pretty slick."

"You'd better text Amber and Elisa to let them know where we are." Becca flips her phone open, quick-keys them, and waits for a reply.

"Oh. They're already over there. I'll go get them if you want. So you won't have to face your secret admirer."

"More like a stalker. Yeah, okay. Go get them."

Becca grins and jogs toward GameRage, leaving me alone with my thoughts. What is with this Fletcher guy? Why would he in any way think that I'd be interested in him? I replay the scene in the van, the one where I was so mad at Anders, and hurt, and how that stupid Fletcher said something about me being on my period. What a dork! Come to think of it, I've seen him around school. He's older than I am, so we don't have classes together, but I've seen him during lunch. Where else? Maybe in gym? There are a lot of guys doing gym when I have my class. Or maybe he's in a sport. Didn't somebody say he plays football? No, doesn't seem the football type. He's built too slightly, sort of thin but muscular. He has nice forearms. Maybe he plays tennis. His hair is that coppery new-penny color, which I've always liked, not really Ronald McDonald red. And he has really nice green eyes, almost transparent, like sea glass. But still, he's a total dork. I want nothing to do with him.

Becca comes bopping around the corner, with Amber and Elisa behind her. "Oh my God," Elisa squeals, which is very unlike her. "I cannot believe it. Fletcher Berkowitz asked you to the dance."

"Why is that good?"

"Oh, I don't know. He's only the cutest sophomore guy in school, and he's on the academic decathlon team, and he's the student producer for Panther TV."

"Sounds like somebody has a crush."

"Well, all this drooling over a guy is great, but we need to get to business," Amber says, sounding bored. Maybe she has a Fletcher Berkowitz obsession too.

"I suggest we get smoothies before we start doing any hard work." Elisa adjusts her backpack, which seems to be a permanent part of her body. "I'm hot and thirsty."

"Juice Ranch," we all say in unison.

Juice Ranch has any kind of fruit imaginable in any combination with frozen yogurt. And you can kind of pretend it's healthy, which is nice. The only thing I don't like about it is that it's got this cheesy Western motif, and all the decorations are lassoes and pictures of cowboys and stuff. Even the cups have little cartoon ropes painted on. Anyway, we get our drinks and sit in a booth underneath a sad-looking deer head mounted on the wall.

"That creeps me out," Amber says, gesturing to the trophy. "It looks really depressed."

"You'd be depressed too if somebody took off your head, stuffed it, and mounted it on a wall," Becca says.

"Hopefully, we'll never know." Amber takes a noisy sip

from her Raspberry Round-Up. "So, what's the latest Queen Geek adventure?"

"Twinkie collection is going well," Elisa reports, consulting her Palm Pilot. "We have thirty-two boxes and several dozen loose Twinkies."

"Loose Twinkies," Amber snorts, choking on her smoothie. "What, do they put out on the first date?"

"I'm ignoring you." Elisa shakes her head, then continues. "I think we should wait for maybe another week, then get all the stuff together and send it. And we should do something to let the TV stations know we're doing it."

"Becca's all on that," I say. "She's the mistress of press releases."

"My parents worked in films," Becca says matter-of-factly. "So, I have lots of experience."

"Lots of experience with what?" Amber laughs at her own lame joke. I'm noticing this is a pattern.

Becca continues. "National Invisible Boy Day will be coming up soon too, so we need to get on that. Since all we have to do is ignore people, it shouldn't be that much work."

"T-shirts?" Elisa fishes a pencil from her backpack and draws on a napkin. "I had a great idea. We draw a girl next to a boy, and he's like, half disappeared because she's ignoring him!"

"How do you draw something half not there?" Amber asks.

"I don't know. You're the artist."

"I write poetry."

"That's artistic." Elisa has pursed her lips and she and Amber are having a stare down. The forlorn deer head looks on, dejected, as if to say *Can't we all just get along?*

"T-shirts might be tough. Expensive too," Becca says. "Why don't we just make signs? Or maybe bumper stickers? You can do those right on your printer."

"Sayings?" Elisa is ready to jot down anything brilliant that comes out of our mouths.

Nothing comes out.

"Okay, we'll think about that one." Becca sucks the last drops from her Banana Bronco and crushes the cup. "The dance. We still need some amazing ideas."

"*Pirates of the Caribbean,*" Elisa offers, ever mindful of any way to connect to her almighty Johnny Depp.

Amber drums her fingers on the red-checkered plastic table. "Maybe we could do something with pirates, but with other stuff too. What do you associate with islands and the ocean?"

"Seasickness," Elisa blurts out.

"Oh, that'll bring people in." Amber throws a straw at her. "I meant something positive."

"How about the rain forest?" Becca starts talking faster. "Yeah. We could create this huge canopy of trees, and get bird sounds, and make the gym into a forest—"

"Putting aside the fact that it took hundreds of years for the rain forests to grow, how do you think we could afford to do it?" Elisa shakes her head. "I still like Johnny Depp."

Amber laughs. "Oh, and *he's* not expensive."

"Well, we can't really get *him*," Elisa replies. "I just mean that type of décor. Maybe pirate games."

"What? Walk the plank into a tank of sharks for a dollar?"

"Stop being so negative, Amber!"

"Hey, hey! Peace!" Becca has to practically throw a smoothie on them to cool them off. Who knew something as meaningless as a high school dance could fuel a civil war? "Let's concentrate."

"Why not a tropical rain forest island with pirates?" I slurp loudly on my smoothie. "*Gilligan's Island, Survivor, Lost*. Tropical rain forest islands are hot."

"We don't want to just follow a trend," Becca says hesitantly.

"If we combine two trends, is that following a trend or creating a whole new trend based on existing trends?" Elisa asks, cocking her head to one side and staring absently at the deer head.

"That gave me a headache," Amber mutters. "How could we do something like that? We don't have the money to do anything that elaborate."

Becca is warming up to the idea. "It's not a formal, so we could do a costume thing. Everybody could wear beach wear, waterproof stuff. We could have a hula lesson!"

"We could hide gold doubloons all over the gym! I mean, you know, those chocolate coins, not the real thing," Elisa says, still stuck on her pirate fantasy. "And if you find one, it's a free soda or something."

"Back up," Amber says, waving her hands in the air so vigorously that all her silver bracelets jingle. "How can we make an indoor tropical island?"

"Oh, that was a stupid idea." I swirl the stuff at the bottom of my cup so I won't have to have eye contact with anyone. "Sorry I brought it up. It just sort of popped out—"

"It's exactly what we need." Becca has a look of determination on her face that I've seen before. I know it means we will create an indoor tropical island, no matter what. "No one's ever done anything like this. It'll be an accomplishment that people will be talking about for the next four years! It will put us on the map!"

"And how do you propose we actually make it happen?" Elisa asks.

"There might be a reason no one has ever tried it before," I offer. "Big trees, sand, rainstorms, man-eating plants—"

"Details, details," Becca says, brushing off our concerns with a smile and a wave of her hand. "Man-eating plants could be optional. This can be worked out. Shelby's dad is a scientist, and my parents have worked with people in movies for years. I'm sure we can get some special-effects stuff together and make it happen."

"Your parents were in movies?" Amber asks, more excited than I've ever seen her. "Do they know Johnny Depp?" So she's a Depp worshipper too.

Becca ignores her. "Okay, so we all put our fantastic brains to work figuring out what the mechanics are of creating a lush tropical paradise, and I'll put my parents on it too."

I'm just wishing I'd kept my brilliant mouth shut.

The conversation dissolves into more typical high school topics: boys, teachers, projects none of us have done, reading most of us have skipped. I have to admit that since I met Becca and we started this whole Queen Geek Social Club thing, my schoolwork hasn't been as good as it was. It's really hard to concentrate on things that don't matter in life when you have exciting stuff like guys and indoor tropical islands to worry about. Algebra just doesn't cut it. I make a mental note to put in some time on schoolwork tomorrow.

"Our first dance committee meeting is on Monday," Becca says as we clean up our table and get ready to go. "We have to convince everyone else that this is a great idea."

Elisa slides out of her chair and hitches up her backpack in one move. "Who else is on this committee anyway?"

"Well, we know for sure that Fletcher Berkowitz is on it," she replies, winking at me.

"Don't start."

"Huh?" Elisa frowns at me, then Becca. "What's that about?"

"Fletcher joined the committee because Shelby is on it. I think he has a thing for her."

Amber snorts as she follows us out into the mall. "Great. What happened to the Swedish dude?"

"He's Norwegian," I say through gritted teeth. "And he is a jerk."

Silence follows. Sometimes other girls know when you don't want to talk about it. It's the unspoken girl code: If someone hurt you really badly, it takes a while before you want to tell that story over and over again. Eventually, you do, but when it first happens, you just want people to leave you alone with it. How we are all able to figure this out, I don't know, because we can't even seem to talk to our own parents about the simplest things without having a fight with them. Must be hormones or something.

Amber and Elisa split off from us and decide to go to a movie, but Becca and I go outside in the cool spring afternoon to wait for my dad to pick us up. Sitting on a bench near a water fountain, she kicks her legs mindlessly against the seat. "Maybe you should give Fletcher a chance."

"I don't want to have anything to do with guys right now." I've started kicking the bench too, but not gently. "I want to be single and not tied down. Guys are stupid."

"That may be true. But they look good in pants."

"That is one of the dumbest things you've ever said."

"Oh, just wait," she grins. "I'm sure I'll come up with even dumber stuff than that."

After a moment, I ask, "So, this indoor tropical island thing. I have no idea where that came from. I think we should just stick to the pirate theme, that's cool. But this is just too complicated."

She shakes her head. "Shelby. You know what they say? If you never shoot for the stars, you'll always end up with your head in the sand."

"Who says that?"

"Somebody. Anyway, I know a way to do it already. We just need some specialized help from some friends of my parents, but it's not all that hard."

"So you're going to try to get the dance committee to agree to it, get the school to agree to it, and then find some way to get the mist and sand and trees inside our gym?"

"First of all, it's not that *I* am going to try anything. It's *we*. And as Master Yoda says, 'there is no try, there is only do or do not.'"

"Thanks, Obi-Wan. I'll remember that when we're getting expelled."

12

DANCE COMMITTEE FEVER

(or The Confusing Cloud of Boy-Dust)

Sunday is devoted to homework, which, because I haven't really been paying attention for several weeks, is harder than it needs to be. I get through it with only minor interruptions from my dad, who keeps poking his head in to see if I want to talk, which I don't. Euphoria, on the other hand, cannot take a hint.

"Shelby, I wish you'd let me help you with this," she whines as I struggle over some complex graphing problem. "This is like the alphabet to me."

"But then I wouldn't learn how to do it, and you won't be there when I take my finals, will you?" I erase yet again, cursing the flimsiness of graph paper.

"That's a good point. But I hate to see you struggling. Still, maybe I can make you something to eat."

"Sure," I say, mostly to get rid of her. "How about a sandwich? Egg salad?"

"I'm on it." She rolls away, humming the *Star Wars* theme. I cannot get away from that stupid movie.

Just as I'm really starting to make some progress on the algebra (that is, I'm not erasing everything I write), the phone rings. "Hello?"

"Shelby?" A male voice. My fists clench involuntarily. "Hey. It's Fletcher."

"How did you get this number?"

"Calm down. Becca gave it to me."

"Becca?!" That rat! "Hmmm. So what do you want?"

"Wow, nothing like the little pleasantries of conversation for you, huh?" He chuckles, a deep kind of manly chuckle that I sort of like despite myself. "Don't get all upset. I'm not calling to ask you out. You've been real clear with your opinion of me since we met."

For the first time I feel sort of guilty about hitting him with the pillow. But then angry Shelby comes back, pummels nice Shelby on the head, and shoves her into a closet. "Well, I'm glad you picked up on my subtle signals. Good for you. What are you calling for?"

"Yeah. Well, I talked with Becca about the dance committee, and she told me about your idea, about the island thing."

"Yeah, that was stupid. I don't know why she's so fixated on it now."

"I think it's brilliant." He coughs uncomfortably, as if he is choking on the compliment. "Sorry. I didn't mean to be nice to you. This is really a business call. I want to talk to you about the nuts and bolts of the whole thing, assuming we can get that through the dance committee."

"Uh-huh." I continue erasing my graph paper, look down, and notice that I have doodled Fletcher's name in the margin! Is he practicing mind control? I must remember to severely punish my right hand with a paraffin wax dip and a dose of toxic green nail polish.

"So anyway, I wondered if maybe I could come over and we could talk about it today, before the meeting tomorrow." He sounds tentative. "Of course, if you'd rather not let me see your home, I'd totally understand."

"What does that mean?" I snap my pencil in half.

"Oh, I just know how it is sometimes. With parents and . . . um . . . alternative living arrangements. You might be sensitive about it, that's all. So, we could meet—"

"No. You come on over. I have nothing to hide. What, do you think we have trained monkeys flinging their poop around our house or something?" Trained monkeys? Poop? Clearly I'm dehydrated.

He laughs, a full-on belly laugh with a tiny squeak in the middle, which is sort of charming. "No, no. I just mean that Becca told me about your living situation, and—" Becca again! I'm really going to have to think of something good, revenge-wise.

"Just hurry up and let's get this over with. I'll e-mail you directions and my address. What's your e-mail?"

"FBInvader at nerfnet dot com."

"I'll send it to you. Can you be here in an hour?" I carefully tear the piece of paper with his name on it from my homework and rip it into teeny-tiny bits.

"Sure. I'll bring my research."

"You've done research?"

"Oh, yeah. It's what I do. Bye, C-Shel." He laughs again.

"That's my screen name! How did you—"

"Like I said, it's what I do."

"I don't like you."

"I know."

I hop on my computer, fire off an e-mail (complete with insults), and then jump up and immediately begin primping. I just want it known that I'm only primping in self-defense. What I mean is, the better looking a girl is, the more influence she can have on dumb, clueless boys, so it's in my best interest to look devastating.

Euphoria comes in with my sandwich and asks, "What's going on?"

"Somebody's coming over. A kid from school. We're working on a project together."

"Oh. Should I make another sandwich?"

"God, no. If you feed him he might never leave."

"A he? Really?"

"Don't get your circuits in a twist. He's a total jerk. I'm only seeing him so we can work on this project for the dance committee."

"Hmmm." She sets the plate down. "That's not what I'm sensing."

"Go away."

"Higher-than-normal perspiration rate, pulse elevated, and I think I smell perfume."

"Please go build a friend with spare parts and leave me alone."

She sniffs indignantly. "That's the thanks I get for making you a sandwich."

After I've changed clothes three times, curled my hair and then straightened it, and applied and wiped off several shades of lipstick, I feel ready. My next order of business is to chew out Becca.

"Hi there," she says as she answers her cell. "So? Anything new?"

"As if you didn't know, traitor."

"What?" She plays innocent. "I don't know what you mean!"

"Fletcher."

"Yes?"

"He called me. You gave him my number."

"Did I?" She pretends to think about it for a second.

"Oh, wait. Maybe I did. It seems to me a young man did call asking about you. Was that Fletcher? I'm shocked." She yawns.

"Okay. Just be warned. This is not the last you've heard about it."

"Oooh. I'm trembling. When's he coming over?"

I check the clock. Only thirty minutes left? I've been primping for half an hour? "Pretty soon."

"So, do you look ravishing?"

"Flawless. Want to come over?"

"I wouldn't want to butt in. You go it alone. But you have to call me after he leaves."

"I just want you to know that the only reason I got girled up is because I want him to be even more painfully aware of what he can't have."

"I believe that."

"You do?"

"Sure. Anyway, enjoy. Call me later." The phone goes dead.

I'm left alone with a warm egg salad sandwich, wads of lipsticked tissues, and an internal struggle. I am, despite my mean attitude, kind of intrigued by this Fletcher guy. I mean, don't you have to be pretty confident to ask a girl out after she's assaulted you? Well, confident or just plain dense. Hard to tell.

I try to work on my algebra again, which is pointless. I keep glancing up at the clock, and every time I look, it's only five minutes later than the time before. I realize that this is a sign of obsession, and since I've just recently been obsessing about Anders, I'm starting to think maybe there's something seriously wrong with me. I've always treated boys as a hobby, sort of like collecting baseball cards or rocks. But a disturbing trend is beginning to become clear: I'm starting to participate in this boy thing with more than a casual interest. I am not at all comfortable with this.

I mean, guys are nice, and they're people too, but I like my independence. I don't want all my thinking muddled by a pretty face or a nice set of forearms. Or the smell of sandalwood. I make a vow to myself that I will be very cautious with regard to this guy, Fletcher. I'll be civil to him, but I won't fall for him, because even if he is a great guy, I am my own person. And I have the Queen Geeks to think about! I mean, I don't have time to—

The doorbell rings. What? I glance up at the clock again, and it's five. How did that happen?

"I'll get it!" I scream, tearing out of my room.

Euphoria is already rolling toward the door. "Where's the fire, honey?"

"No fire. Just trying to be polite. Could you go hide in the kitchen?"

"That's nice. What am I, chopped liver?"

"Have you ever even seen chopped liver, Euphoria?"

She ignores me and grumbles away. I take a deep breath, open the door, and there is Fletcher Berkowitz. "Hey," he says, a little awkwardly. "Thanks for inviting me over."

"It's purely work. Plus, you invited yourself." I sound very cold. That's good. "Come in, please."

"You look great." He walks by me a little too closely, and I catch a scent of something kind of musky, but subtle. The smell is always the first thing to make you stupid.

"Thanks. Let's sit down in the living room." He follows me, and I can sense that he's watching me walk. I feel hot all over.

"Want something to drink?"

"Sure. Soda's good. Regular, though. No artificial sweeteners."

"Health nut, huh?"

"Not a nut, really. I just don't want brain tumors."

I press the intercom button. "Euphoria, could we have two regular sodas, please?"

"Coming."

I sit on the velvet sofa, right in the middle, so he can't really sit next to me without it looking weird. He takes the hint and plops down on the loveseat.

"You have a maid?" He looks surprised. Wait'll he sees her.

"Kind of. My dad made her, though."

"Is your dad Dr. Frankenstein or something? Spare body parts in the garage?"

"Oh, no. You gotta keep the spare parts in the freezer."

She rolls in, and I watch Fletcher for a reaction. Nothing. He takes the soda from her claw, sips it, and says, "Thanks."

As she rolls away, I'm puzzled. Why no reaction? Does everybody he knows have a robot? "So you want to talk about the tropical island thing. As I said, I think it's a dumb idea, and I don't think there's any way we could really pull it off. Think about it—mist, sand, trees, water. To do it right, we'd have to make a huge mess. Plus, the school won't want the liability, and—"

"Okay, hang on. First of all, the school has insurance. Think about football. If they let kids do that, why would they object to a little water? Second, I think we can do this, on a small scale of course, without it being dangerous at all, only fun. Let's go online and I can show you what I mean."

"Uh . . ." My brain and my mouth suddenly aren't speaking to each other. The computer is in my bedroom. The thought of Fletcher going into my bedroom causes massive panic, and I feel myself going all red. "We're not online."

"You just e-mailed me directions to your house!"

"Yeah, but it went down right after that." Lame, but workable. "Why don't we just stay here and talk?"

"Fine." Fletcher sips his soda and stares at me over the rim of the glass. His highly annoying yet beautiful green eyes remind me of a cat's, and somehow I feel like the mouse. "I found a site based in Florida where they actually do these huge themed party events with weather and everything. So if we have the right equipment, I think we could do it."

"What's the right equipment?"

"Wind machine to create a tropical breeze, a sprayer for the rain forest mist, some kind of liner so we could pour sand in the gym without it getting everywhere. Then of course, for effect we'd want lights and sound. I was even thinking of big tropical fish tanks, but that's mostly just window dressing. I think we should work it like a haunted house, with pirates and scary stuff in the rain forest. You know, the haunted Isle of the Panther People or something. Becca says her parents have connections with people in the movie industry, so I think we should take advantage of that, of course."

"So you have it all planned out, huh?"

"Not totally." He sets his glass down on a coaster, then smiles. "There's still the matter of that date."

"I am absolutely not going out with you." I take a gulp of my soda, choke on it, and gasp for air. Nothing like a near-death experience to encourage romance. Fletcher, alarmed, catapults off the couch and savagely beats me on the back, trying to force the killer soda to leave me alone. "I'm okay," I finally croak, swatting at him.

"Sorry. I thought you were dying or something." He retreats to the loveseat, his territory, leaving me to recover any shred of dignity I may have pretended to have when he walked in. "If I'd known the mere mention of a date with me would kill you, I wouldn't have said anything." He grins wryly. "I just have that effect on women, I guess."

"Don't flatter yourself." I almost pick up my glass for another drink, but since that's proven to be nearly fatal, I can't use it as a prop anymore. "We should probably talk about the other stuff at the dance too, like decorations and advertising and music."

"We can go over all that with the committee tomorrow." An awkward silence fills the room, and we both stare at the carpet. "Okay, well, it's obvious you are not interested in me as a date. How about as a friend?"

This throws me off guard. Honesty! Tricky! "I don't see how we can be friends, Fletcher. You're a guy."

"So you don't think guys and girls can have relationships other than romantic ones?"

"I highly doubt it."

"Bet me."

"What?" This guy is insane. Good. One more point against him in my big running potential-boyfriend score-board. "Bet you? What would we bet?"

He pauses, and then, with a self-satisfied smile, says, "If you will try to be my friend, and only my friend, I will bet you a hundred dollars that we'll be able to do it, no strings attached, no romance. I'll bet I can be as good a friend as Becca."

"A hundred? What, are you made of money? I can't afford a bet like that!"

"So you're saying you expect to lose, expecting that we can't be friends. Does that mean you think we'll get romantically involved, so you expect to lose the bet? Or would you win?" His eyes twinkle in that way that makes me want to slap him.

"No! I'm not saying that at all!" Infuriating! I cannot wait to take his money. It will *so* prove to him that women are smarter than men. And that is clearly something I need to prove to Fletcher Berkowitz, who thinks he is being so clever in manipulating me to go out with him. Pathetic! Still, I have to give him points for being original. I stand and offer my hand. This is sure to be the easiest hundred dollars I could ever earn. "We'll see if you can be as good a friend as Becca. We absolutely cannot share clothes, though."

"Fair enough. Some ground rules. First, you do have to spend time with me, or the bet won't be valid. I mean, we need to prove that we *aren't* romantically involved and that we *are* friends, and we can't do that if we never see each other. Second, the time frame. I think this will all be sorted out before summer, so if by the time school's out we aren't romantically involved and we are friends, I win the bet. Deal?"

I know he's trying to trick me, but the great thing about being a Queen Geek is that I *know* he's trying to trick me. And because I know this, I can double-trick him. And get rich in the bargain. I almost feel sorry for him.

"Deal," I say. *And, might I add, you have no idea what you're getting yourself into, Mr. Fletcher Berkowitz. No idea.*

* * *

After Fletcher leaves, I immediately call Becca. "So?" she asks.

"What?"

"So? How was it?"

"Fine." I am doodling in the margins on my homework again, only this time I'm doodling dollar signs. I tell her all about the bet, and about how he played right into my trap, and about the hundred dollars. She laughs. "What is so funny?"

"Nothing. I just think it's great how you two work together. It should be an interesting dance committee meeting tomorrow."

"Well, if he can help us achieve greatness with this indoor haunted pirate tropical island thing—"

"And he knows how to do it?"

"He says we need some stuff from your parents' friends, but yeah, he seems to have a good idea. He's done some research."

"Great. Oh, I'm faxing the press release tomorrow before school, so hopefully we'll get some TV crews here for the big Twinkie send-off on Wednesday."

"Okay. Well, I gotta go. If I don't get some homework done, I may not even be allowed to go to the dance."

After I hang up, I consider Becca's obsession with television reporters. I think she's seriously overestimated the media's interest in what high school kids do in their spare time, even if it involves supermodels and snack food. I guess compared to all the other things we do in high school, it's more interesting, but that's not saying much. I hope she won't be disappointed when the world yawns over our monumental effort.

I pack up my books at about ten-thirty, and unfortunately, none of the algebra problems solved themselves. All I have to turn in to Mrs. Pettinger is a tattered piece of graph paper with dollar signs and violently erased versions of Fletcher's name.

I pretty much go through the morning unconscious, which actually makes it much easier. I highly recommend it if you've never tried it. The only bright spot is a card waiting on my desk in first period English. The front features a panicky cat hanging by its claws to a high limb on a tree, and inside, the card reads, *"Can't wait to hang out with you!"* *Oh, we'll be hanging out*, I think. It almost seems unfair to play poor Fletcher, but money is money, and guys deserve all the knocking down they can get, I figure.

Finally, lunch comes and it's dance committee time. The meeting is in the ASB room, which usually looks like a tornado came through and rearranged everything. A sweatshirt hangs from the fluorescent-light fixtures, and several pencils are sticking suspended from the spongy ceiling tiles. I guess ASB gets boring if they have time to throw pencils in the air. No wonder the school activities are crappy.

Several kids with perfect teeth and that carefully put-together look that looks like it's not put together are milling around near the whiteboard, while several other less god-like kids are sitting uncomfortably on folding chairs. Becca is milling with the popular crowd, which for some reason bothers me. Fletcher walks in just behind me and gives my arm a squeeze. "Hey, did you get my card?"

"Yeah," I nod. "Thanks for that. I always like to start my day with a little animal cruelty."

"Uh—" He is speechless! It's a miracle!

"Okay, everyone." Superblonde Samantha Singer, one of the dance committee hotshots, claps her hands and motions for everyone to sit down. "Thanks, everyone, for coming today. We have a lot to talk about, so let's go around the room and introduce ourselves!"

Becca scurries over to sit next to me, eyes Fletcher on my other side, and then arches her eyebrows. When it's our turn, Becca goes first. "I'm Becca Gallagher, and my friend, Shelby, and I are here representing the Queen Geek Social Club. We have a lot of ideas we think will—"

"Thanks," Samantha stops us with her blindingly perfect smile. She totally skips over me, and points to Fletcher. "And of course, we have Fletch Berkowitz—" *Fletch*? "—and you all remember his amazing fall football season. So good to have you here with us, Fletch."

"Thanks, Sam." *Sam?!* He's one of the pod people! I had no idea. Now I think maybe he's hanging out with us to eat our brains or something. "I did want to bring up an idea.

I've been brainstorming with some people, and we think it would be cool to have a haunted tropical rain forest at the dance. Since it's Caribbean and all."

Dead silence fills the room. "Could you explain that a little more?" Samantha blinks, trying to comprehend an idea that doesn't involve chicken wire and papier-mâché.

"Sure." Fletcher stands up and easily takes charge. "Instead of focusing on the whole Caribbean thing, like with the pineapple drinks and hula skirts, it would be cool to do something totally different. We've researched it, and it is possible, with some donations and some funding, to set up a haunted island paradise, and to decorate the gym like it's a beach, with maybe some pirate stuff thrown in since Johnny Depp is so huge right now."

Becca squeezes my arm so hard I think she's going to cut off the circulation. "He's stealing our ideas!" she hisses.

"Well, maybe we can get together later and you can show me the plans," Samantha purrs smoothly. "If it's doable, it sounds like a real selling point. Any comments?"

The conversation veers off toward talking about expensive hair extensions getting drenched, and several girls complain that wet taffeta doesn't wear well. But when Samantha points out that this is to be a more casual dance, not a formal, and mentions that one-piece bathing suits would be appropriate, a lot of the guys especially seem very enthusiastic.

Chatter starts to heat up about pirate décor, and Becca finally does interject with Elisa's idea of hiding chocolate gold coins for prizes, so it's a treasure hunt. Samantha sort of stares through her until Fletcher pipes up, "I think that's a great idea!" and then Samantha magically thinks it's great too.

With five minutes to go before the end of lunch, the meeting breaks up, and everyone drifts out into the commons to grab something resembling food. Except that neither Becca nor I can eat anything, because we are both consumed with fury. "How could he do that?" Becca keeps saying over and over.

"I don't know. I guess I shouldn't have told him so much." Now I'm sort of wishing I'd beaten him senseless with that pillow.

Fletcher trots to catch up to us as we steamroll out of the ASB room. "Hey!" He matches strides with us, unaware that he is courting death by being within arm's distance. "Wasn't that great? They loved your idea!"

Becca stops dead in her tracks, turns slowly to face Fletcher, and says, very evenly, "Yes, Fletcher. They loved *our* idea. So why did you feel the need to present it as if it were *your* idea?"

The smile drains from his cute, freckly face as he becomes aware of his monumental boo-boo. "Oh." I see him working it out in his mind, trying to figure out how he dug himself into this hole. "But I thought if I brought it up—"

"You thought if you brought it up, Samantha Singer would just fall at your feet and lick your shoes," I spit out at him. "Nice. So you stole our plans so you could impress Malibu Barbie, huh? Well, that's a great start to our friendship, isn't it? I guess neither of us is going to win that bet, because at this point, I don't see us being friends, and I wouldn't go out with you if you were the last guy on earth."

He grins sheepishly. "Even if our dating meant repopulating the earth for all humanity?"

"Especially not then!" Becca and I hustle off, leaving Fletcher in a confused cloud of boy-dust.

"Amazing." Becca, furious, practically runs toward her next class.

"I cannot wait for National Invisible Boy Day," I mutter as I follow her.

Wednesday, the day of our Twinkie send-off, dawns with a steady rain, something we don't see too much of in Southern California. Because of this, I think most people who live here get brain stall when there is moisture; it certainly explains the high number of traffic accidents and detentions on rainy days. It also explains, I guess, why my high school has no sheltered areas and why we all look and smell like wet dogs whenever it even sprinkles.

Despite this, we all drag in at lunch to Ms. McLachlan's room (thankfully unlocked and empty) and wait for Elisa to show up with her report. I'm happy to see large cardboard boxes filled with the clown-colored cartons of snacks, and as more and more girls come into the room, the boxes stack higher and higher. Elisa finally races in, huffing and puffing, and flings herself into the nearest empty desk.

"I cannot believe it!" she wheezes. "We must have collected, like, three hundred Twinkies. At least!"

We are, in fact, surrounded by golden cream-filled goodness. Since I'm in a bad mood, I figure I'll be the bearer of bad news: "How are we going to pay to ship all these things to that modeling agency?"

Silence. No one thought of that, I guess. Becca, who usually has an answer for everything, stammers, "Well, I thought—I mean, couldn't we—" and before she can finish, the door opens again and a tall, pantyhosed stranger enters.

Everyone knows when someone doesn't belong in the high school environment. Only certain adults fit there: the worn-out, grumpy, exhausted teachers with their ties or tasteful pumps, tired of being talked over every day; the parents, who usually look nervous and scared and unsure of themselves or angry to the point of exploding; the administrators, either cocky, threatening or cool, but with that air of mystery that comes with an office and a nameplate. This person is none of those three. She is perfect.

"Hi," she says, her voice deep and friendly. Definitely not a teacher. "I'm Chantal Nelson from Channel Ten News. I got your press release."

The room goes totally silent for half a second, and then everybody is chattering. Becca tries to get everybody to calm down, but finally has to resort to a wolf whistle. "Hi," she says, flashing her best public-relations smile. "I'm Becca Gallagher. I sent the press release."

"Great." She pokes her head outside and motions for someone to follow her. A burly, bearded camera guy comes in after her, shaking water out of his hair, grumbling about "human interest." "This is Bruce, our photographer. So, Becca, we just want to ask a few questions, and then we'll just film your meeting."

"Oh. Okay. But Shelby here is really our spokesgeek." She pulls me in front of her so quickly that I nearly fall over. "I need to take care of some shipping details, so why don't you talk to her?"

Of course, this had to happen on a day when, as I said, I look, feel, and smell like a wet dog. I'm sure this will come through on television; they say you always look ten times bigger and smellier on TV. "So, Shelby, tell us about this Campaign for Calories. What's it all about?"

Brain stall. I guess the rain did it to me, too. "Uh. Well, Campaign for Calories is a thing we're doing to help fatten up supermodels."

"We?" Chantal Nelson, television reporter, asks, acting as if she cares.

"The Queen Geek Social Club. That's us." I motion to the rest of the girls, who are all staring. They look like a herd of big-eyed deer. "Say hi, Queen Geeks."

They come to life, snap out of their stupor, and all wave and hoot and holler.

"Great." The woman smiles with huge white teeth the size of Scrabble tiles. "Can you tell us why you're doing this?"

Why *are* we doing this? An excellent question. Because Becca told us to? Hmmm. That wouldn't sound very good. Think, think . . . "Because we feel it's time for high school girls to stop thinking they have to look perfect to be happy."

"You do?" Perfect Chantal frowns slightly, as if I've told her some very bad news. "Why?"

"Because we don't *need* to look perfect to be happy," Amber says, standing up. "We can be just who we are. That's enough."

Perfect Chantal seems stuck. I don't know what she expected, but I guess it wasn't us. "Well, that's a unique point of view. What do you hope to accomplish by mailing off all these goodies?"

Elisa jumps up. "We found the agency with the least favorable body-fat-to-height ratio, and we're sending all the snacks to them. We hope they'll feed the models." All the other girls laugh, and camera guy Bruce busily films us all.

After a few more pithy questions, Chantal goes outside and we see her doing her little lead-in or close-out thing that the news people do. "I wonder what she's saying?" Elisa asks, craning to read lips out the window.

Amber strikes a dramatic pose. "Probably something like, 'There you have it, ladies and gentlemen. The fate of the Western female world lies in the delicate hands of these budding activists, a blooming garden of flowers who wish to—'"

"You sound like a tampon commercial," Becca calls from the back of the room, where she is busily scrawling addresses on labels. "Could some of you TV stars help me lug these boxes to my mom's car after school? And will McLachlan let us keep them here until then?"

"Let me call my dad," I offer. "We have the Volvo wagon. The Jeep won't have much room."

The photographer turns off his light, and I see them turning to leave, so I quickly duck my head out the door. "Hey, is this going to be on TV?"

She turns toward me, smiles and says, "I think the piece might run tonight at eleven. In fact, I think it might be picked up by the networks. It's such a cute story. You girls are precious."

"Yeah, thanks. You too."

She doesn't quite know how to take this, so she just throws me a little wave and tip-taps away on her high heels, dodging puddles and clusters of freshman boys who ogle her without even trying to conceal it.

Dad picks us up and we load the Twinkie boxes into the Volvo (even into the front passenger seat and beside the two of us in back); Becca calls her mom to be sure she can stay over so we can watch the news. "This is great," Dad says as he steers through the leftover drizzle on the way home. "You girls might make a big impact."

"That would be cool, huh?" Becca is grinning from ear to ear, and she has been since lunch was over.

"That's just because you want to be Empress of the World," I whisper.

"No I don't. I want to be Queen Geek of the World." We both start giggling like we're about five years old.

"You two okay back there?" Dad calls from the front seat.

"Yeah, yeah. We're good." To Becca, I whisper again. "So, what if it does go on the national news? What then?"

"I don't know. We'll figure it out when it happens. For now, let's just get these things to the post office and off to what's-her-name's modeling agency."

Dad kindly battles afternoon traffic to get us to the post office (and kindly foots the bill for mailing several hundred Twinkies, which is a lot more than you might think) and we finally end up at my house, huddling in my bedroom with a plateful of Euphoria's chocolate chip cookies, counting down the minutes until the news is on.

"If everybody watches it, we could be famous," Becca says between cookie bites. "I mean, people might even come to the school to see how we do it."

"See how we do what?"

"The club."

"*We* don't even know how we do the club. We just get together and stuff happens."

Becca sighs loudly. "It doesn't sound very good when you

say it that way." She throws the rest of her cookie on the plate. "Yuck. How many of these have I eaten?"

"I stopped counting when I could see the bottom of the plate." Unfortunately, there is very little but plate left, which means we managed to inhale all those yummies. Oh well. "I think we need to really ramp up the Invisible Boy thing."

"Not before the dance!" She sits upright, a horrified look on her face. The look is somewhat softened by the big smear of chocolate across her lower lip.

"Sure, why not? It will make them appreciate us more." To be honest, I am seriously wanting to torture Fletcher, and this is the only reason I'm pushing for the event to happen soon. It's a way to get even with him while making it look like a positive political activity. Plus, I'm really mad about the disintegration of that bet; I had plans for that hundred dollars. "I think we should do it in two weeks. That gives us a little time to plan, and leaves a week before the dance."

"And then we're dangerously close to finals and the end of the year."

That's hard to believe, really. I mean, it seems like we just started school, that I just met Becca. To think about the year ending is not something I want to tackle at the moment. Who knows where somebody like Becca spends the summer? Paris? The Swiss Alps? I'm sure she won't stick around here. But I decide to think about that tomorrow.

Becca has moved to my computer, a sure sign that she's

serious about moving forward with our plan. "Do you have a file started yet for Nibid?"

"What's tha—"

"National Invisible Boy Day. Nibid. I get tired of saying it."

"Oh. Yeah." I tap a few keys, and my folder opens. She starts a file and begins to type furiously. "What are you doing?"

"Typing our manifesto. Could you get some milk and give me a minute?"

I leave her with the glow of my computer monitor giving a radioactive shine to her face. In the kitchen, Euphoria is using a built-in drawer in her midsection to hold the items she's emptying from the fridge. "It looks like a science project in here," she mutters as she throws a can of old spaghetti sauce into the bin with a bang. "Since your father is a scientist, he ought to know the harmful effects of bacteria."

"Maybe they're an experiment. You shouldn't throw them out—it might be the cure for cancer or something."

She pauses for a split second, and I see her thinking about it, but then she laughs her mechanical chuckle. "You can't fool me, missy. If he'd wanted it saved, he probably wouldn't have put it in the fridge."

I grab the milk jug. "Can't pull anything over on you, huh?" As I pour two huge glasses, I say, as casually as I can, "So is Dad over this dating frenzy?"

"Hmmm. Do you think pickles go bad?" She's eyeing a moldy-looking jar of green gook.

"Uh . . . I don't think I'd eat them, so yeah, pitch 'em."
To stall for time, I rummage for a tray to put the glasses on.
"So? Dad? Dating?"

"Oh. No, I think he's done for a while. That skinny
teacher got scared off, I think. He got too stressed." She
pulls out a Tupperware container full of something foul-
looking. "Hmmm. He needs to invent something that will
clean the refrigerator."

I don't say out loud that he did, in fact, invent something
that cleans the refrigerator, because I think she'd find that
insulting. Still, happy with the news that Dad seems safely
date-free for the moment, I take my milk to my room to see
what new conquests Becca has engineered.

"Ah!" she exclaims as I push the door open with my
elbow. "At last! My evil assistant!"

"Why do I always have to be the evil assistant?"

"You look better in the sequined tights. Anyway, here's
what I came up with. Get comfortable."

After I've snuggled up in my bed with my milk and cookies, she continues in her most authoritative voice. "Green
Pines Queen Geek Social Club invites you to participate
in National Invisible Boy Day. For one day only, boys
will not exist to girls! We don't see them! We don't hear
them! We don't acknowledge their existence! Be free of
them for twenty-four hours and see what a difference a day
makes!"

"Beautiful." I sigh. As she continues to proofread, I imagine the day. Fletcher comes up to me; I ignore him. He is

puzzled; I ignore him. He begs for forgiveness; I yawn and ignore him. By the end of the day, he is driven insane by my total lack of interest in his existence; he loses his mind and is sent off to St. Bongo's Home for Wayward Boys, never to be seen again. Well, maybe that last part is a little extreme. Maybe he could come back for high school reunions.

"Oh my God, it's time for the news!" Becca screams and jumps up from the computer and we dash into the living room. The news has just started, so we have to sit through several pointless stories about kittens being rescued, kids who are born conjoined, and water-skiing squirrels. Finally, they get to our story.

"Ah! There you are!" Becca squeals as the picture on the screen narrows to include just my face.

"Do I really have that many zits? I had no idea."

"The camera adds ten zits, everybody knows that. Turn it up!" I frantically punch at the volume button, and we catch some of newswoman Chantal Nelson's commentary: "These are clearly girls who know what they want, and it isn't a size ten figure." A shot of Elisa bending over her backpack fills the screen, making her back end look ten times bigger than it really is, which is fairly large.

"Oh, that is just not fair," Becca mutters. "Not cool."

"And their hope is that one day, all models will be of a 'normal' size, thus changing forever the idea that models must be beautiful."

"What?" Becca screams, then throws a pencil at the television screen. "She got it totally wrong!"

"Are you surprised?" I ask. "I mean, she's one of them. If she exposes our secret plot to make them more human, the ones who aren't will have to go back to the mother ship."

The piece ends with some of that dopey music they play when the squirrel water-skis, and shots of us girls all laughing and packing up Twinkies. They also happen to catch Elisa eating one, which really doesn't help put us in a good light.

"Okay, well," Becca slumps against the couch. "At least she got our name right."

"Great. So now everybody will know that we're the ones who want models to stop being beautiful and be more like us."

"Sure, you could look at it that way," Becca answers. "Or you could say, 'Well, why do any of us have to be beautiful? And what does that mean anyway?'"

"Too deep for me. I'm heading for the cookie plate." I jump up and run toward my room.

With a joyous squeal, Becca is hot on my heels.

13

NATIONAL INVISIBLE BOY DAY

(or What You Can't See Can't Hurt You)

The television spot is the talk of the school on Thursday, and it feels good to be a celebrity, even if it does mean that people keep taping Twinkies to my locker. Since the Queen Geek Social Club seems to be on a roll, we call a special meeting for lunch under our tree, with just Amber and Elisa and me and Becca, a little party to celebrate our being media darlings.

Elisa digs a big plastic bottle of fizzy yellow liquid from her backpack, and four plastic champagne glasses. "It's just lemon mineral water with food coloring, but I figured we could pretend," she says as she pours us all a glass of bubbly.

Becca raises her glass. "Here's to the Queen Geeks. May we be fruitful and multiply!"

We all clink our glasses (which sounds more like a plastic thunk) and drink our toast. Elisa wipes the bubbles from her lips and says, "And I'd like to add, here's to the Twinkies that will make a difference in some poor supermodel's life. Once they taste fat, they'll never go back!"

"Yeah, you know from personal experience," Amber sniggers. "I saw you sneaking one on TV."

Elisa goes red. "Well, that was just a sampling. I wanted to be sure they hadn't been tampered with. We don't want to get sued."

"Okay. So our next move is Nibid."

"And that is?" Amber gives her a confused squint.

"Ignoring boys, you know. Making them invisible."

"I do that anyway. No big challenge," she says, yawning. "And they return the favor."

"The dance is only three weeks away, so we'd better do the ignoring day fast so we can stop ignoring them and they can ask us out," Elisa reasons. "I, for one, do not want a repeat of last year's eighth grade grad dance, where the only person left to go with was Jeff Hall, and he asked me and I went because I felt sorry for him."

"Yeah, and he did that robot mime dance in front of the whole eighth grade," Amber crows. "That was awesome!"

"Awesome if you weren't his date," Elisa mutters. "I got teased about that for weeks."

Munching her way through a wilty salad, Becca says emphatically, "We do it next week."

"Too soon!" I squeak. "We don't have time to get ready. How can we get everyone on board? Get the word out?"

"Oh, like that's a problem. Just start a cell phone gossip chain," Amber says. "Haven't you noticed how some stupid piece of gossip goes all around the school in less than a day? Why is that?"

"Uh . . ." Elisa squints at her, confused. "This isn't gossip."

Amber whacks her with an empty chip bag. "No, it isn't, genius. But if we make it sound like it is gossip, it will go around the school quicker than head lice at a preschool party. So we need to make it gossipy."

"About a person?" Becca asks, leaning against the tree. "That could be tricky. Who would our gossip be about? Who's had anything bad happen, love-life-wise?"

All eyes turn toward me. Great.

"Oh, no," I say, stuffing my lunch bag back into my backpack. "I'm not going to be the topic of hot gossip for the next week."

"Don't flatter yourself. Gossip only stays fresh for a day or so." Elisa has retrieved her Palm Pilot and is jotting some notes on it. "Okay, so I have access to a hundred and twenty-five numbers here and I can send a simultaneous message to all of them. Then they'll pass it on, and pretty soon it's like the flu—everybody's gotten it. But what's the message?"

We all sit quietly, pondering this crucial question. Well, I was pondering why I had to be the one singled out to be the designated loser and focus of the chitchat virus. Just as I'm thinking of convincing arguments to make the gossip be about someone else (anyone else, really), Becca comes up with one of her brilliant strategies. Really, her talents are wasted in high school. She should either work for the government or become someone's mother.

"Okay. I've got it." She shushes everybody and gestures for them to come near. "We text everybody that Shelby has a terminal illness. And to raise money, we're asking all the girls to participate in Nibid."

"That is absolutely immoral. I look healthy as a horse, not to mention that it's really tasteless. No terminal illnesses." Honestly, the things some people will do for a little success. It makes me queasy.

"What if Shelby needs some kind of surgery?" Amber offers.

"How about we don't lie to people?" I suggest. I mean, lying always leads to trouble, in my experience. I could just see this ending up with me on a gurney somewhere, being put under while some dude in a surgical mask asks, "And which testicle are we removing, Mr. Jones?" No thanks. "It really needs to be something that has some small particle of truth in it."

"Well, you broke up with Anders," Elisa points out. "That's tragic."

"I didn't break up with him. You can't break up with someone you never dated. We just got our signals crossed."

"A contest!" Becca shouts. "A contest! Like the radio stations do. If you're caught doing it, then you might get some really amazing prize, like a new car!"

Elisa laughs. "Where are we going to get a new car, or an old car for that matter?"

Suddenly, I receive one of those amazing ideas that usually only happen when you're asleep, and you can't remember the idea itself, only that you didn't have pants on when you got it in your dream. Okay, maybe that's just me. Anyway, I get this great idea, like a jolt of lightning through my head. "We tell them that if they participate, they get a thousand dollars."

A stunned silence greets me. After I listen to the rewind of what I just said, I can see why they look at me like I've been inhaling Krazy Glue.

"Okay, that's dumber than the car idea," Amber snorts. "Let's give them money if they participate?"

"Right. But only if they come to the dance with a special ticket we'll give them for participating, and then they get the opportunity to reach into a barrel for the thousand dollars."

Becca wags her finger at me. "I think I'm getting this. So we ask them to do it, spread a rumor that if they do it they can get a special ticket to make them eligible for the drawing, but then no ticket ever wins, right?"

"No, a ticket has to win," I say. "But by the time the dance comes around, and we do the drawing, they'll have forgotten all about the money."

"Oh, I don't think so. Not with the serious money-grubbing we've got around here." Elisa shakes her head in dismay.

"How about a date with a movie star?" Becca asks nonchalantly, as if she has movie stars sleeping at the bottom of her purse.

"Like?" Amber asks.

"Like maybe Brandon Keller." She looks down at her nails, as if to appear humble. "My parents happen to know him. I told you they worked in movies."

"So you could get someone a date with Brandon Keller, the television star? The romantic stud of the world? Everybody's book-cover fantasy?" Elisa scoffs. "I don't think so. But if you want to try and tell people that, I'm all for it. It'll come back on you if it gets screwed up."

Becca throws an arm around Elisa as the bell ending lunch rings. "That's why I like you. I know I can count on you to watch my back."

"So we text everyone we know, spread rumors, and get everybody to do this next Friday?" Becca asks. Amber and Elisa nod as they gather up their stuff.

"Wait," I say. "Shouldn't you check in with Brandon Keller before you commit him to a date? I mean, he probably has other stuff going on, like making huge blockbuster movies."

"Leave that to me," Becca says breezily as she saunters off to class.

During fifth and sixth periods, I tell as many girls as I can about the upcoming ignorefest and possible date with a hot-tie movie star. Many of them stare at me in disbelief for a second, then ask, "So what do you have to do? And how do you get a ticket?"

By the time I meet Becca in front of the library after sixth period, she's bouncing with joy. "I cannot believe how many girls are in, just this afternoon! I wrote a note and passed it all around to every girl, and by the time we left, they were all asking me how they could get the tickets!"

As we walk through the grass toward the street, I men-tion the thought that's been plaguing me all afternoon. "What if they just *say* they did the Nibid thing, but didn't, and then they get a ticket?"

She shrugs. "Well, we can't watch all of them. But at least of few of them will do it, and that's enough. It will make an impact. Maybe we should make them wear stickers too."

"Okay. Stickers that say 'I'm ignoring you because it's National Invisible Boy Day,' something like that?"

"Right. We can print those out without a problem. Big, pink stickers." She gleefully chuckles at the thought of all the girls on campus branded with our badge of honor. "On a less interesting subject, I have a project due in Social Sci-ence, so I'm going to have to get home and put some time in on that tonight, and tomorrow after school Mom's driving us up to L.A. to get some of the stuff we need for the haunted island. We're staying over."

"Where do you get haunted-island-making supplies?"

"You go to the special-effects people, the ones who make

that stuff in movies." Becca skips along, confident that everything, even things as massive as a haunted island and a date with a movie star, will be taken care of in the same way that picking up milk at the 7-Eleven is taken care of. I wish I had her confidence, her absolute belief that whatever she wants will happen.

So, I guess, I focus on the stuff I know I can do, like stupid schoolwork. "Well, you want to come over for a little while and read *Romeo and Juliet*? We have to finish Act II by tomorrow."

"Only if you'll be Romeo." She grins wickedly. "Or maybe we could call Fletcher."

"Don't mention that name!" I am still really mad at him for taking our ideas, and I don't think I can forgive him, even if he does have extra-sexy green eyes.

At home, Euphoria putts in with a pitcher full of delicious iced lemonade and a plate of her absolutely best cookies, the peanut butter ones with a chocolate kiss in the middle. This is a sure sign that something is wrong.

"Uh, what's with the royal treatment, Euphoria?" I ask as she attempts to leave the room without comment.

"What? Oh, just felt like practicing my baking skills. Don't want them to get rusty, you know. Ha. Rusty! Get it?" She laughs, a high-pitched, chittering laugh that sounds like nerves to me.

"What's wrong?" I ask as Becca dives for a cookie.

"Nothing's wrong, why would anything be wrong? Nothing's wrong." She says it so fast I barely register anything except the word *wrong*, which means something definitely is.

"Is it Dad? Listen, don't freak out. I'm okay about the dating thing, if that's what it is." I pour some lemonade into a glass and try to act as calm as possible. It's really weird when you have to keep a lid on your feelings in front of your robot so you won't upset her.

"Oh, come on, Euphoria," Becca mumbles over a mouthful of cookie, "you can tell us. We can keep a secret."

"Well, all right." She rolls over to us, and whispers (as best a robot can whisper, which is something like the low hum of a blender), "I *am* a little nervous, really. It's because . . . well . . . your father has decided to bring in another robot."

"What?" I practically spit out my lemonade. "Another robot? To *replace* you?"

"Oh, no, no." She pretends to fan herself, something I think she picked up watching *Gone with the Wind* too many times. "To help him in the lab, and outside. And I've sneaked a peek online, to see what he's doing—"

"Euphoria! Did you sneak into Dad's online folders? That's like going through somebody's underwear drawer!"

"I know, I know," she chatters. "I feel so bad about it, but I needed to know. So I found out that it's probably going to be a combination leaf blower/mower and vacuum with a computer interface that makes it programmable. And he's got a really cute processor!"

"Unbelievable. Euphoria has a boyfriend." Becca shakes

her head and grabs another cookie. "Even the females who aren't human let their lives revolve around guys."

"Well, I'm happy for you," I say, patting her claw. "I hope it works out."

"Oh, so do I!" She hums some tuneless song as she rolls merrily into the kitchen. The phone rings, and since she's too love-struck to answer it with any kind of sense, I pick it up.

"Hello?"

"Hi, Shelby. It's Fletcher." I hang up the phone immediately. It rings again.

"Who was that?" Becca asks.

"The Thieving Freckle Jockey." The phone continues to ring, and to avoid Euphoria picking it up, I answer. "Listen, Fletcher, I don't want to talk to you. Ever. You stole our ideas and I hope you and Samantha Singer will be very happy—"

"Will you stop talking for one moment?" he interrupts me. "Just listen for a change. I called to apologize. I really didn't mean to steal your ideas. I told Samantha they were your ideas, and that I was just presenting them, and I also told her that there is no way I can take her to the dance. Because I'm taking you."

"You are not taking me anywhere!" I slam the phone down again. "The nerve of this guy! How dare he think I would care if he takes the blond bubblehead to the dance or not? I couldn't care less. He can take whoever he wants to any stupid dance that comes up."

Becca claps slowly. "Very convincing. Oscar-worthy."

"Huh?"

She sighs heavily, then leans forward, smiling at me with a sheepish grin. "Shelby, you like him. You really do. If you didn't, you wouldn't be so mad at him."

"Some friend *you* are." I grab a pillow from the couch and pound it with my fist. "How can you say I like him at all? He drives me crazy!"

"Exactly my point." Becca grabs her *Romeo and Juliet* book and waves it at me. "Lots of times people end up falling for the person they think they hate the most."

The phone rings again, an annoying ring that I know belongs to Fletcher Berkowitz. I can just tell. "Hello?"

"Shelby, listen, before you hang up—"

"I'm listening." I pound the pillow with my fist. Poor, poor pillow.

"Oh." He pauses, as if the fact that I am agreeing to talk with him is totally unexpected, which it probably is, given the fact that I practically blew his head off last time. "Okay. Well, I want to explain something to you. I kind of fit into that crowd, the Samantha Singer crowd, but I'm not one of them."

"Sort of like you're a spy or something? An alien walking among the humans?" The snide tone in my voice is exceedingly mean.

"Kind of. I'm not saying they're bad people, I just don't think like them on a lot of issues."

"Oh, so you just sort of hang out with them out of pity?

To let them bask in the glow of your greatness? Well, I think I'll pass." Oooh. That was good. Maybe a little too good. Do I really want to chase this guy away totally?

"Fine." A slight twist of anger is added to his regretful tone of voice. "If you're too narrow-minded to actually listen to me, then I guess we don't belong together anyway."

"Narrow-minded?" I practically scream. "How can you call me narrow-minded? I'm in the most liberal, most progressive club on campus! We're trying to make a difference, to open people's minds!"

"Except that if somebody doesn't fit into your little cookie-cutter world of what we should all be, then they're narrow-minded, huh?" Fletcher chuckles, but it sounds sad. "Well, great reasoning. You sound just like the rest of them. Except with a better vocabulary. See you at school."

The line clicks dead, and I feel like my heart might explode. "What happened?" Becca is next to me on the couch, her hand on my arm. "You look terrible. What happened?"

"I think I just blew it."

Saturday comes, and it's so boring that I actually look forward to working on school stuff. Becca is gone to Los Angeles with her mom to get the haunted-island-making supplies, and I just feel like burying my head under several feet of hard, uncomfortable concrete. That isn't readily available, so I settle for eating more cookies.

Euphoria pops into my room every once in a while and checks on me, trying to cheer me up. "Shelby, maybe we could go outside and play some croquet?" She buzzes excitedly. "I think the new gardener robot is due to arrive today."

"If you really want to get a glimpse of him, just roll on outside and wait." I look at my Life Management worksheet and realize that I've colored all the reproductive organs black. This won't help my grade. "Did Dad go to pick him up?"

"I think so," she says breathlessly as she rolls to the window and pulls the blinds aside. "The car's still gone, though. He left really early, before you got up."

"Do you know where your hottie bottie is from?"

"That's not a very nice thing to call him," she says, but she titters in a girlish way anyway. Seeing a robot lovestruck is not something I would recommend to anyone.

"What if you two don't hit it off?"

She whirs and clicks in a disapproving way. "Shelby, we're not like humans, you know. We all get along."

"I seem to recall a scuffle with a certain garbage disposal."

"That was only because the disposal was defective," she huffs as she takes the hint and rolls out of the room. "No need to bring up the unpleasant past. Do you need anything?"

"Just a new personality," I mumble as she leaves.

When Dad does finally get back with the lawn bot, Euphoria is pretty disappointed. I don't think she realizes that not all machines have her conversational skills. She tries to talk to the gleaming hulk of aluminum tubing and electric wire, but it just sits there, burping up blades of grass. Dad is in the driveway tinkering with it, with Euphoria standing around pretending to dust the garage.

"So? How's the new lawn boy?"

"Ah," he sighs, frustrated, as he wipes sweat from his forehead. "I got it from Dr. Merton, one of his little tinkering projects that didn't quite work. I was hoping to fix it, but I can't quite get it to do what I want it to."

"Maybe you should let me try," Euphoria purrs.

"Subtle as an armored tank," I whisper to her as I walk back to the house.

My cell is ringing; it's Becca. "You will not believe this. We actually ran into Brandon Keller at lunch. He's totally in for Nibid."

"You're kidding."

"Yeah, I'm kidding. But it sounded good, huh?" Her laugh crackles on the cell phone line. "Anyway, we got the wind machine, fog machine, rain tree, lights, and a sound system that will probably break the windows. Plus, and this is the best, a real movie pirate ship."

"You got all that in the Jeep?"

"Naw. Borrowed a truck. Mom can actually drive a truck better than she drives the Jeep. She just runs over anything in her way."

"Efficient." Back in my room, I close the door, hoping to avoid more gossip about the lawn mower from Euphoria. "He didn't call back."

"Did you think he would? Hang on." I hear a squeal

of tires and horns honking, and then Becca says, "Just don't flip him off, Mom. I'd like to make it home in one piece. Anyway," she says, back to me, "maybe you need to call him."

"Me call him? No way! What's the point of Nibid if we make our lives revolve around guys?"

"Right. But aren't you thinking about him and nothing else?"

"No," I lie.

"Right. So, I guess you're good. See you tomorrow, and we can get together to see if this stuff works. Can you come to my house?"

We decide on eleven, I hang up, and I sit on my bed and steam for a while. I am not obsessing about him! How dare she suggest that I spend all my time thinking about Fletcher? It's ridiculous. But then, when I really look at my thoughts over the last few days, I have to admit: He has been at the top of the list a lot of the time. Maybe he hypnotized me.

It gets dark, and Dad is still in the driveway hammering away at Mr. Grassroots, or whatever his name is. "Hey, Dad. Want to eat something? Maybe Euphoria can stop ogling the new guy long enough to whip up some spaghetti."

Euphoria's lights flash indignantly in the twilight. "Well, I don't need to be told twice," she says as she rolls to the front door. "I wouldn't want to inconvenience anyone."

"Not working, huh?"

"Nope." Dad throws an old greasy rag onto the cement.

"He's stubborn. The primary problem is the programming, and I just can't get it right. Plus, he's kind of rusty." He looks into the pink-orange sunset that is spreading across the tops of the palm tree silhouettes. "Looks like it's time to put him to bed, though. Want to help me stow him in the garage?"

"Euphoria would probably be happy to take care of him," I murmur as we push the heavy, clunky metal man toward the back of the building. "I think she's in love."

"Really?" He loops a length of nylon cord around the machine and ties it to a hook in the wall. "I think you're reading that into her. She's not programmed for that."

"Not like humans, huh?" I help him close the door; he locks it and puts an arm around my shoulders. "Dad, I'm not sure that bit of programming was a good idea."

"Love?" He laughs and walks me toward the door. "Love is always a good idea."

"Sounds like a greeting card."

"Thanks. I practice." He stops before we go inside. "We never really talked about all that dating stuff, did we?"

"Honestly, Dad, I'm done with dating for a while."

"I was sort of talking about me."

"Oh. Yeah." In my teenaged, self-obsessed mind, I had totally forgotten about the whole Dad-dating crisis. "Well, we don't have to talk about it. If you feel ready, you do it. It's your life."

He smiles at me, kisses me on the forehead, and opens the front door. "But you're a big part of it, and you'll always be a big part of it. Don't forget that. Oh, and if you do happen to start dating again, I want to meet him."

Figures. Of course, at this rate, I don't think it'll be something I have to worry about.

When I get to school Monday morning, I see that the Queen Geeks have been busy. Or at least one of them has been. There are huge butcher-paper posters everywhere (and I mean everywhere, even the girls' bathrooms) that read *NATIONAL INVISIBLE BOY DAY—FRIDAY*. And on almost every flat surface (including the sidewalks) there are screaming acid-green fliers advertising a date with Brandon Keller for one lucky girl who ignores boys on Friday.

When I get into English, the whole room is buzzing about it. "Samantha Singer told me!" Taffy Burton chatters to Jennifer Crist. "I mean, if she thinks it's for real, it must be!"

"Wow," Jennifer answers. "A date with Brandon Keller. I don't think I'd live through it."

One of the acid-green fliers is posted on Napoli's front board, and as she starts class, she points to it. "I gather from all the talking that you all saw these today." The class settles a bit since it seems she's going to talk about something interesting. "So what do you think?"

"About what?" A girl in front asks.

"About this National Invisible Boy Day. Is that a good thing, or is it insulting?"

Silence. Nobody, including me, had thought at all about whether it was good or bad. It just was. "Shelby, Becca. Aren't you all in charge of this event? Can you tell us why you're doing it?"

Becca stares at me, wide-eyed, coughs, and points to her throat, leaving me to field the questions, as usual. "Well—" I start. Dustin, my old reliable harasser, pipes in: "It's probably because they're all lesbians and they don't like guys." This gets an appreciative chuckle from several other boys.

"Is that it?" Napoli asks without batting an eye.

"Uh, no." Becca has found her voice at last. "It's because we're tired of girls always focusing so much on guys. It's like we have no lives without them. Is that really fair? Shouldn't we be finding out who we are first?"

Nobody says anything, including me. Napoli shrugs, and says, "Good point. I guess if Juliet had thought about that, she'd still be with us today. Well, maybe not. It was the 1500s . . ."

With that, we're off on Shakespeare again, the Friday event forgotten for the moment. I sit through my classes for the rest of the morning thinking about what she said: Is ignoring boys really the way to go? Or are we just sort of masking the real problem?

When I bring this up to Becca at lunch, she does her donkey honk and almost chokes on her sandwich. "Please! The real problem is that we don't think of ourselves enough. This will give us a chance to focus on us for a change. Pass the nachos."

"So, what was the supply trip to L.A. like?" I munch on celery as Elisa and Amber trundle over from the food cart.

"We got everything we need except the pirate ship, and that's coming next week."

"Pirate ship?" Amber eases herself, cross-legged, onto the grass. "With or without pirates?"

"I think we have to provide our own," Becca says. "We had to really pull some strings to get that one. It's not totally huge, just big enough to hold about ten people at a time. It's a smaller version of one they used in a movie. And yes, Johnny Depp was in it."

Elisa chews dreamily on some disgusting mess from a plastic container. "When's the dance?"

"Two weeks." I cringe at the thought of going to this stupid dance, dateless. But all in all, it will be better. I'll get to dance with my friends, hang out, just be one of the girls—

"Ben Lamb asked me." Becca is picking through her lunch bag very thoroughly, as if she doesn't want to meet any of our eyes. "I said yes."

"I'm going with Oscar Andrade." Amber sweeps her long hair dramatically. "He's a poet."

With a sinking feeling in my stomach, I look at Elisa, my last, best hope. She grins and says, "Jeff Hall."

"That dork?" Amber squeals. "I thought you said you'd never go out with him!"

"He grew and his voice changed." Elisa hums busily as she packs her gross container of bird intestines or whatever it is back in her bag. "He's not that bad now."

"So I'm the only one without a date?" I look at each one accusingly. "This is unbelievable! What happened to Queen Geeks together forever? To ignoring boys?"

"Just for one day," Elisa says apologetically. "I mean, we don't want to ignore them forever. They're cute."

The bell rings, and Amber and Elisa scatter quickly, leaving me and Becca alone. "Listen, you can come with us," she says. "It's totally—"

"Thanks. I can just wear my nun outfit and come as your chaperone." I pick up my trash and throw it toward a can and miss. I don't even pick it up. "Whatever. I hope you all have fun. I guess I'll be there, making sure you do."

"Hey!" Becca calls after me as I run toward the girls' bathroom. I fly into a stall, shut the door, lock it, and sit for a little bit. I'll be late, but who cares? I'm a loser. Lateness is the least of my worries.

Even as I sit there moping, I turn my head and there it is: one of those acid-green fliers inviting me to ignore boys on Friday. Well, for me, every day from now on is going to be Friday. But not by choice.

The actual National Invisible Boy Day Friday finally arrives. Everywhere I walk, girls are wearing hot-pink stickers, and boys are standing around looking sad and lonely. It's kind of satisfying in a way.

Becca finds me in the commons before first period, and jumps up and down. "Can you believe how many people are doing it?" she hisses excitedly. "Look at all the pink stickers! Look at all the stupid boys looking like they have no clue what to do now!"

"Yeah, it's pretty inspiring," I say, not sounding very inspired.

"It is. And I think—oh. Oh, uh . . ." Before she can finish beginning the sentence, someone taps my arm. I turn, and it's Fletcher. Great. At least I get to ignore him.

"Hi, Shelby. Listen, I know you're ignoring me, and that's cool. I just wanted you to know that I still like you, even if you did act like a total jerk to me on the phone. I totally forgive you for that, by the way. I'm telling you this today because I know you won't say anything back." I won't look at him, and instead I'm humming some '80s tune ("Walking on Sunshine," I think) and pretending that I'm incredibly fascinated by the birch tree I'm standing next to. "Okay, then. Just wanted to check in. Bye." He kisses me on the cheek. The nerve! I am almost ready to pop him, but then I wouldn't be ignoring him! What a jerk! What a sneaky jerk!

"That was so . . . so . . ." Becca tries to be sympathetic, but she starts laughing. "That was really funny. And smart. I know you want to hate him, but you've got to admit, that was classic. Too bad he's not a girl."

Becca has arranged for the Queen Geeks to have a table at lunch where we can give out tickets to girls with pink stickers. Right from the start, we get mobbed. "Isn't this cool?" Elisa exclaims, jumping up and down as she gives out blue tickets.

"Uh . . . yeah." Becca is staring distractedly across the crowded commons. A huge gang of immature freshman boys (Dustin among them—big surprise!) surrounds a group of girls and keeps taunting them with low-level insults to try and get them to talk. "C'mon," she says to me.

"Hey, ladies," she says to those girls, who are all wearing stickers. "Do you hear something? Sort of like an annoying buzz? Maybe it's flies."

"No, I think it's probably just static," one blond girl says as she waves the air as if trying to clear it. "Interference."

"Nice," one of the boys in the knot says. "Let's go find some chicks who are worth looking at."

They walk away, and the girls sitting in the circle with their pink stickers wait until the boys are out of hearing range. Then the blonde says, "Guess that bothered them, huh?"

"I sort of enjoyed it," a pink-haired girl in a black sweat-shirt says, grinning. "Hey, aren't you guys in charge of this thing?" she asks us.

"Yep," Becca answers brightly. "Queen Geek Social Club, ladies. Feel free to come to our meetings anytime. Wednes-days at lunch, Room E7."

"How do we get our tickets for the date drawing?" the blonde asks. "I am so in love with Brandon Keller!"

"I've got 'em right here." Becca pulls a strand of blue carnival tickets from her pocket and gives them out. Each girl scrambles to get hers and to give Becca the stub, which she places in a big manila envelope. "The winner will be announced at the dance, so good luck!" she says as we walk away.

"Look how many girls have pink stickers!" She opens the envelope, and I peer in. Hundreds of little blue ticket stubs are piled inside. "This thing is huge!"

"Maybe it's because they all think they're getting a date with Brandon Keller."

"Maybe," she says. "But either way, they did it. That's what counts."

By the end of the day, Becca's envelope is crammed full of blue ticket stubs.

Elisa, Amber, Becca, and I go to Becca's house after school on Friday to celebrate our amazing victory. Three of us cram into the back of her mom's Jeep, squished so close that if we did get in an accident, we wouldn't get hurt because we couldn't move enough to hit anything. Thea has the top down too, so it's sort of like riding in the bag of a vacuum cleaner. Not that I've ever done that, of course.

"So it went well?" Thea yells over the Beatles CD that's blaring from the stereo.

"Yeah," Becca screams. "It was awesome."

"Now what are you going to do?" Thea stops the Jeep at a light and turns down the stereo. This would be okay except that Elisa keeps singing "Sgt. Pepper's Lonely Hearts Club Band" in my ear, and it's not a pretty thing to hear. "I mean, you were successful, so now you have to outdo your-selves, don't you?"

The mood suddenly turns a little down. She's kind of right. We now have set a standard for ourselves that we have to live up to, or we'll disappoint people. Wow. It kind of makes you wish you were mediocre, really.

However, Becca cannot be brought down. "Well, this dance thing is going to be the icing on the cake. It will per-manently put the Queen Geeks on the map." She turns to Thea, who has now gotten on the freeway and is dodging in and out of lanes like a NASCAR racer with failing eyesight. "Where are you storing all the supplies?"

"Out by the pool." She laughs. "Who knows what the neighbors think?"

We get to Becca's house without an accident (amazing) and crash in her game room (equally amazing, as I've said before). Amber sets up the billiard table, racking the multi-colored balls in their little triangle like a pool shark. "Mere-dith, Pepsis for all!" Becca calls into the intercom. "And any chocolate you can find handy!"

"It must be cool to have a servant," Elisa says wistfully as she sinks into the tan suede sofa.

"Meredith isn't a servant." Becca frowns at her as if she's said something tasteless, which I guess she has. "She's . . . like part of the family, except that her job is to get stuff for everybody else. But she has her own room and everything, and it's not like she's chained in the basement after hours."

Amber chalks a cue stick, blows the blue dust off the end, and eyes the balls. "Guess it all depends on your point of view, doesn't it?"

"I guess." Becca checks the hall to see if Meredith is coming with the drinks yet. "But she can leave if she wants. She's not a slave. She gets paid very well too."

"So should we talk about the dance?" I try brightly to change the subject, which is interrupted by Amber's spectacular break on the pool table that sends several balls flying in various directions.

"Fire in the hole!" Elisa shouts as she dodges a purple projectile. "Amber, you should not be shooting pool without a license."

"Hey, I'm just an amateur." She lays the cue stick cautiously on the edge of the table. "Looks a lot easier on *Celebrity Billiards*."

Meredith brings the tray of sodas and a big bowl of M&Ms in weird pastel colors: gray, pink, pale turquoise. "What's with the gray candy?" Amber asks as she grimaces at the bowl.

"Mom did a party a couple of weeks ago, and the people color-coordinated the candy to the décor. She got the extras." She grabs a handful of candy, pops it into her mouth, and chews noisily. "Tastes the same."

Elisa helps herself, picking out only the pink ones. "So, as for the dance, are you seriously going to give somebody a date with Brandon Keller?"

"Mom called him when we were in L.A. last weekend," Becca says, as if it's the most normal thing in the world. "He said he'd do it."

A stunned silence falls on the gray M&Ms. "He said he'd do it?" Amber says slowly, as if she must have misunderstood.

Becca starts talking before she's finished chewing up the weird-colored candy, which grosses me out. "Mom was his godmother. It's no big thing. They're just people too, you know."

"But they're people who are cuter and richer than us!" Elisa exclaims.

"Speak for yourself." Becca swigs her glass of soda. "Once this dance happens, people will be asking Brandon Keller if he knows *us*."

14

THE BIG DANCE

(or Yo Ho Ho and a Bottle of Humble)

To say that the next two weeks of preparation for the dance were time-consuming is like saying the *Titanic* had a little water retention problem. Even though we were approaching the end of the school year, the planning and sheer physical labor involved in making a haunted tropical island in a high school gym absorbed any time I might have had to do schoolwork, eat, sleep, or think about boys.

Which was just as well, really. I mean, I would've been thinking about either Fletcher or the long-lost Anders, whom I suddenly seem to see everywhere I go on campus. He usually just waves to me, and if he's with Ilsa, he sort of looks the other way. Fletcher, on the other hand, has no problem being seen or communicating. He leaves notes for me all the time, he sends me text messages, he knows my schedule and follows me around.

On Monday the week of the dance, Samantha Singer calls an emergency meeting of the dance committee. Fletcher plops down next to me, and I look the other way. He pretends we're speaking to each other.

"So," he whispers excitedly. "Ready to put that island together?"

Becca leans across me. "Could you please just leave her alone? Isn't it clear that she doesn't want to talk to you?"

This is the first time Fletcher seems at all dented by my absolute indifference. He looks startled; he sits back against the folding chair, crosses his arms, and doesn't say anything else. Why do I feel slightly disappointed?

Samantha clears her throat politely. "Okay, so, we're all meeting Wednesday after school to start putting the island together. Fletcher? Want to give us more details?"

He looks at her, then looks at me, then looks at the floor—as if gum-spattered vinyl is going to give him the right answer! "Uh . . . this was really Becca and Shelby's idea. They should tell you about it."

An audible gasp is heard. Okay, maybe I'm making that up . . . but in my mind, there was definitely an audible gasp. Becca's wide eyes show her astonishment too, and when Fletcher sits down, still not looking at us, she stands up. "Well, yeah. I have all the stuff in my backyard, except for the pirate ship, which should be here tomorrow, early evening. We'll be here to get it set up, and then Wednesday, if you're all here to help, we can get the rest of it put together over a couple of days."

There is more chatter about decorations, dress code, and signing up people to work the door and such, but I can't focus on anything but Fletcher. After all his attempted glory stealing, for him to simply back off and admit to the group that it was our idea took some nerve. Why did he do it, I wonder? And of course, the answer echoes back from the teeny-tiny dark corner booth of my mind: *Because he likes you, dork.*

After school, what I've come to think of as the primary four Queen Geeks go to my house for our last afternoon of relative freedom. Even though Elisa and Amber aren't on the committee, we've recruited them to help structure the epic entertainment event that will be the spring dance, so whether they like it or not, they're part of the action. They have mixed feelings.

"I'm not sure I want to work. I sort of wanted to get to know Jeff Hall," Elisa says glumly as we trudge through an unseasonably hot afternoon full of haze and pollen. She sneezes for about the twentieth time since we started walking, and blows her nose in such a way that wild geese from Canada answer her. "But with allergy season coming up, I suppose it's just as well I can't spend a lot of time with him. Nobody likes to kiss someone with chronic postnasal drip."

Amber, on the other hand, has blossomed into something of a flirt since she got involved in the dance thing, and with poet Oscar Andrade as her escort, she's really excited about it. "He's really cool," she croons in a very un-Amber-like, positive way. "He's got a dirt bike."

"A dirt bike? That's not very artistic," Becca points out as she kicks an empty paper cup out of her way. A little dust devil blows across the sidewalk. "Of course, I guess here, it's more practical than a sculpture garden."

"It's a good thing it's so hot, really," I remind them. "A sprinkler system is much more fun when it's hot and dry."

"Santa Ana winds," Elisa says, shaking her head and sneezing again. "Every year, they bring evil and allergens."

"You're so dramatic," Becca says. "Let's talk about something more interesting. How about Shelby's love life?"

"No, please," I groan.

Amber jumps right on it. "Yeah. I heard Fletcher sort of offered you his soul in exchange for a date, huh?"

"Uh, that's a little bit of an exaggeration. It was only his *mortal* soul, not his *eternal* soul. Actually, we made a bet. I guess I'm going to lose it, but so is he." I try to change the topic of conversation, which I figure will be unsuccessful, but when you're about to be subjected to uncomfortable friendly advice, you've got to at least try. "So does everybody have their outfits for the dance, or should we go thrift shopping?"

No one has to answer, because Becca's cell phone chimes out. "Hello?" She stops walking abruptly, and Elisa, in mid-sneeze, runs smack into her backpack. Becca waves her away. "Really? When? No way. That is too awesome. Hang on, Mom." She covers the phone with one hand and says "Brandon Keller is coming here on Friday. He's staying over at our house!"

Amber shrugs her shoulders, Elisa starts coughing and turns kind of blue, and I smile broadly. If I can swing an invitation to stay over at Becca's while the TV stud is there, that will absolutely flip Fletcher's wig.

"Mom? We're gonna need to haul all that stuff from the backyard to school on Wednesday afternoon, okay? Can you get some guys to help you? Great. I'm going to Shelby's right now, but can you come get me at about seven? Cool. Love you too."

Elisa has overcome her respiratory distress. "Brandon Keller is going to be at your house?" She grabs Becca's arm so hard she squirms to get away. "I have to meet him. It's a lifelong dream."

"You're only fifteen. How can you *have* a lifelong dream?" Becca shrugs her off. "Listen, you guys, he's just a person. I grew up around him. I told you, he won't want to be treated like he's a freak or something. If you all come over and drool over him, he'll feel weird, so maybe you shouldn't come over."

We all holler at that, and promise to be good if we're allowed in his presence.

When we all finally drag into my house (thankfully air-conditioned), Euphoria brings in a tray full of icy lemonade and a plate of cookies. "Ah," Amber says, biting into an oatmeal raisin, "Here's to success! Not to mention a back-room lip-lock with Brandon Keller!"

Fletcher doesn't call, which sort of surprises me after his oh-so-dramatic sacrifice of ego. But he's a guy, so I don't have to understand what he does or does not do. Wednesday finally comes and the school day drags on. Finally, it's after school and the real event of the day can begin: the construction of the island.

Thea is already in front of the gym with a huge truck and eight very large men with various piercings and tattoos. "Where does your mom meet all these guys?" I whisper to Becca as one, who looks like a redwood tree with legs, walks by carrying a piece of equipment that is three times his size.

"Movie sets, theaters, art galleries." She sighs as we watch her mom boss the burly men around. "It's like living with a really popular older sister. Sometimes I really miss having a normal mom, you know, one who's into knitting and cookies and stuff instead of belly dancing and tattoos."

They've decided to put the haunted island on what we call the porch, the open-air court that's fenced in behind the interior of the gym. We come face-to-face with the pirate ship, which Becca assures me was used in a Famous Hollywood Movie (due to legal restrictions, she says she can't tell me which one). It is pretty spectacular; although not the size of what I'd imagine a real sailing ship to be, it's still big, and looks like it's made of old, rotting wood dripping with Spanish moss. I can't resist, so I touch it as it glides by; it's resin, fake, just like all the cheeseball snowman decorations people put on their lawns at Christmas.

"So what's the haunted part of all of this?" I ask Becca as we grab two big boxes of beads and jewels and head for the gym.

"Brandon's got some of his acting friends coming up to be the spooks," she says as she balances the box on her knee. "We'll have some real Island of the Damned action happening on board. Some awesome special effects. I don't want to tell you everything, because then it won't be a surprise."

"I can't believe you made this happen." I trail along behind her, like I do in everything, it seems.

"*We* made it happen," she corrects me as she shoves a hip against the double doors into the gym. *We*. Right.

Things inside look, in a word, amazing. The decorating committee had gone into overdrive. Jewel-colored banners and pirate flags lit by flickering tiki torches (battery-powered) wave above small carts with red-and-white-striped awnings where signs advertise Island Smoothies, Good Luck Charms, Madame Hula's Crystal Ball Readings, and my personal favorite, Jerk Chicken. I wonder if Fletcher will hang out there all night. Well, at least I know he won't be with me.

The members of the piercing-and-tattoo brigade are hoisting lights and plugging stuff into huge power boxes. The pirate ship heaves into place, and a truck full of sand pulls around to the back of the gym and starts dumping. Kids are jumping around in the sand like they're all of two years old. The hardest part is trying to figure out a way to help the muscle-bound dudes who are now somehow erecting a rain forest with hidden sprinklers next to the brand-new beach that is gleaming where we usually play racquetball. We all just sort of stand around and watch, because they obviously don't need our help.

Big fake palm trees and greenery come from nowhere and the men set them up on a grid, fluff them a little, and they suddenly look like a lush tropical paradise. Thea watches all of this, darting around and clapping her hands like the good fairy on caffeine. Or green tea. Or whatever.

Where's Fletcher?

Nine o'clock rolls around and the rain forest and sprinklers still aren't all hooked up. Most of us have had at least a partial drenching, which was kind of fun at first, but we all feel tired of the island way of life. "It smells like wet dog and glue," Amber says, wrinkling her nose.

Thea, still looking fresh and dynamic, sweeps over to us and puts her arms around me and Becca. "You girls look absolutely done in. Let's call it a day. We'll just meet here again after school tomorrow to finish up." She motions to the burliest of the burly men, a side of beef in pants. "Felipe? Why don't you all come over to the house and shower. I'm sure you're all just exhausted. We so appreciate your work here, don't we girls?"

Felipe just sort of grunts and motions to the other men, who begin to pick up random pieces of palm tree and electrical conduit. "They're not staying at our house, are they?" Becca hisses at her mom as we walk out.

"Well, what did you want me to do?" Thea hisses back.

"They're working for free, you know. I had to call in a lot of favors to do this for you, Becca. Do you have any idea what these people make in a day on a film set?"

"Yeah, yeah," Becca says, rolling her eyes. "It would pay for my braces, if I needed them. I know."

"I did meet them through your dad. At least he was good for something," Thea chirps brightly. Becca stops abruptly, causing both Thea and me to nearly take a tumble into a pile of fake ferns.

"Do not talk about Melvin like that."

Melvin?

Thea crosses her arms and faces her daughter. I am feeling like I'm caught in the middle of a brewing storm with no way out. After all, she is my ride.

Amber and Elisa, meanwhile, have other transport, so they make their excuses and scurry out of the gym, looking back to see if Becca and Thea have started to riot. Instead, Becca is about ten paces ahead, marching furiously toward the parking lot.

"She's so dramatic," Thea huffs as she follows her daughter. Gee, I wonder where she ever got that personality trait? We drive to my house in absolute silence that is thick with accusations. Becca sits, arms folded, and refuses to wear her seat belt. When Thea screeches into my driveway, Becca finally says, "Well, if I make it home in one piece, I guess I'll see you tomorrow," which kicks off another screechfest between the two of them.

I just go inside, go straight to my room, strip my clothes off, and flop into bed. I only barely notice Euphoria settling in for the night with a murmured, "Well, it would be nice if *someone* bothered to say hello."

Thursday. School? What school? Who cares? Honestly, it's a miracle I'm even passing anything at this point, and there are a couple of classes I'm not totally sure about, which I am conveniently forgetting to mention to my dad. At lunch, Becca and I drift over to the gym, just to gaze longingly at our brainchild. No Fletcher.

Becca seems to have overcome whatever problem she had yesterday, which is what she usually does. Nothing bothers her for long. "Yeah, yesterday was weird," she says as we walk toward the food cart. "We had, like, ten sweaty guys sharing a bathroom. Luckily, they were all in the other part of the house."

I mumble something in response.

"So?" Becca asks as I barely eat my disgusting rice-and-black-bean burrito. "Why are you so depressed? This is our crowning achievement. Everybody at this school is going to know who we are after this, and probably people for years to come will talk about this. Why aren't you happy?"

"I don't know." I throw my lunch in the trash without eating much of it.

After school, we all bolt over to the gym as quickly as possible. I watch one of Thea's beefy helpers as he positions a wind machine, turns it on briefly, and nearly knocks Amber on her backside.

The rest of the place is a theme park. The pirate ship looks like it's beached against the outside door, and a hidden sound system is blaring Caribbean jungle tunes peppered with moaning and creaking. Even by daylight, it sounds creepy. But with someone cute, it would really give you an excuse to get close, wouldn't it?

"Do you have your bathing suit yet?" Becca waves a hand in front of my face. "Hello? Anybody home? Seriously, this lovesick stuff is tired. Can't you just call him?"

"Call who?"

She doesn't even answer, just rolls her eyes at me and walks away. How rude. As if I can read her mind . . . okay, well, I did know who she was talking about, but I wasn't about to let her know that.

By about ten o'clock, the gym looks ready to go. The lights focus on the pirate ship and make it look like a wreck bathed in moonlight, and the tall palm trees seem to sway in a tropical breeze. The movie guys even thought to pump in some plumeria and eucalyptus scent, so it really feels and smells like a rain forest. It literally seems like our gym just fades into a tropical paradise, like it dropped into the Bermuda Triangle and came out the other side. I can only imagine the horror the gym teachers must be feeling at this moment. But sand on the basketball court is the least of my worries.

"Who wants to take a walk?" Thea calls out. Those of us still left (including Becca, Amber, Elisa, and a few of the die-hard ASB types) line up next to a big wooden post with an aged-looking skull on top, and a sign that reads *Abandon All Hope, Ye Who Enter Here*. Yeah, well I already did that, like, days ago. I didn't need any pirates to make my life a disaster.

"Now, of course, we don't have the actors yet, and Brandon promised they will be spectacular," Thea gushes. "But we do have all the other effects, so come on in and enjoy!"

With a soundtrack of bird and monkey calls, we tread cautiously along a path and immediately feel like we're in a rain forest. It's like school just disappeared, and for a moment I'm caught up in the excitement of it. Something whizzes past my ear, and I duck. "What was that?"

"Huh?" Elisa is behind me, and suddenly screams. "A spider! There's a spider in my hair! Get it out!" She's flailing like a puppet on a string, while Amber and Becca crack up. The big hairy spider, meanwhile, goes on its union lunch break and recedes back into the palm trees. "Not funny!" Elisa murmurs as she pats her hair back in place.

The path is a lot longer than you would think, given that it's in a school gym. It seems like we walk for at least ten minutes. It gets darker too, and I start to get kind of creeped out. Becca grabs my arm, pulls me back a bit, and points silently to something moving in the trees. "Watch," she whispers.

Amber is a few paces ahead, and as she steps on a branch lying on the path, something rustles and moves toward her. She turns and finds herself nose to nose with a moldy skeleton in pirate garb. Screeching like a monkey, she slaps at the skeleton pirate and runs away, knocking Elisa flat in the process.

"This is some fun," Becca nods. "We will be so totally famous."

We walk for another five minutes or so and finally end up at the pirate ship, where Thea tells us that tomorrow hordes of scary actors will be spooking the heck out of all our friends. The finale is when the beefy helper guys turn on the rain forest sprinklers and drench all of us.

"I wish I hadn't worn my white T-shirt," Amber mutters as she crosses her arms across her chest.

Friday I do something I never, ever have done my entire school career: I skip school. Dad is gone, and Euphoria is absolutely enraged, but she can't do much about it since Dad never programmed her to beat me or anything. She does make me burnt toast and runny oatmeal, which is I guess her way of registering disapproval.

Becca calls me at about ten, and is frantic. "Where are you?" she yells. I hear the rush of people scurrying to class. "Why aren't you at school? Are you sick?"

"Not really." I'm lying with my head over the side of my bed, staring up at the glow-in-the-dark stars. "Just sick of . . . everything, I guess."

"This is no time to throw in the towel!" She dashes into the bathroom, judging from the multiple flushing sounds. "You've got to be here tonight. I mean, it's the end of all our great work this year. It'll be the best dance the school has ever seen!"

How can I explain? Even to my best friend, I don't know how to say it. Instead, I just say, "Yeah, I'll be there. I'm not sick, I'm just tired. Don't worry."

I can hear in her voice that she doesn't quite believe me. "Okay. Well, do you want me to come to your house with Brandon before we go to the school?"

"Brandon?"

"Uh, you know, the mega–movie star friend of my mom's who's donated a date tonight so we could promote our club? Hello?"

"I'll be there. But I'll just come by myself, thanks. See you at about five."

"Hey, but I wanted to—"

The call gets dropped, or she hangs up, but either way, the line of communication is down. Something has happened to change me, not her, and I know it. It's like there's a big wall between me and the rest of the world suddenly, and even something as totally cool as an outrageous dance and changing the school culture for the better don't bring me out of my funk. Maybe chocolate would do it. No, probably not.

I spend the day watching cartoons. Every cartoon I watch, and I am not exaggerating about this, features a tall, skinny guy with green eyes and auburn hair, almost as if the god of the boob tube decides to punish me by teasing me with tiny animated versions of Fletcher Berkowitz. And on top of that, I have to deal with Euphoria coming in about every half hour to let me know that I am wasting approximately 1.2484395 percent of my total estimated life span (rounded up).

"Four-thirty, Shelby. Time to get ready for the dance." Euphoria brings in a tray with a nice green salad, a glass of mineral water and lime, and a dinner roll. "Eat light," she advises. "Nerves make humans throw up."

"How do you know I'm nervous?"

"Please. Do I really need to answer that?" She's dissing me. My own robot is dissing me. What kind of world is this?

Anyway, I do get ready, even though I don't feel like going. Becca calls five more times: to tell me she's at the airport, that she's spotted Brandon, that her mom is hugging Brandon, that she just hugged Brandon, and that they're on their way home. I'm guessing I'll get another call when Brandon uses the bathroom.

I look in the mirror before heading out. Blue-and-green batik sarong tied over a one-piece bathing suit in deep turquoise; turquoise necklace in silver that my dad got me for my birthday; hair tied in a ponytail; subtle but effective makeup. Why do I feel so ugly? Sighing, I shove my feet into some beaded flip-flops and head for the door.

Euphoria stops me, of course. "You're wearing beach attire to a dance?" she asks as if I've committed a federal crime.

"It's a beach party theme." I grab my bag and take one last look in the hall mirror. If I weren't me, and I saw that girl, I'd buy her some antidepressants and chocolate. Or maybe chocolate antidepressants, like spiked M&Ms. Why hasn't anyone thought of that?

"Oh." She senses my lack of enthusiasm, and tries to make me feel better. "Well, you look very bitchy."

"Do you mean *beachy* by any chance?"

"Isn't that what I said?" She buzzes and clicks in confusion.

"Never mind." Opening the door, I feel butterflies start to wake up in my stomach. Nervous? Why? The most exciting thing that will happen at this dance is that I might get drenched or find a chocolate pirate coin. Whoopee. "See you later. I'll probably be home late since I might have to help clean up. I'll call when I'm on my way home, though."

"Call me every half hour after eleven," she answers, calling as I walk down the driveway, "I won't sleep till you get home!"

"You don't sleep anyway," I mutter as I throw her a lazy wave good-bye.

It's nearly five, and the dance doesn't start until seven, but I have nothing to do really, so I figure I might as well go and help get the last-minute preparations in order.

Walking gives me a chance to think a little bit about my situation. Boys are a bother. As I decided at the beginning of the year, I do not want to be tied down by anybody, because it's just not worth it. I mean, eventually they'll leave you anyway, and why get all attached and then find out that it was all for nothing, when you could put your efforts into other, more important things, like . . . uh . . . knitting, or cooking, or games. Or school. Yeah, school! I could throw myself into my schoolwork next year; in fact, I could even do summer school to get ahead. I should be a total book nerd, somebody who everyone else comes to for help. I could just get straight As, and I could—ah, who am I kidding? I don't even *want* straight As. I've always felt they were a sign of weakness and the result of a lack of social skills.

The Queen Geeks! Maybe I could make that my focus. I mean, Becca has huge plans, I'm sure, for next year. I could just pour myself into the club, make it my life's work, and become the geekiest of the geeks. I could get a geek medal of honor, maybe even star in documentaries about geeks. How pathetic.

A horn honking snaps me out of my dismal fantasy. It's Amber and her mom, whom I've never met; they pull over and Amber leans out the window. Her long, dark hair is braided with plumeria and she has on a jewel-toned swim-suit. "Hey! Want a ride?"

"No thanks." I don't think it's fair to expose people to my dark thoughts and depressing attitude, especially before a party. "I'll just walk. It's not that far."

"See you there!" She waves excitedly. What a difference from when I first met her! She was too cool for anything, all artsy and dark, and now she's wearing a lei around her neck and hanging out of car windows. At least some of us have changed for the better.

When I get within view of the school, it's like I stepped into a transporter out of *Star Trek*. The front of the gym is decorated with tiki huts and torches, and a Polynesian drum group is unpacking its gear. Becca is bent over a treasure chest and is arranging fake jewels, game tokens, and a skull.

"Hey, anybody we know?" I ask, pointing to the bones.

"I thought maybe it was you." She stands up, dusts off her own red wrap skirt, and crosses her arms defiantly. "What's with the silent treatment?"

"Sorry," I mumble. "Just kind of feeling blah. Didn't want to bring you down too."

"What are friends for?" She gives me a hug and suddenly sparkles again. "Okay, so come in and see the gym. It is absolutely amazing!"

We walk in, and I have to admit, my jaw drops. The place doesn't even look like it belongs in a high school. "It looks like a movie set."

"It kind of is," she says, leading me to what looks like a fifteen-foot cave lit from within with some ghostly green light. "Mom's friends come through once again!"

"Is there something in there?" I peer into the entrance.

"Guess you'll have to find out!" she grabs my hand and runs toward a row of cabana tents in bright-colored stripes of emerald, royal blue, violet, yellow, and orange.

"What is this?" People are buzzing around the tents, stacking boxes, setting up—in one case, a huge spinning wheel like in a casino.

"It's our Pirates' Market! We have a fortune-teller, a game of chance, booths where you can get ale (which is really just soda) and snacks, and a souvenir booth."

"Yeah, I noticed the Jerk Chicken cart earlier," I say pointedly.

Becca ignores me. "Elisa's over there. She made, like, a thousand of these cool pins with our club name and a picture of Johnny Depp!"

"Wow. Hope she doesn't get sued. And won't your buddy Brandon be offended that we didn't steal *his* likeness instead?"

"No. He's cool. Wait till you meet him." She checks her watch. "Wow! We're running out of time. Do you want to work in here or help in the ticket booth?"

The idea of being around all this merriment makes me queasy, so I opt for the booth. She takes me outside again, where the steel drummers are tuning up, and locks me into a little glass cubicle with some girl who looks like the lead member of the Junior Accountants Club. "Hi," she says curtly. "I'm Alice. Please don't breathe on my cash box. I'm very concerned about infection."

Great. So I'm stuck in a cube with a germ freak, a roll of tickets, and change for a twenty. Could life get better?

"Hey, Shelby." Oh, yes. Life could get better.

"Hi, Anders. Hi, Ilsa. You guys want tickets?" They're cuddling as if they share a hip.

"Yes, two please," Anders says as Ilsa tugs at the red bandana around his head. "You're going to the dance too, right?"

"I'm hoping not to." I furiously tear two tickets and shove them through the little hole in the window. "Here you go. Have fun. Be sure to visit the haunted pirate island."

"That's not in the script," Alice hisses at me from the side of her mouth.

"Don't talk to me or I might sneeze on you." She does sort of huddle against her side of the cube and seems inclined to leave me alone.

"Well, hope to see you inside," Anders calls cheerfully as Ilsa adjusts her very revealing sequined tank top. "Ilsa is a mermaid. Isn't that clever?"

"Yeah." I smile robotically. "Great. Have a nice day." I never noticed before that Anders sounds a lot like the muscle-bound *Terminator* guy. I wonder if he always sounded like that, or if I'm just more annoyed with him now?

Alice is fuming, yet terrified that I might infect her, which I can use to my advantage. I pretend that I have a violent cough, and I see her cringe and huddle a little closer to the side of the booth.

I sell a few more tickets, and as it gets closer to the official start of the dance, the crowds become thicker and thicker until finally it feels like Alice and I are in a foxhole trying to dodge dollar bills. "Wow, this is a really popular dance," she says breathlessly. "I think I might be getting an asthma attack."

"Because it's a popular dance?" I scoff as I throw quarters out the little window to make change for a couple.

"No, because you're taking up all the oxygen in here." She loosens her collar and hands perfectly aligned dollar bills to a kid on the outside. "You know, it seems to be slowing down. Perhaps you should take a break."

"Yeah." Wow, even crazy Alice doesn't want me. As I get up, a few people in the line outside the booth protest, but I wave at them and say something about virulent diarrhea, which shuts them up.

It's seven o'clock, and the crowd is milling around, but inside, the music is pounding already. The Polynesian musicians are playing brilliantly, that kind of music that makes it impossible for you to be sad because it sounds so much like sunshine and sparkling water. Except that I am sad anyway.

I hear Becca's voice amplified, which is sort of scary in a I'm-the-queen-of-the-world kind of way. "Everyone who has a blue ticket stub from our National Invisible Boy Day, please be sure to have it ready. Brandon Keller will be arriving very soon! We'll be doing the date drawing at eight-thirty sharp, and then Brandon is yours for the rest of the evening!"

A massive female scream erupts from the gym. Guys stare, frightened, at the sheer sound volume of the girls. "Geez," one guy near me says, "you'd think this guy was, like, in the movies or something."

"He *is*, you moron." His friend shakes his head. "Let's go check out the haunted island. I heard it's totally awesome and scares the chicks."

That perks me up a little. The island, *my* island, is totally awesome. Maybe I'm not useless after all.

Inside, the gym is bursting with people. Colored streamers float above and the caves are now populated with kids hanging on them, sitting on them, and, if I look toward the back, making out in them. I see a vice principal heading that direction, so the making out won't last long, but the place looks amazing anyway.

Becca, Elisa, and Amber are standing on a stage under the basketball hoop, and it's all decorated to look like a jungle hut with two wicker chairs draped with Mardi Gras beads. Hanging above the chairs is a butcher-paper banner that reads *Caribbean King and Queen* and on a low table, two leis and two crowns are perched, waiting to be awarded to whoever is voted the royalty of the fling.

Becca spots me and waves frantically for me to climb up onto the stage. "Hey!" She grabs my hand and pulls me up, forgetting the stairs, then gives me a huge hug that crushes her plumeria necklace and sends a delicate scent into the air. "Brandon and Mom will be here any minute. Isn't this exciting? It's so successful!"

"Where's Samantha Singer and her pet weasel, Fletcher?" I scan the crowd, but don't see the red hair or the tall, blond mannequin.

"Haven't seen either of them. I thought Samantha wanted to announce king and queen, but if she doesn't show up by eight, I'm doing it." Suddenly squeals and then a roar of approval and clapping rush like a wave from the front door

to the stage. "Brandon must be here." She motions frantically to the DJ, who abruptly ditches the CD he's playing
and switches to a hip-hop version of the theme song to
Brandon's show, *Life with Brandon*.

The crowd parts, a sea of sarongs and bathing suits and
board shorts, and a guy in sunglasses, a white linen shirt,
and Dockers struts up the aisle flashing his best movie-star
smile. A groping field of female hands stretches toward him,
and he touches fingertips as he walks by, leaving swooning
girls in his wake. It's truly disgusting. You'd think the guy
found the cure for cancer or something.

"And here he is!" Becca screams into the microphone, trying to be heard over the shrillness of Green Pines' loudest
girls. She waves to Brandon and extends a hand to help him
onto the stage, but he just jumps it like it's nothing. Show-off.

"Hey, San Diego, what's up?" he yells. He's met with a
swelling scream that even the guys join in on. "Welcome to
Caribbean Madness! Have a great time, and remember, at
eight-thirty, I'm gonna pick a ticket and whoever it belongs
to is my date for the night. Let's party!"

The DJ amps up the music, the crowd claps and screams,
and the dance is officially in full swing. More people keep
flooding in, the principals look nervous, and the music
rocks. Couldn't be better. So what do I do? Think about
going home to my robot.

Becca dances next to me, bumping into my hip in time to
the music. "Let's go!" she yells at me. "Have some fun!
Loosen up!"

"I'm so loose I might fall apart," I say, too softly to be heard.

Amber seems glued to Oscar Andrade and she's all smiles. "C'mon, Shelby," she shouts. "It's your party!"

Becca is chatting with Brandon, staring up at him as if he's the most amazing thing ever created. She doesn't have time to deal with my bad mood, and I shouldn't make her deal with it, either. I jump off the stage, thread my way through the growing crowd, and suddenly somebody grabs my arm. It's Becca.

She motions for me to follow her since there's no way we could be heard over the music. We end up at the far end of the caves, sheltered a little from the constant heartbeat of the tunes. "Listen," she says, breathless. "What's up with you?"

"I don't feel good. I'm going home." I turn to go, and she grabs me again.

"You cannot go, Shelby. I won't let you."

"Really? What are you gonna do, send Brandon Keller to rough me up with a manicure?"

"He's here as a favor. Don't be a jerk." She's looking at me as if she doesn't really know what to say. We've always been able to talk before, but now . . . again, there's that wall. I guess I should've known it would happen eventually. I've never really had a great, good friend. I don't know why I expected to have one in high school.

"I gotta go." Elbows out, I move out into the sea of bodies, trying to swim for the door, but Becca blocks my path.

"I know why you're like this."

"Like what?" Annoyed, I try to dodge past her, but she won't let me. Stupid tallness.

"You're mad because Fletcher didn't keep pursuing you, and you wanted him to. And now you're upset that you blew it when you really liked him."

"That's such crap! I never liked him!" I jerk my arm away, biting the words off like hard candy. "You wouldn't know anything about it, since you've got your movie star and all." I know this is a stupid argument, and that I sound like a real idiot, but it's all I can think of to throw at her at the moment.

"Okay." She puts her hands up in a gesture of surrender. "I'm not going to try to convince you that you really do like him. I'm also not going to tell you it doesn't matter, because obviously it does. Now, mope if you want, but I think it's embarrassing. But I will say this: No matter what guy you like, and which guy likes you, you are always a Queen Geek, and that should be enough for anybody. Case closed." She walks away, and quickly gets lost in the ocean of bobbing heads and waving arms.

A lightbulb goes on in my head (or maybe the spit-swapping couple blocking the stage lights just moved slightly), but either way, I get this tingly feeling all over. I don't have to feel this way over a guy, even a guy as admittedly perfect for me as Fletcher Berkowitz. I've wasted so much time over the past few years trying to convince myself that guys aren't important, that relationships don't matter, that I don't need anybody, and that I'm totally happy alone. Maybe that's not true anymore, and maybe I'm not totally happy. But all in all, I do have friends, and that's worth a lot more than a hot guy with freckles.

"Time to announce the king and queen!" Becca screams into the microphone as the song ends. The crowd surges forward toward the stage, and from somewhere a spotlight hits Becca. She squints and puts her hand up to shield her eyes. "I have in my hand your votes for King and Queen of Caribbean Madness. Is this the coolest dance or what?" Shouts and stamping of feet bounce off the walls of the gym. "Could I have some music, please?"

The DJ puts on some generic love song and Becca dramatically tears open the envelope. "And your queen and king of the spring dance are . . . Samantha Singer and Fletcher Berkowitz!"

Just when you think things can't get worse . . . the music gets louder and a rustling in the crowd turns into applause and hoots and hollers. I see Becca onstage looking for me with a worried expression on her face. The spotlight finally finds the happy couple as they walk regally to the stage, jump up, and graciously accept their Hawaiian flower crowns.

"Thanks to everyone who voted for me," Samantha gushes. She is perfect, of course; her blond hair is done up in a complicated hairstyle that, if I attempted it, would look like two octopi having a street brawl. Her gold dress clings in all the right places; she looks like a glowing statue of a tropical goddess. How can you compete with a goddess? I know my mythology. I have zero chance.

I try to avoid looking at Fletcher, but my eyes are drawn to him. He's wearing a sage-green shirt and khaki shorts, and he's never looked finer. As Samantha rambles on about how glad she is to be the most popular girl in school, Fletcher shifts uncomfortably beside her. When it's his turn to speak, he just says, "Thanks," and hands the mike back to Becca.

"One more round of applause for our king and queen!" she yells. Fletcher and Samantha take their thrones as the rest of the kids resume partying.

For some reason, I just can't leave, even though I desperately want to. I wander outside to the porch to watch people head up the haunted trail, and find a spot to sit. I watch group after group take their turns getting caught in the romantic mist, frightened by the ghostly actors who pop out of the foliage and the windows of the pirate ship. If I wanted to believe I was stranded on a rain-swept island, I could. At least, the stranded part seems pretty real.

I guess I drift off or something, because suddenly Becca is back on stage trying to be heard above the crowd again. "Everybody, it's time to see who gets a date with Brandon!" she calls, and most of the kids outside start to drift inside, and I follow them. Becca's on stage with Brandon Keller, who is holding her battered envelope full of blue tickets. All the girls push forward to the front of the stage; the guys hang back, looking disgusted and just a little jealous.

Brandon sticks his hand into the envelope, pulls out a ticket, and reads the number: "The lucky winner, and my date for this evening, is number 904503. That's 904503. Who is it?"

A frantic rustle of girls trying to read in the dark fills the room, and seconds tick by with no winner. People start murmuring, groans by the disappointed losers fill the room, and still, no date. "Didn't you get a ticket?" a girl next to me asks. "You're in that club, so you had to get one, right?"

"Oh yeah." I take it out of my purse, just to check. Figures. 904503. I never win anything.

The girl is looking over my shoulder. "Hey. Hey! You won!" She grabs my arm and waves it above my head so I look like a puppet whose operator needs antispastic medication. "Here she is! She won! This girl won!"

Bodies press in on me, forcing me to the stage like a piece of kelp caught in a rip current. I try to swim against them, but it's no use. It's a mosh pit, and I'm the mosh, and it's the pits. About six feet from the stage, somebody decides to pick me up and float me over the top of the crowd, so I'm lying, face up, on the hands of strangers, moving along on a tide of jealous girl hormones.

They dump me onto the stage in a heap, and Becca stares quizzically at me. "Here's the ticket," I say, handing it to her. "No kidding."

I awkwardly get myself to a sitting position, and happen to look over at the perfect king and queen, who are engaged in some animated conversation. Just as I look away, Fletcher and I lock eyes. What is he feeling? Relief? Disgust? It doesn't matter, I guess. He has his perfect queen, and she's not a Queen Geek.

Brandon reaches out, take my hand and helps me up. He takes off his sunglasses and dazzles me with a perfect grin. "Hey, date," he says as he takes me in his arms. "Ready to party?"

Hmmm. Could be worse, I guess. I feel myself let go for the first time in weeks. He smells good too, and gives a pretty good hug. But then he dips me backward, plants this big old movie-star kiss on me that sucks all the oxygen out of my body, and after what seems like about an hour, pulls me back upright.

The crowd screams, guys roaring their approval, girls moaning in envy. I check for drool (on my mouth, not his) and try to focus. So, maybe this date thing won't be so bad.

Becca tries to be heard over the crowd. "Give it up for Shelby, our winner tonight!" It's hard to tell which is louder, the music or the clapping. Finally Becca says over the microphone, "Okay, enjoy the dance, the games, the food, and our fantastic haunted island!"

"Come on," Brandon says, taking my hand. "Let's dance."

The music has gotten mellow and gone from that constant hip-hop rhythm to a slow dance. He helps me off the stage, puts an arm around my waist, grabs my hand, and whisks me off, expertly, into a magic dance. I feel the eyes of all the other girls on me, but I can't really concentrate on that, because the weirdest thing is happening: While I'm dancing with this absolutely gorgeous movie-star guy, I'm thinking about that stupid Fletcher.

"You're a great dancer," Brandon whispers in my ear.

"Thanks."

After a pause, he says, "But you'd rather be dancing with somebody else, huh?"

I pull back a bit so I can see his eyes. "What?"

"I can just tell." He pulls me back so my head is on his shoulder. "You dance with enough girls, you can tell when they're already dancing with somebody else."

I close my eyes and try to just get into the music, but his words keep ringing in my ears. Suddenly, he stops dancing. "Keep your eyes closed till I tell you to open them," he says.

"What?"

"No, no. Just keep 'em closed." He starts to back away from me ever so slowly, and just as I'm about to protest, he's got his arm around me again. Except—

I open my eyes, and I'm dancing with Fletcher Berkowitz.

"Hey," he says softly. "I told you I was going to take you to the dance."

"But—"

He puts a finger to my lips, then holds me tighter. "We can talk later. But just listen to one thing before we finish this dance: I think you're the most beautiful girl in the world, but even if you weren't, I'd still want to be here with you."

"But—"

To keep me from talking, he plants his lips firmly on mine, which is the one time I've not minded somebody telling me to shut up. "Oh, by the way," he says when we come up for air, "I think I might owe you a hundred dollars."

Okay, so maybe I do need other people, maybe even a hot guy with freckles. But while I'm on that subject, I just want it to be known: I will always be a Queen Geek, and that's enough for anybody. And though it seems like Fletcher and I might become romantically involved, I'm not going to collect on that bet. I like to keep my options open.

ABOUT THE AUTHOR

Laura Preble is a journalist, singer, teacher, and writer from San Diego, California. *The Queen Geek Social Club* came to her in a three A.M. dream, and she has written one other young adult novel, *Lica's Angel*. Her husband is jazz musician Chris Klich, and they have two children, Austin and Noel.

MAKE SURE YOU CATCH
THESE AWESOME TITLES
FROM

berkley jaM books

COMING OCTOBER 2006
PROM NIGHT:
MAKING OUT
BY MEGAN STINE
0-425-21179-7

COMING NOVEMBER 2006
SECRETS OF A SOUTH
BEACH PRINCESS
BY MARY KENNEDY
0-425-21196-7

WWW.PENGUIN.COM